A POSSE OF PRINCESSES

Sherwood Smith

ISBN-13: 978-1-934648-27-8
ISBN-10: 1-934648-27-2

Trade Paperback Reprint Edition

July 1, 2008

A Publication of
Norilana Books
P. O. Box 2188
Winnetka, CA 91396
www.norilana.com

Printed in the United States of America

A POSSE OF PRINCESSES

YA Angst

an imprint of

Norilana Books

www.norilana.com

Other Books by Sherwood Smith

Crown Duel
Inda
The Fox
King's Shield
Senrid
Over the Sea: CJ's First Notebook
A Stranger to Command (prequel to Crown Duel)

Acknowledgments

With grateful thanks
to my beta readers at Athanarel,
and to Tamara Meatzie
for her generous help in proofreading

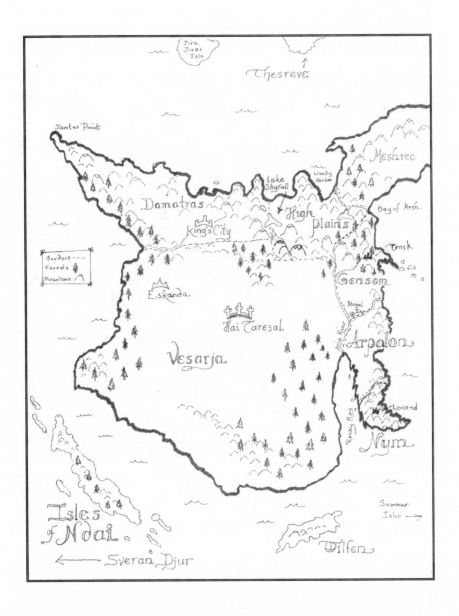

A Posse of Princesses

SHERWOOD SMITH

ONE

From the tower lookout in the royal castle—highest tower in all the kingdom of Nym—Princess Rhis peered down through the misting rain at a messenger on the main road.

This rider slumped in the saddle of a long-legged lowlands race-horse that was now plodding up the steep road, occasionally hidden by tall stands of deep green fir. The messenger had to be from the lowlands. Anyone raised in Nym's mountains knew that the only animal for the steep roads was a pony. Their sturdy bodies and short legs fared better on steep slopes. The rider's cloak was crimson, a bright splash of color even in the gloom of a rainy afternoon. None of Nym's royal messengers wore crimson cloaks. This one must be an equerry from the Queen of faraway Vesarja, she thought, and turned away from the window to resume pacing around the little room.

Once, many years ago, the old tower had been a lookout for Nym's warriors, no longer necessary since the kingdom had established magical protection. Now the small, stone tower room had become Rhis's private retreat.

Her parents considered themselves too elderly to climb all those stairs any more; her older brother, Crown Prince Gavan, was too busy, as was her older sister, Princess Sidal. And Gavan's wife, Princess Elda, was too stout—even if she'd approved of frivolities such as spending time in tower rooms, which she didn't. Something she mentioned rather often.

Rhis loved the lookout. It was cozy, and had a nice fireplace (with a magical firestick in it that burned evenly all winter long), a comfortable cushioned chair, a desk, a small case containing all her favorite books, and a tiranthe—the twenty-four-stringed instrument that Elda insisted only lowly minstrels played. Here Rhis could practice and not disturb, or disgust, anyone. Here she could sit and read and dream and watch the ever-changing weather and seasons over the tiny mountain kingdom. She could also write wonderful ballads.

At least . . . she hoped they were wonderful. Would be, some day. Maybe.

She stopped pacing and frowned down at the paper on the desk, close-written with many, many scribblings. She loved music, and stories, and ballads—especially romantic ballads. All her favorite books contained wonderfully romantic stories about people in history who had gone through terrible adventures but had succeeded in finding their True Love.

When she'd begun her first ballad, it had seemed easy. All she had to do was picture a forlorn princess, one who was tall with brown hair—someone a lot like herself. Only instead of having a cozy retreat, this princess was locked up in a tower room, she wasn't quite sure why yet, but for some horrific reason, which would require her to escape secretly down all 538 steps, slip out into the treacherous snows of winter, and away—meeting a prince along the road.

Rhis frowned. She knew what kind of prince the princess had to meet. He had to be brave, and good at overcoming vast numbers of evil minions, but he also had to be kind. He absolutely must like music—especially ballads—but he had to be a good dancer. He had to look like. . . .

That was the part that she always got stuck at. Rhis dropped onto her chair and reread her verses about the mysterious prince. Every line began with "The best" or "The greatest" or "The finest"—he had the darkest hair, the bluest eyes, he was the best dancer, but still, somehow, he seemed so . . . um, boring.

With a heavy sigh she dipped her pen and struck out the latest words that just a while ago had seemed so wonderful. What were *the bluest eyes*, anyway? Were eyes the silver-blue of the morning sky bluer than the dark blue of evening?

Blue eyes were stupid anyway. Everyone in ballads either had eyes of emerald or sapphire or amber. How about something *really* unusual, like red eyes? Or yellow and purple stripe? But would those be handsome? Rhis frowned and tried to picture a fellow puckering up for a kiss . . . handsome lips, handsome nose . . . and right above, a pair of yellow and purple striped eyes? No. Well, how about red? But what kind of hair would look handsome with red eyes? Not red, certainly, though her favorite color was 'hair of flame', which sounded more romantic than anything. But crimson eyes and hair of flame? He'd look like a measle.

Not blond either, she thought. She didn't want a blond prince, for the people of Damatras far to the north were supposed to be mostly light haired and paler than normal people, and everyone knew they lived to make war.

How about—

A tinkling sound interrupted her thoughts, the summons bell that her mother had magically rigged so that the servants wouldn't have to climb the tower stairs, either.

Rhis's first thought was of the messenger, but she dismissed that. No one ever sent her messages, except for dull letters from Elda's younger sister, Princess Shera, and those always came with the green-cloaked messengers from the kingdom of Gensam.

Rhis wrinkled her nose. It could only mean that Elda wanted her—and always for some dreary task, or lesson, or duty, and if she dawdled too long she also incurred a lecture given in that sharp, annoyed tone of voice that never failed to send servants whisking about their business, and made Rhis feel two years old.

Rhis's feet knew all 538 of the worn tower stairs. She skipped down, dashing out onto the landing at a run. A glimpse of pale blue caused her to veer, and she narrowly missed running down Sidal, who tottered, struggling with a stack of books in her arms.

Rhis reached up to steady her sister's pile of books. "I'm sorry," she said contritely.

Sidal recovered her balance, and peered over the topmost book. "A slower pace, perhaps?"

Rhis grimaced. Elda was forever lecturing her on always using a sedate step, as a princess ought. "I will," she promised. "But I was in a hurry because someone rang the bell." She looked around for one of Elda's maids.

Sidal smiled. "I did. Papa just received a letter from Vesarja. It seems that Queen Briath Arvanosas has invited you to attend the ceremonies arranged for Prince Lios, who is officially being appointed Crown Prince."

Rhis clapped her hands together. "Oh! Oh!"

Sidal tipped her head in the other direction. "They are in there discussing it now."

"Oh, Sidal," Rhis breathed, dancing in a circle around her sister. "I've never gone anywhere, done anything—"

"I think," Sidal said in a quiet voice, her eyes just slightly crinkled, "you ought to go in and hear what they have to say."

Rhis whirled around. Sidal was like Mama. She never raised her voice, or said anything unkind, but when either of them dropped a hint, it was always to the purpose.

Rhis knew at once what Sidal was hinting at: Elda was in the audience room.

Despite her promise to be more sedate, Rhis fled down the carpeted hall, her pearl-braided hair thumping her back at every step. She slowed at the corner just before the audience chamber, took in a deep breath, and with proper deportment walked round the corner.

A waiting servant—Ama, mother to the upstairs maid— saw her, bowed, reached to open the door, then paused. She pointed in silence over one of Rhis's ears, and Rhis clapped her hands to her head, found a strand of hair floating loose. How Elda would glower!

"Thank you." She mouthed the words as she tucked the hair back.

Ama smiled just a little, and finished opening the door.

The first voice Rhis heard was Elda's.

". . . and she has, despite all my efforts, no better sense of duty than she had when she was five years old."

Rhis stepped in, her slippered feet slow and silent.

The audience chamber was not the most imposing room in the castle, but it was the most comfortable. It had rosewood furnishings and gilt lamps and the stone walls were covered by colorful tapestries. The king did most of his work there, often joined by Rhis's mother, when she could.

King Armad was seated in his great carved chair, a fine table loaded with neat stacks of paper at his right hand. At his left side, in an equally great chair, sat the queen, a book on her lap, her pen busy on a writing board. She looked up and smiled at Rhis then returned to her work.

"Is there nothing you can attest to in my daughter's favor?" the Queen said in her calm voice. Rhis felt her face go hot. She was reassured to see the humor narrowing the Queen's wide-set gray eyes, though her mouth was serious. "You have had the training of her for ten years."

Elda flushed, her round cheeks looking as red as Rhis's felt. "I have tried my very best," she said. "What she does well is what she wants to do well—singing, dancing, and reading histories. No one dances better, but a great kingdom like Vesarja will require more of a future queen than dancing, or knowledge of which clans fought which back in the dark days, before Nym became civilized!"

"This is true," the king said.

Elda added, with her chin lifted, "As for what matters most, my own daughter—scarcely ten years old—knows her map better, and the rates of exchange, and can recite almost half the Common Laws. If Rhis knows twelve of them, it would surprise me."

The king spoke, still stroking his beard. "But your daughter knows that she will one day rule Nym, after my son. Is Rhis's character bad? Or her disposition?"

Rhis bit her lip. She longed to point out that Elda's disposition was none too amiable—and she'd married a prince. But she stayed silent, fuming to herself.

Elda gave one of her annoyed sighs, short and sharp. "Her habits are lazy. She would rather loll about in her tower room, piddling with her song books, than apply herself to appropriate studies. Her disposition is not bad, for she does not argue or stamp or shout. She simply disappears when she does not agree with what she ought to be doing."

The king looked up at Rhis. "Is this summary true, child?"

Rhis gulped. She wanted so badly to shout that Elda was not being fair. Rhis was *not* lazy—she kept busy all the day long. She simply didn't see the reason to study those dull laws and tables, since she wasn't going to rule.

Yet Papa had not asked if Elda's words were fair. Only if they were true.

"Yes, Papa," she said in a subdued voice.

Her father stroked his long silver-white beard with one hand, and lifted the other toward Queen Hailen.

The Queen said, "We will discuss it further."

Everyone from high degree to low knew that Elda was a princess, born and raised in Gensam, and Rhis's mother was just a magician whose family had been farmers. They knew equally well that when King Armad was gone, Rhis's mother would sail east to the Summer Islands to teach magicians and Gavan and Elda would rule Nym. Still, no one—including Elda—ever argued with Queen Hailen.

"Very well," Elda said, and walked out, scarcely giving Rhis a glance.

"Come, child," the queen said, rising to her feet. "I have worked the morning away. Now I need to stir a bit." As she passed the king she bent a little and laid her hand briefly on his old, gnarled hand.

The king smiled at them both, then returned to his work. Rhis glanced back doubtfully. She hadn't really thought about how *old* her father was. She knew that after a long single life, refusing every match, he'd been nearly fifty when Queen Hailen was sent to replace the old Royal Magician, and he fell in love with her almost at once. Gavan and Sidal had been born each year following the marriage, but another fifteen years had passed before Rhis was born.

She seldom saw her father, except for formal occasions. Now, as she and her mother passed out onto the roofed terrace, she wondered how she could not have noticed how frail he looked.

The door closed behind them. Rhis turned to discover her mother studying her. She was now fully as tall as her mother. Who had aged too, Rhis realized, looking into her face; there were tiny lines at the corners of her mouth and eyes, and her brown hair, so neat in its coronet, was streaked with gray.

"Is Papa all right?" she asked in a whisper.

"Your father's health is good, and his mind is quite as strong as it was when he was young," the queen said, smiling a little. "I confess it would hearten him very much to see you well established."

"Well, I do know what my duty is," Rhis said, trying without success not to sound resentful. "I've always known that Gavan and Elda will one day rule, and after them Shera." Rhis thought of her thin, small niece, Elda's daughter, who was so good and perfect—who studied all the time, and never smiled, or laughed, or made jokes. Despite the fact that Elda never failed to hold Shera up to Rhis as an example of what she ought to be, Rhis sometimes felt sorry for her niece. "Sidal will be Royal Magician. And since I did not want to go away and study magic, my duty is to marry to the benefit of Nym." On impulse Rhis pleaded, "Oh, but is it so wicked to wish for adventure and romance first?"

"Wicked? No one could say it's wicked." The Queen laughed softly. "Perhaps the wish for adventure is, oh, a rash one, as adventure is seldom comfortable for anyone undergoing it."

Rhis smiled. She had embroidered the saying she thought so wise, taken from one of her ballads:

Adventure is tragedy triumphed.

"And romance, for those who wish it, is not unreasonable. It can also lead to disaster, if one makes it an end in itself."

Rhis held in a sigh. How many lectures had she endured from the sharp-tongued Elda on the follies of young girls and love?

A hesitation, a quick glance, then her mother said, "This invitation is a splendid opportunity. It will be a chance to practice courtly behavior among others your age, and to hear the wisdom of your elders in another kingdom. You could learn much."

Rhis curtseyed. "Yes, Mama." She peered out through the misting rain toward the green mountain slopes. In the distance a waterfall thundered. Now that she'd gotten over the surprise, this invitation was beginning to sound more like a duty—and not very romantic at all. The invitation sounded more like a summons.

"But . . . you wish that this unknown prince had come courting you here, am I right?"

Rhis stared at her mother.

"You remind me very much of my sister, who was even more romantic than you," the queen said, still smiling. "At least you can be practical when it is necessary. Consider this: if you were to marry Prince Lios, you would be living in Vesarja. How else can you find out if you can adapt to their ways?"

Rhis exclaimed, "Oh! I see. But why are they inviting me? No one knows me—I've met no princes. In fact, I've hardly met any boys my age."

Her mother made a quiet gesture of agreement. Nym's rulers did not keep court. They met frequently with the guild council, and Elda and Gavan spent the summer and autumn months each year traveling about the country, the better to truly see what the various provincial governors were doing. Last year they had taken their daughter—as future queen, Elda explained, Shera ought to get to know her important subjects—but Rhis had been deemed unnecessary.

The Queen said, "Your father knows Queen Briath, for they are closer in generation. He thinks that she has invited every young lady she deems eligible so she can look them over at once."

Rhis turned to her mother in silent dismay. "So it *is* a summons!"

The Queen's eyes crinkled—just like Sidal's. "What that really means is that there will be parties, picnics, ridings, dances, and all manner of wonderful festivities planned for the young people. You can be sure that if there are princesses and girls of suitable high rank invited, there will also be boys who very much want to meet those princesses. Even if you and Prince Lios do not take to one another, there will be many opportunities to find another boy you might like better—and you'll have the time to get to know one another. And meanwhile, you will be an ambassador for our own kingdom. Good relations with our neighbors is important."

Rhis laughed. "Being an ambassador might not be romantic, but the parties and dances sound like fun!"

Queen Hailen patted her cheek. "I think it will be. Flirt all you like, but remember you cannot marry until you are at least twenty. That might be a comfort."

Comfort, Rhis thought indignantly.

Her mother went on with a smile, "At sixteen we often make vows about the rest of our life, but the truth is, the rest of our life usually looks very different at seventeen, and even more different by eighteen. Enough talk! You have a long journey ahead, so you must prepare. And part of that preparation is to listen to Elda. She knows a great deal about the etiquette of court life. This is something I know nothing of, which is why she undertook to teach you, and not I."

Rhis bit her lip. She did not want to complain about Elda, but she did not look forward to extra lessons.

Her mother took both her hands in her cool, strong fingers. "Part of being a ruler is to recognize that everyone has something of value to offer. What isn't as valuable can be . . . overlooked."

Overlooked. Did that mean that the Queen knew as well as Rhis did that Elda was a sour-pie?

The queen gently squeezed Rhis's hands. "I see you understand what I mean."

It was all she said, but suddenly Rhis felt a lot more grown up. "All right, Mama," she promised. "I'll learn as much as I can."

TWO

Once the decision had been made that Rhis should go, Elda took over the organization of her journey. With her customary brisk and indefatigable energy, she not only insisted on doubling Rhis's lessons in proper royal etiquette, she also made certain that Rhis would travel with an entourage fit for a princess of Nym—complete to a new wardrobe.

This last item made all the tedious lessons, and lectures, worthwhile for Rhis. For the first time, she realized what being rich *meant*.

Though no one would know it to look at them all in their sturdy castle that had for several centuries held off ferocious winter winds, and equally ferocious warriors, Nym's royal family was wealthy. Queen Hailen only had a single jeweled and embroidered velvet gown not because they couldn't afford any others, but because she only wore it once or twice a year, and thought it impractical to order more. She was more proud of her mage's robes anyway—those she'd earned, she'd told Rhis once.

Nym was small, mountainous, wealthy—and not the least romantic any more.

Rhis could recite Nym's history without much thinking about it. Its gemstones were world famous, and its mines—most of them made by magic centuries ago by the mysterious Snow

Folk, whose descendents lived in the fog-shrouded Summer Islands to the east—difficult for anyone but the people of Nym to find and exploit. Many had been the attempts over the years to conquer Nym, and failing that, to raid the caravans that left twice a year to sell gems. For ages they had been protected by the tough mountain fighters who had honed their abilities in Nym's interminable clan feuds, but after the country was united, the king had chosen to protect his interests through magic rather than bloodshed.

Rhis had learned her history, but until now the only part of it that had interested her were the old romances. Not that there were many, but those few had been fairly spectacular—night-time raids, escapes, abductions (planned by the princess in question herself, so it would go right)—and most of them happy. She didn't like the ones that had come out tragically.

Finally the last day arrived. Everything was packed, and loaded, and guards picked, and all the servants that Elda thought appropriate for a Princess of Nym were also ready. This included a lady's maid, something Rhis had never before had. Elda had declared that she would choose a proper lady's maid, but unexpectedly Queen Hailen had intervened, and saw to the selection herself.

Rhis did not say anything, but she was secretly glad. Elda's own lady's maid was a prim, sour-mouthed woman who spied on servants and royalty alike, reporting wrong-doings—real or assumed—to Elda. Instead of getting another such person (who would, no doubt, write awful reports back to Elda on every mistake Rhis made) she was introduced by her mother to a quiet, calm-faced woman named Keris, with a sweet voice and unobtrusive ways.

And so, at last, night fell. A terrific storm raged outside the castle. Rhis lay in her bed listening to the wind howl and rain and hail clatter against the windows. The rain itself didn't disturb her. Anyone who grew up in Nym knew that mountain weather, though fierce, seldom lasted long. But she was so excited she couldn't sleep—and even if the night had been balmy and silent, she suspected she'd still be lying awake.

Finally, when the distant bell rang the pattern for midnight, she gave up trying and clapped on her glowglobe. She could at least read for a while, and daydream.

She was just reaching for a book when she heard a soft tapping at her door.

She dashed across the cold stone floor. "Who's there?"

The door opened, and to her surprise a tall silhouette in pale blue emerged from the dark hallway and walked into the light room—her sister Sidal.

"I came to wish you a safe and happy journey," Sidal said, sitting down on the bed beside Rhis.

As long as she could remember Sidal had been tall and competent and a little remote, busy with her magic studies. At an early age she had showed magical talent, and had trained hard in order to take Mama's place when it became necessary. Rhis had also shown talent—but she'd never had her sister's interest in the hard work of becoming a mage.

"Sidal," Rhis asked doubtfully. "Do you think I'm silly to wish for romance?"

The silvery light of the glowglobe glinted in her coronet of soft brown hair. Sidal was not pretty—no one in the family was considered pretty. They all had long faces and strongly marked bones—but right then, while she was looking out at the rain-washed window, Rhis thought privately that she was beautiful. "I think," the princess-mage said slowly, "that it depends on what you mean by romance."

"Oh, like the ballads. Overcoming great odds to find your true love, or doing great deeds to save him. 'Adventure is tragedy triumphed!' Or he does great deeds to win you. Something dashing and heroic," Rhis explained. "For love."

"Not great deeds." Sidal gave a tiny shake of her head. "Too many great deeds translate out to be great pain for those who lost."

"Except it's always villains who lose," Rhis said quickly. "They deserve to lose. When the heroes lose, then it's a tragedy, and I *hate* tragedies."

"The villains would think their losses tragedy," Sidal said with a rueful smile. "Of course there are truly evil people in the world. The emperor of Sveran Djur is reputed to be one, and I believe it, for he has done terrible things with his magic. But there are so many others who set out with the best intentions, or what they believe to be the best intentions, and find themselves on the opposing side of others who also have the best intentions. The people on each side, in their own ballads, appear as heroes, and the other side as villains."

"I know. And Elda's told me many times how rulers agree that no one can rule a kingdom and be a mage. That Mama had to sign a certain type of treaty, and cannot rule after Papa dies. All just because of that emperor." Rhis sighed. "That doesn't sound romantic. It sounds nasty."

"Wars and fighting and using magic for coercion are always nasty."

"Well, I don't want that. Since I have to marry anyway, I just want, oh, to fall in love, or have a wonderful prince fall in love with me. And no *terrible* fighting," she added hastily. "Just something exciting! Like in a ballad. Maybe a duel or two, or some chases, but nobody gets hurt."

Sidal laughed, a soft and sympathetic sound. "Sounds like you want a stage play sort of life! And there's nothing wrong with that, as long as you remember what I'm sure Mama told you as many times as she told me when I first went away to magic school—"

"I know." Rhis recited:

> *"Fall in love*
>   *with heart, not head,*
> *to trouble you're led.*
> *Fall in love*
>   *with heart and mind,*
> *then true love you'll find."*

She couldn't help but feel a little impatient, for she'd already endured last-lectures from Elda all during supper, and even afterward.

Sidal got to her feet. "Then I'm sure you'll have a wonderful time, and that's what I want most for you," she said, smiling. "But . . ." She twisted a fine opal ring off her finger, and slid it onto one of Rhis's. "Just in case. No one need ever know. If you do find yourself in trouble, and need me, then touch this stone and say my name three times."

Rhis glanced down at the ring, and closed her other hand over it. "Thank you, Sidal," she said. "Do you foresee trouble?"

The tall princess-mage bent down and kissed Rhis on the forehead. "No one ever foresees trouble, unless she is looking for it," she said. "So if you don't use the ring-magic, I will know that you are having a wonderful visit and that you don't need it. It would be terrible if trouble found you, and you had no one to help you. Never mind. Just wear it and think of me when you are dancing," she said, caressing Rhis on the cheek. Then she went swiftly out the door and closed it.

Rhis clapped off her glowglobe and snuggled under her quilts, thinking about the ring, and about Sidal. Did her serious sister have a romantic side after all?

Feeling very confused, Rhis let her thoughts drift into her own dreams, and then into sleep.

She woke up to streaming sunshine and a promising new day. Remembering her trip, she raced out of bed and into her dressing room where Keris, the new maid, had her new traveling gown all laid out and ready for her. The rest of the room looked empty, with all her trunks packed and gone downstairs to the stable.

After a hasty breakfast, she danced into the audience room to kiss her father good-bye, for he was already at work. The rest of the family accompanied her to the courtyard to see her off. She embraced them all, winning a smile from her mother when she gave Elda a spontaneous hug. "Thank you for bearing with me, Elda," she said happily. "I'll do my best to make you proud."

Elda's cheeks flushed red, but she smiled a little. "Dignity, Rhis. Remember, a *worthy* prince looks for dignity and dedication to duty above all in his future queen."

That sounds just like my boring brother, Rhis thought, but all she said was, "I'll remember!"

Then Rhis climbed into the coach, waved from the window, and they were off.

Rhis watched her home until the road down the mountain took them around a great slope and the mighty stone castle slid from sight. It was not a handsome castle, Rhis thought, watching the last tower disappear from view. In fact, most would probably consider it gloomy, for it had been built to withstand weather and marauders. Elda, who had grown up in the more peaceable Gensam, had once said, "A palace is quite different, child. Built not just for beauty but for comfort."

Rhis grimaced, for the first time thinking about what those words meant. She'd grown up with all those narrow stairways and stone rooms and cold slate floors, so she was used to them. Would a visitor think them barbaric? Maybe it was better that no prince had shown up to court her!

Anyway, *now* she'd see a real palace. Impatience gnawed at her as she realized just how long a trip lay ahead of her. Though Nym was small on the map, it would take several days to wind down through the treacherous mountains—if the weather held. If the weather turned truly severe, as it sometimes did, she could be held up a week or more.

She wished that she could travel about by magic, as Sidal and her mother did. But people other than mages seldom traveled by magic, because apparently it was dangerous, and sometimes had nasty effects. And you could only go one at a time, to specially designated destinations—either a place, or, more rarely, a person.

Rhis looked down at her ring. Would it be dangerous for Sidal to transfer directly to Rhis, wherever she might be? Rhis considered her sister, who had professed not to like dangerous circumstances—but who was obviously ready to face them if necessary.

People are surprising, she thought, settling back in the cold coach, and pulling a soft woolen quilt up around her chin. *Even the ones you think you know.*

A long series of days followed, each much alike, as the coach made its way steadily northward. The journey out of Nym did not take weeks, for the weather stayed relatively mild. They descended steadily through the fir-dotted heights, down into pine forest, then at last reached the Common Road along the coast of Arpalon. They sped along the rolling hills, under a variety of trees Rhis had only seen pictures of. The roads were paved and smooth, and the journey seemed less arduous. Though still quite long.

The inns they stayed at were comfortable, but after the first exciting night of sleeping away from home, they all blended together into a series of big wooden buildings with nice beds and fine meals, all supervised by the quiet, efficient staff that Elda had sent to protect Rhis. These servants also kept her from talking to anybody on the road, nor did they tell anyone who she was. The days when Nym's royalty were routinely kidnapped for fabulous ransoms if they left the protection of the mountains were not all *that* long in the past.

Rhis knew these things, but she still found traveling to be very dull. She caught glimpses of people who looked interesting, from far-away places, as she was conducted straight to her room at night—and then to her carriage in the morning, after her lonely breakfast.

She had begun the journey resenting the fact that Elda had arranged for her to meet at Gensam's border her younger sister Princess Shera, but by the time she'd made her way north without speaking to a single person except the quiet Keris, she was looking forward to Shera, despite how boring her letters had been.

Shera was a year older than Rhis—it was she for whom Elda's daughter was named. When Rhis turned six, not long after Elda married Gavan, Elda had insisted that it would be seemly for the two princesses to start a correspondence. She had supervised each of Rhis's letters, saying, "It's as well you learn early how royalty carry on a correspondence, for you never know when you might need it."

So Rhis had had to write, in her very best handwriting, formally phrased letters describing her studies—and not much else. Just once she'd said something about her favorite ballads, but Elda had been horrified. "You have to remember that to the rest of the world, Nym is a country full of wild people. No one in those old songs was the least bit civilized." So Rhis had had to recopy the letter, leaving out her favorite subject.

The letters she received back were neatly written, and very, very uninteresting. Elda had obviously told the truth: civilized princesses really did just brag about their studies, and proper interests, like growing flowers. Rhis was always glad when winter came, preventing messengers from getting through too often, slowing down the exchange.

By the time Rhis and her entourage had left the coast and were riding along the great river Aria, with no one but vigilant, respectful adults to talk to, she longed for someone close to her own age—even someone whose letters had been full of deportment lessons and the varieties of flowers in the castle garden.

When at last they neared the border of Arpalon and Gensam, Rhis was so looking forward to seeing Shera she felt she could talk about roses and starflowers all day, if only she could *talk*.

They were to meet at the ancient Royal Inn on the border, where many treaties and royal marriages had been negotiated in the turbulent past.

The word 'inn' was misleading, Rhis decided when she saw the huge building with its numerous windows and fine columned archways. A great many well-dressed people strolled about, and for the first time she was glad of her entourage when they rolled up the carriageway to the splendid courtyard. Nothing in Nym was this fine! People stared so when she emerged from her carriage, but no one smiled.

She walked inside quickly, glad to follow Mistress Ranla, her father's courier, who was the leader of the entourage. A brief glimpse of a spacious area full of fine furnishings and handsomely dressed folk strolling about was all she got before she was conducted up a grand, sweeping stairway to another storey, and then to a suite of huge rooms where nothing was made of stone. The walls were smooth wood painted a warm cream color.

She sank down onto the nearest chair, as servants and retainers curtseyed and moved about arranging things. A few moments later a girl her own age approached with a cautious, uncertain step. She was much shorter than Rhis. She had a round figure, a moon-shaped face, and the honey-brown skin common to their end of the continent, with a rosebud of a mouth. Her hair was a rich chestnut brown, glinting with red highlights, and it had natural wave that made long bouncy curls that Rhis envied at once. Her gown, light green trimmed with pearls and dark green ribbons, was at least as fine as the finest of the gowns in Rhis's trunks, and it made her brown eyes look greenish, contrasting delightfully with her reddish hair.

She gave a correct nod as Rhis rose to her feet. "Princess Rhis?" Her voice was high, with a slight lisp.

"Princess Shera?" Rhis said, giving the same nod.

"My parents bid me welcome you to Gensam," Shera said in a carefully modulated voice. "I trust our journey together will be pleasant."

Rhis knew what to say to that. "Thank you. In my turn, I am to convey greetings and thanks from my parents to yours, and from your honored sister, Princess Elda, as well."

The conversation proceeded like that for a short time, each girl admirably formal and dignified and very, very proper. Rhis was glad of her lessons with Elda. At least she wasn't making a fool of herself. But by the time a quiet servant had brought in hot chocolate and biscuits, Rhis was feeling the strain of so much dignified, formal conversation. At the thought of two more weeks of it, she found herself wishing that she would be alone after all.

When next Shera spoke, it was to praise the inn's garden. Rhis half-listened to the slow, lisping voice enumerate the fine early blooms and important plants that she had found in her five days' stay while waiting for Rhis's arrival. Since very few flowers grew in cold, high Nym, Rhis didn't recognize half the names she heard, and she couldn't help her mind wandering.

She was choosing her fourth biscuit—she wasn't hungry, but at least it gave her something to do with her hands—when she happened to look up, just as Shera started to yawn.

The princess closed her jaw at once, her eyes watering slightly.

"If you are tired, Princess Shera, it will not discommode me if you wish to retire to rest," Rhis said politely, hoping to get rid of her for a time.

Shera's round face went bright pink. "I'm not tired—" she said quickly, then she turned even redder.

Rhis stared. Was it possible that Shera was as bored as she was? How to find out, without making some terrible mistake in etiquette that would disgrace her family—her entire kingdom?

"Not tired?" she repeated in her most polite voice.

"Well, a little, maybe. There was music last night, and perhaps I stayed awake too long to hear it," Shera said, just as politely.

"Do you, ah, like music?" Rhis asked, even more politely.

Shera's eyes widened slightly, an expression of surprise and delight, but then her face smoothed into blankness, and she said very formally, "Fine music is a very appropriate diversion."

Rhis almost choked on her biscuit. Elda had often said that, in just the same voice: *Fine music is a very appropriate diversion*—meaning, of course, that ballads and the like were most definitely not 'fine music' or 'appropriate.'

"Princess Elda says that often," Rhis said slowly, watching Shera's face.

At the mention of Elda's name, Shera's little nose wrinkled slightly, then her face smoothed and she languidly picked up her hot chocolate cup, her fingers held precisely in the approved position.

Rhis took a deep breath. "I," she said bravely, "happen to like ballads. And I know that those are not considered fine music."

Shera hastily lowered her chocolate cup. She gulped once or twice, her eyes tearing again, and Rhis clapped her hand over her mouth in an effort not to laugh.

"Ballads?" Shera squeaked, her big greeny-brown eyes going wide and round.

Rhis nodded firmly. "Love them. *All* of them."

"Do you . . . know . . . *Prince Aroverd and the Snow Woman?*" Shera asked, her voice high, and not at all modulated.

Again Rhis nodded firmly. "All twenty-seven verses. And I know the older version—"

"—*The Snowlass and the Toadfield,*" Shera breathed.

The girls stared at each other.

"My favorite part is when she turns the invading army into toads," Shera said.

"I like that part, but my favorite is when she pushes the evil Red Mage into the swamp and stops the prince's runaway coach before it sinks—"

"Oh, I love that part too." Shera gave a fervent sigh. "I used to pretend I was the Snow Lass, going on adventures, and having princes wanting to marry me."

Rhis dared one more thing. "I can play it on the tiranthe," she said quickly.

And again Shera's eyes widened in delight, but this time she forgot to smooth out her face. Instead, she clasped her hands together. "Oh, I *do* envy you," she said. "We could never learn to play anything."

Rhis grinned. "Elda told me that only entertainers play. A princess might strum if a boy professes to like music, but only to look decorative, and that proper princesses summon entertainers when they want real music. But proper princesses don't ever want ballads. So after I learned the chords from a tutor, and she sent him away, I learned in secret from the cook's nephew, who comes home every winter from his group of traveling players. Of course I wasn't allowed to pack my tiranthe for the trip."

Shera grinned back. "Shall we call for one?"

"Let's," Rhis said, adding, "I'll buy it for the trip, and teach you what I know!"

THREE

Within a very short time the girls had established a good understanding.

"My letters," Rhis said apologetically. "Elda had to read them before she would let me put them in the courier bag."

Shera grimaced. "And my governess had to read mine. But when Elda wrote to me, it was always to tell me how much you were learning, and how grateful you were for her lessons, and how I ought to work hard to be just like you."

"That's what she said to me about you," Rhis exclaimed.

"Mama is always twitting me about my behavior," Shera said, curling her legs beneath her in a fashion that would have caused gasps of dismay from Elda. "I guess I take after my Uncle Kordey, who Mama always calls *that frivolous, dream-touched, undutiful brother of your father's* when no one else is around. Try as I might, I just couldn't measure up to Mama and Elda."

"In your letters, all you talked about was your garden," Rhis said cautiously.

"It was the only place I could be alone," Shera explained. "Planning elaborate gardens is now fashionable, so I could write about it. But actually I left all the planning to the head gardener, and I really spent as much time as I could there to dream and sing," Shera admitted with a quick, merry grin.

"I have a tower," Rhis confessed, liking her sister-by-marriage more with every exchange. "That's where I keep my books, and my tiranthe. Elda's too stout to go up there, and her awful maid Sazu refused to climb all 538 steps."

"Sazu," Shera said, wrinkling her nose. "How I remember her! She used to spy on me, and report every mistake to Elda and Mama. It's her sister who I have as governess, and let me tell you, if nothing pleasant—besides meeting you at last—happens on this trip, at least I will have this time away from her."

"Poor Elda," Rhis said, her conscience giving her a pang of regret. "Tried so hard to turn us into proper princesses. Well, at least we'll know how to behave when we get to Hai Taresal and meet Queen Briath, because I'll wager anything *she* doesn't play a tiranthe or daydream in her garden."

"No," Shera said. "But we won't be going to the capital. Didn't you get word? No, I guess you couldn't, for the letter arrived just before I left home, and you would have already been traveling. We're to go to Eskanda, which is Crown Prince Lios's own place. The celebration will be there."

"Is it? But we'll still be meeting the Queen, won't we?"

Shera shook her head. "Papa says she never, ever leaves Hai Taresal."

Rhis tried to picture the map. Hai Taresal, the capital of Vesarja, lay right in the center of the kingdom where two great rivers met, a city whose beauty was legendary. She remembered vaguely that Eskanda lay in the north-western quarter of Vesarja. "I wonder why they changed it? We'll have a lot farther to travel."

Shera shrugged. "And we can enjoy every moment of it. As for why, who knows? But this I'm sure of: if the Queen stays behind, all the older, stuffy courtiers will probably stay too, unless they have daughters to try to marry off, which means that things ought to be much more fun in Eskanda."

Rhis gave a sigh of pleasure. "So it will be all people our age? How wonderful!"

Shera wrinkled her nose again. "Well, don't count on that, for I know that Iardith will be there, and probably we'll find others like her."

"Iardith?" Rhis remembered the name from her lessons. "Princess Iardith of Arpalon?"

"That's the one." Shera fluttered her fingers on either side of her head. "You're lucky that your father and the king of Arpalon are mad at each other over some trade agreement, because *you* haven't had to meet Iardith."

"What's wrong with her? Is she evil?"

"Oh, nothing so interesting," Shera said with a laugh. "She really is a perfect princess—and if you don't happen to notice all her perfections, she will tell you about them. But only in private. In public, she's just as sweet and dignified and proper as Elda and the others could wish. We don't have a hope of attracting Prince Lios's attention while she's there, which doesn't matter to me—much—because I've been twoing with Rastian, the son of the Duke of the Northern March, for eight months and seventeen days—ever since I was formally introduced at Mama's court." She waved her hand vaguely northward.

"Is Iardith very beautiful, then?"

"Very," Shera said. "Hair blacker than midnight with no moons, and glossy, and never messy, though it is quite long, and light brown eyes—the boys who like poetry call them *topaz*, how disgusting. She has long, dark lashes, and perfect features, and a perfect figure, and she dances perfectly, and uses her fan perfectly, she has perfect manners—when others are around.

And she knows more than you do—as she will tell you, ever so nicely—about every fashionable subject, whether flowers or artists." Shera sighed, rolling her eyes. "When she came to visit us for my mother's birthday, every one of the fellows at court acted like puppies around her. Disgusting!" She grimaced. "Even Rastian got a little silly after she started looking at him over her fan and blinking those long and perfect eyelashes. I thought she looked like a cow, but the effect on Rastian was like he'd walked into a wall."

"Did you get mad at him?"

"I certainly did. He pointed out that I haven't yet met a prince who is quite that comely, and if I did, and I got silly too, he'd forgive me, so I forgave him. But still, it was lowering because she did it on purpose. When he followed her right out of the room and into the garden, she looked back at me and gave me *such* a nasty smirk."

"I suppose she's already met and fascinated Prince Lios, then?" Rhis asked.

"She couldn't have." Shera poured out more chocolate for them both. "Didn't you know? He's only just returned from overseas, after years and years. Now that he's the heir, he had to come home—and stay home."

"I don't hear anything," Rhis admitted. "That is, about people. I can tell you what father thinks of every ruler's trade policies, and I can also tell you a lot about what Mother thinks of the various royal mages in each kingdom, but they don't talk about people as people, and Elda, of course, thinks mere gossip quite improper. A princess, she says—"

"—Needs only to behave with dignity and grace, and the worthy suitor will recognize her merit." Shera pinched her nose. "Didn't I hear that one a million times! But in a court there's gossip, especially from those who travel, and so I hear things.

Not much about Lios, but then," she added triumphantly, "neither has Iardith, since he's been so long gone."

Nevertheless, Rhis felt the last of her dreams of attracting the unknown Prince Lios fade away. Who would possibly prefer a tall, angle-faced beanpole with hair the color of a wooden plank to such a paragon as Iardith? She shrugged, resolving not to let it bother her. "Well, as my sister said, quite rightly, at least there will be dancing, and picnics, and lots of fun."

Shera nodded vigorously. "And lots and lots of music!"

While the girls chattered far into the night, ending with playing and singing of their favorite songs, their entourages made all the preparations for the long journey to the northwest.

They set out the next day. Rhis asked Keris to put the tiranthe into the carriage, and not pack it. Keris complied without betraying any shock or horror. Once again Rhis gave silent thanks to her mother for putting her into the care of this calm, kind-hearted woman.

The days stretched into a week, and then a second week, as the girls crossed the length of Vesarja, but they were quite happy in each another's company. Rhis had never met an eligible young man in Nym's isolated fastness, so she was quite happy to listen to Shera talk about her Rastian—and of course Shera loved to talk about him.

When they weren't talking they were singing, or playing the tiranthe. Shera learned rapidly. Rhis found out that Shera wasn't really interested in history—or great deeds—only in great love matches, the more fraught with perils and sufferings, the better. Those made the best songs, she pointed out. Sometimes, when their fingers tired of playing and they tired of talking, Shera hummed absently under her breath as she stared out her window. She didn't have a great singing voice—neither did

Rhis—but Rhis discovered she liked listening to these little pieces of melody.

Twice heavy spring rainstorms caused them to halt for a day or two along the road. The last inn had hired musicians and promised nightly dances, and there were plenty of travelers also caught by the rain, so Rhis got her first chance to practice with real partners. The men were mostly older, and none were princes. Rhis was self-conscious, and spent most of her dances looking over at Shera and giggling. Shera did the same. At the end of her last dance, she dared to look up at her partner—a balding fellow with a pleasant face and a silvery beard. He had begun by complimenting her on her grace, but he'd gone quiet soon after. When she glanced up he suppressed a yawn as he stared over her head at the other dancers.

Annoyance flushed through her, but she just curtseyed politely when the dance came to an end, and the man bowed equally politely and then promptly moved away.

She thought about that after she and Shera parted to sleep. Dancing well really wasn't enough, she realized, remembering what her tutor had said. Part of the art of dancing was to converse well with your partner. And—she had to admit—she hadn't even tried to talk with him, but had spent her time peering at Shera and her partner, and laughing when their eyes met.

What will I talk about when I dance with Prince Lios? She burrowed into the pillow, sleepily wondering what he'd be like, and what she'd say, and what he'd say, until she slid into dreams.

Slowly the great forests of the east changed to rolling farmland. The air smelled much different than mountain air—like grass and herbs—and Rhis liked it very much. There were lots of gardens along their route, and Shera, who had learned much from the gardener in Gensam, gave Rhis names and properties of different plants. Rhis found herself gradually taking an interest as they compared size and hues of various blossoms. Reading about plants you've never seen is boring, but seeing gardens in all their brightness and variety was like discovering surprise after surprise. Beautiful surprises.

Finally they turned north, heading toward a more mountainous region. It did not make Rhis homesick—she was enjoying herself too much for that—but she loved the broad trees with their complicated leaves, so different than the ever-present pines of home.

The two days before they reached Eskanda caused the girls much excitement. By then they had gone through each other's wardrobe to determine which gown ought to be worn for their first appearance in company. In Rhis's mind was that mental image of the perfect princess Iardith. She did not really expect to make a stir (much as it was fun to imagine universal gasps of admiration when she first walked into the grand parlor), but she did want to do credit to Nym, so she tirelessly discussed the pros and cons of each outfit with Shera, who had the better knowledge of what was the very latest fad, and what wasn't.

At last their carriage rolled through the gates of Eskanda Palace, a vast structure built of a warm gold-veined marble that glowed in the westering sunlight. The sun was also reflected off hundreds of arched windows, which made the palace look like it was decorated with firestones. A magnificent garden of grand proportions made Shera draw in her breath in admiration. This kind of garden, she pointed out later, was only achieved after at least a hundred years of being constantly tended.

The garden was pretty, but Rhis saved her attention for the people. Not that many were in view, except for liveried servants moving back and forth. The courtyard was quite empty when their carriage clattered to a stop. The girls stepped out onto a mosaic pattern made of a variety of bricks of different shades. As they shook out their gowns they were approached by an impressive man who wore the blue and white of Vesarja's royal family. Otherwise, Rhis thought to herself, she would have thought him some royal relative.

He stopped to briefly address the girls' outrider, then came forward with stately step and bowed low. In a sonorous voice he said, "Prince Lios bids me welcome you to his home, Your Highnesses. If you will consent to follow me, I will show you to the quarters prepared for you."

"Thank you," Shera said in a small voice.

Gensam might be a lot more sophisticated than Nym, Rhis thought, but Vesarja and its royalty were even moreso. She kept resolutely silent as she followed behind the dignified steward.

Once inside, she stared in silent amazement. She'd thought the Royal Inn at Gensam's border fine, but it was nothing compared to this palace.

No stone was in evidence, except in carved columns supporting stairways, each of which was wide and curving. Those were all marble. The ceilings far overhead were splendidly painted with graceful decorative figures of intertwined plants and birds.

They progressed down several very long halls, up three flights of stairs, and at last the steward threw wide two carved doors and they walked into a large circular parlor with four great windows that looked out over the garden. The ceiling here was made of inlaid wood, in complicated geometric patterns. On the walls hung painted still lifes, and the furnishings were all carved and polished darkwood, with pale blue satin coverings.

"When you are ready to join the company, Your Highnesses," the steward said with another low bow, "here is the bell pull. A runner will conduct you."

He soon withdrew, and Shera said, "At least we don't have to disgrace ourselves stumbling about getting lost." She dashed to the window. "Oh, it's fabulous!" She whirled and clasped her hands. "I don't think I ever want to leave!"

"But we haven't met the people yet," Rhis said, feeling a tight sensation in her middle.

"Let's do it quickly," Shera said. "Before we lose our courage."

They found that the adjoining rooms were bedrooms, each with its own little bath chamber and dressing room. Keris was already in the one that had been selected for Rhis, laying out the gown she'd chosen for her first appearance.

Rhis's heart thumped as she got ready. She forced herself to sit patiently as Keris brushed out her long, straight hair and wove into it white ribbons embroidered with silver.

At last she was ready. Her gown was a very deep midnight blue, edged at neck and sleeves with silver-embroidered white lace. Shera appeared, wearing yellow, white, and gold, all trimmed with contrasting ribbons. Her rich curls hung down charmingly, only decorated with two tiny bows, one holding a lock just above one eye, the other at the back of her head. The girls admired each other, and then Shera reached for the bell pull.

The liveried runner, a very young girl, knocked a short time later. With a solemn face she bowed and silently indicated that they follow her.

Another long walk through increasingly splendid surroundings brought them at last to another set of high, carved doors. This time another liveried steward threw open the doors, and after a quick whisper from the runner (Shera didn't seem to notice, she was so busy peeking through the doors, but Rhis did) he announced the girls: "Their Highnesses Princess Rhis Lanvred of Nym, and Princess Shera Tevoriac of Gensam!"

Rhis stepped inside first. Her eyes were dazzled by what seemed to be thousands of crystal chandeliers. She realized that one wall in the chamber was mirrored, throwing back light and glitter, then she dared a glance at the assembled people.

Young faces, both male and female, stared back at her, some with smiles, some blank, some curious. Jewels gleamed in hair and on clothes, and here and there a fan waved slowly. She didn't have time to look any longer, for first she had to proceed down the length of the room toward an elegant chair higher than the others.

From this distance all she could see of Prince Lios was dark hair and a tunic of silver brocade.

"Oh," Shera breathed softly next to Rhis.

The girls walked toward the dais. Rhis looked at her toes, feeling intensely shy. But when they reached the end of the room, she forced her chin up, spreading her skirts and making the curtsey proper to a royal heir who was also her host.

Then she looked into dark-lashed eyes the color of chocolate, framed by glossy dark hair. Prince Lios smiled, a dashing smile in a face so devastatingly attractive that by the time Rhis had straightened up from her little curtsey, she had fallen happily and quite painlessly in love.

FOUR

She felt, she realized later, as if a boulder had dropped out of the sky and klonked her on the head—except nothing hurt. She just felt stunned.

Without once speaking she followed behind Shera, who was continuously looking about and whispering behind her fan. Not that Rhis heard a word. She was still seeing that handsome smile, those dark eyes framed by long dark lashes. Shera apparently recognized a few people, for she exchanged some words of greeting, and once or twice a wave of her fan and a smile. Rhis stood in the background, sneaking peeks back at Prince Lios whenever she thought that no one was looking her way.

He didn't look back at her after that initial smile, for which she was more grateful than not. Oh, it would have been nice if he'd taken one look and sent everyone away—or even if he'd stolen peeks at her, as she did of him—but she was incapable of doing anything but gawk helplessly. What could she possibly say to someone so handsome?

After a time a discreet bell sounded, and everyone moved off in one direction.

Servants sprang to open doors, and they passed through into a wonderful dining room built on two or three levels around an indoor stream, which appeared under one wall and disappeared out under another. In the middle was a waterfall-fountain, around which tables were set. Little trees and ferny flowering plants grew alongside the stream, lending their fragrance to the air.

The tables were all small, seating four. Shera and Rhis hung back, not sure what etiquette dictated here, until they were approached by two tall boys who looked older than Rhis.

"Your Highnesses," one of them said, bowing. "Welcome to Eskanda. Will you join us for supper?"

Shera smiled, her relief obvious. "Gladly!"

Rhis managed a tiny nod.

"This way," the first said. He was neatly though plainly dressed, a little taller than medium height, with a friendly face and his plain brown hair tied back instead of elaborately braided or decorated with gems. "Let us introduce ourselves. I'm Dandiar, Prince Lios's personal scribe, and this is Lord Halvic Barael, a cousin of the royal family."

"Very distant," Lord Halvic said with a grin. He was short and stocky, with a shock of dark red hair that probably would have stuck out like a brushfire if it hadn't been braided.

"Our job is to greet the newcomers," the scribe explained as he indicated a table near the stream.

"I like this job," Halvic added with a suave bow, before seating himself. "When the newcomers are ladies, and not more fellows."

Shera giggled, and Rhis grinned.

"We can also explain anything you'd like explained, and maybe tell you a few things to make it easier to get used to all these people," Dandiar went on. "For instance, the Prince decreed that no one uses titles. If everyone goes around *your highnessing* one other, they'll sound like a pit of snakes." He exaggerated the 's' sound, making both girls laugh. "So though I

greeted you as 'Your Highnesses' when you came in—all very
proper—from now on I'll call you Shera and Rhis." He looked
from one to the other, his friendly light brown eyes slightly
questioning.

"If truth be known, that's what we do in Gensam—when
we're not before my mother," Shera said with a smile. "She
insists on proper formality. And Rhis, up in those Nymish
mountains, only has her family to talk to and I don't think they
'Your Majesty' each other."

Rhis shook her head, not wanting to add that Elda had a
habit of using her full name and title when she was angry with
Rhis.

"There are some who don't like the informality," Halvic
said, as a servant came up and set dishes before each of them.
"But they comply."

While this was happening, Rhis stole quick peeks around
the room, and noted that Prince Lios was seated next to the
waterfall. At his table was a very tall boy dressed in black
velvet, which made quite a contrast to his long light blond hair
and pale skin. With them was a short girl with a very haughty lift
to her chin, and a fabulous gown of gemmed brocade, but she
was scarcely noticeable compared to the fourth, who had to be
Iardith. Her black hair flowed in a serene fall almost to the floor,
as ordered as her green velvet gown with its deceptively simple
silver embroidery. Her skin was the color of hot chocolate, with
a dusky rose tone beneath it—unlike Rhis's dull weathered-
wood brown. Iardith's long-lashed profile was toward Rhis—she
faced the prince—and she was as spectacularly beautiful from
the side as from the front.

With an inner sigh Rhis withdrew her gaze, noting that
those tables around the waterfall had been seated and served
first. So that was obviously the favorite place.

"Another rule." Dandiar's voice recalled her attention. "At breakfast and midday people may eat when they wish, and it's very informal. But at supper, we eat together, here, four to a table." He waved at the young ladies, then at himself and Halvic. "And you're supposed to eat with different people every night. In order to get to know everyone the more quickly."

Rhis wondered if Iardith obeyed that rule.

"Not that it's strictly enforced," Dandiar added. "But it is what Lios wants."

"Well, I'm for that," Shera said practically, picking up her fork and knife. "I'm here to have fun, and the more people you know, the more fun it is."

Rhis gave her little nod again, then took a bite of food. It was fish, in some kind of delicate sauce—delicious. Suddenly her appetite woke up, and she applied herself to the meal with more attention.

Conversation flowed around her, mostly Dandiar talking about the palace. He explained where everything sat, and Rhis tried to pay attention, but her mind kept wandering back to that table by the waterfall. She only permitted herself two more peeks, but both were sufficient to show that Prince Lios was thoroughly engrossed with Iardith, who managed fork, fan, and hair with a dainty grace that made Rhis sigh inwardly with envy and wish she'd practiced far more, instead of sneaking off to play ballads and read books.

When she turned her gaze away the second time, it was to find Dandiar watching her. She felt her cheeks redden, and bent her attention to the last of her food.

"Up there with the prince," Dandiar said easily, "are Princess Iardith of Arpalon and Lady Mera, daughter of the Duke of Wilfar Island. The fellow is Prince Jarvas of Damatras."

Shera's eyes went round. "Damatras?"

Dandiar's smile turned ironic at the corners. "Supposedly the war is over, and the two countries are at peace."

From what her father had said about that, Rhis didn't believe that the Damatrans were ever really at peace, but she didn't want to say it.

Dandiar looked her way, as if waiting for her to speak, but she just went on eating, trying hard to emulate Iardith's fine manner.

Shera shrugged. "I don't know. All I hear about is how much they like squabbling with everyone else. But I don't have to worry about that, I'm glad to say." She grinned unrepentantly. "That's the nice thing about not being the heir."

"So what would you like to hear about?" Dandiar asked. "The latest gossip?"

"We know all that," Halvic added, with a quirk to his brows.

Shera brightened. "Of course! Who's twoing with whom, and who is feuding with whom? I don't want to make any blunders," she added. "Besides, I like gossip."

"So do I," Halvic said, with a laughing glance at the scribe, who just shrugged and opened his hands. "Let's see . . . Prince Lios is not twoing with anyone, contrary to whatever you might hear. Sefan—heir to the dukedom of Lis—and Cria of Port Kelar are. Plenty of flirtations going on, but those change as fast as it takes to talk about them," Halvic said.

"Speaking of which," Dandiar added, "there's usually dancing directly after supper for anyone who wants. However in three days' time, the official celebration will be initiated with a masquerade ball. The theme is famous lovers, or famous heroes and heroines."

"Ballads," Shera breathed, and she giggled again, hiding her face behind her fan.

Rhis couldn't help a big grin, thinking how appalled Elda would be.

"And Lios," Dandiar said, waving his hand to encompass the entire room, "will manage to dance with every one of you girls."

Supper ended shortly afterward. Halvic offered to conduct Shera and Rhis to the salon cleared for dancing, but Dandiar excused himself, saying regretfully that he had duties.

Shera chose to go dancing. Rhis shook her head, preferring to retreat to her room for quiet. She didn't know anyone yet, and was frightened at the thought of standing around partnerless while Iardith danced (beautifully) with Prince Lios.

She wanted to sleep, but she was still awake when Shera came back well after the midnight bell had rung.

Shera came unceremoniously into Rhis's room and sat on the end of her bed. "It was wonderful," she declared, still breathless. "A full orchestra! They have one every night. Two new dances—I can show you in the morning. Easy, one like the *havan* and the other a step-and-circle dance, quite lovely, but dizzying. The prince brought it from overseas, someone told me. I had nine partners, and I liked every one. That Jarvas only danced once—with Iardith, of course—and spent the rest of the time propped against the wall with his arms folded, glowering at her partners. Only Lios had the courage, or maybe the indifference, to ignore him and dance with her twice. Of course she managed somehow not to look sweaty, or get her hair in a tangle," Shera added with disgust.

"Did she talk to you?" Rhis asked.

"Only to ask, in her most poisonous sweet voice, if we knew about the masquerade." Shera grimaced. "She knows quite well from her visit that my mother doesn't approve of dressing up as other people."

"Elda doesn't either," Rhis murmured. "But don't worry. Keris already found out, and she's hired seamstresses for us. All we have to do is choose who we want to be."

Shera sighed happily, lying back on the bed. "Well, if I'd known that, I could have given Iardith a mighty crisp answer. As well I didn't, though, I guess."

Rhis said in agreement, "Better we just appear in our masquerade costumes, as though we've had them all the time."

Shera grinned, and got to her feet. "That Keris of yours is a real treasure." She yawned. "I guess I'd better sleep, or I'll be pinch-faced and owl-eyed tomorrow, and I don't want that. There's to be horse-racing in the afternoon."

She wandered out, her gown trailing behind her, and Rhis resolutely closed her eyes and turned over.

Next morning, she was up and dressed fairly early. Shera was still soundly asleep, so Rhis rang for a runner to take her to breakfast.

"Can you explain the palace to me?" she asked the boy in livery who came to conduct her. "So I can learn it, and I won't have to ring that bell all the time."

The boy bobbed his head. "Main structure in this shape, your Highness," he said, forming his fingers into a square. "With smaller buildings joining the inside, like this." Now he formed a cross. "Those are all the grand salons." He pointed out each intersection as they walked, and Rhis studied them, memorizing landmarks. After breakfast, she decided, she'd just wander around and try to learn her way.

When they reached the bright, sunny parlor in which breakfast was served, she thanked the runner and wandered out. She found long tables set out on a terrace and more inside for those who didn't want to be in the outside air.

The morning was clear and cool on the terrace. Rhis found a side table with trays of tempting foods to choose from. When she'd made her selection she sat down alone at the end of a table where she could observe the rest of the terrace and the forested garden beyond.

Someone came and asked what she wanted to drink; soon she had creamy hot chocolate to warm her up.

There were very few people up as yet, she noticed. Several sat alone like she did. A group of three girls arrived together, and took a table across the terrace.

Then a slight stir went through the breakfasting people, and Prince Lios strode out onto the terrace, followed by a group of seven or eight, mostly boys. With them was Dandiar. The group circled around the prince, faces expectantly watching to see where he wanted to sit. He waved carelessly at one table just outside the terrace doors, and when the group moved to sit down, he tapped Dandiar on the shoulder and they walked across the terrace to stand by the low carved marble rail.

Rhis munched a biscuit as she idly watched them talking, the taller Lios bending his head to hear what his scribe was saying. She reached for another biscuit—everyone else was watching the two at the rail as well. What would it be like to be courted by Lios? He really was devastatingly handsome, she thought, admiring the cut of his green-and-white tunic that flattered his athletic body. He laughed suddenly, a loud, free laugh, then stopped, and cast a guilty look around. Had this prince been cautioned by tutors just as Rhis and Shera had that civilized people did not make a lot of noise while laughing? Rhis thoroughly enjoyed the idea. It made him seem a little more human.

Meanwhile, Dandiar laughed as well, though his was soundless; she only knew he was laughing because of his shaking shoulders, and the deep dimples flashing in his cheeks.

Servants, Rhis knew, learned how to be soundless—something that Elda approved of. Everybody in their proper place. Rhis had never dared to make friends with any of the few castle girls her own age.

Then the scribe bowed low and moved away, flashing one last smile over his shoulder. The prince grinned back. They were obviously good friends. So maybe 'proper place' wasn't always true any more than 'no proper princess likes ballads.'

Dandiar disappeared inside, and Lios rejoined his company, after smiling round the terrace at everyone—Rhis included. She felt her face heat up, but she managed to smile back. Was there something special in his smile to her? Did he linger just a little longer, or was it her imagination?

She watched him as she sipped chocolate, hoping he would turn and look again. She was so engrossed that when someone sat down across from her she was startled, and nearly dropped her cup.

"May I join you?" a male voice asked.

She looked up at a fellow with dark, curly hair and bright blue eyes.

"I'm Vors Admasos," he said. "You're Rhis of Nym, am I right?" When she nodded, he went on, "Shera told me about you last night. Said you love music. So do I! There's to be a concert after supper tonight. Singers all the way from Charas al Kherval, I'm told. Will you sit with me?"

"I'd be glad to," she said, surprised and flattered.

Vors sat down and dug into a plate piled high with food. "Had a little sword fighting practice this morning," he said. "Lios and a few others. Works up an appetite."

"Sword fighting? Did Lios win?" she asked, and tried not to blush.

"He's good," Vors admitted. "Strong. Good reach. I'll tell you who's really good, though, and that's Taniva of the High

Plains." He whistled softly. "I always heard those plains riders were half-barbarian, and I can well believe it. She rides like a windstorm, and she's death with the two blades." He waved beyond the rail. "There she goes!" He half rose up in his seat. "Got to see if she's barefoot again. Hates shoes. Guess that's formal wear up in those mountains." He laughed as he peered into the garden.

A tall girl with two long dark braids was just breaking off a crimson blossom from one of the flowering vines. She stuck it behind her ear, then moved out of sight at a brisk pace along the garden path. Rhis admired her brightly colored gown, very different from the others, but it suited Taniva's strong figure.

"Not that I mean everyone from mountain kingdoms is a barbarian," Vors said in haste.

Rhis snapped round, looking at Vors in question. Vors stared back at her in obvious consternation—yes, he *had* meant Nym!

"Well, it's been said about us in Nym," Rhis said, trying to decide how she felt about that. A barbarian, she decided, would get mad. But a polite ambassador for her kingdom would . . . turn the insult into a joke? "But I'd never go barefoot. Too cold."

"That's what I like, a girl with a sense of humor." Vors grinned, his face clearing. "Now. Music. Tell me what your favorites are."

They talked for the remainder of the breakfast. Rhis found that he knew very little of ballads, but he was familiar with other kinds of music.

He was nearly done with his food when a shadow fell across the table, and Rhis discovered Dandiar the scribe standing just behind her, a cup and saucer in one hand. "May I join you?"

"Of course," Rhis said, giving him a smile of welcome.

Vors got to his feet. "Tonight," he said to Rhis, and without a glance at the scribe, he walked away, leaving his unfinished food.

A servant appeared and quietly removed the plate as Dandiar sat down. His mouth quirked deeply at the corners.

Rhis stared after Vors, surprised at his rudeness. Was it so terrible to sit down to a meal with a scribe? Then she wondered if she had inadvertently disgraced Nym with her own compliance—but she remembered sitting with him the night before, and no one had given them odd looks. She also remembered Lios's behavior earlier. Though Elda might not approve, *he* obviously didn't think it so terrible to be seen talking to his scribe.

"I'm glad to discover that you can, in fact, speak," Dandiar said, smiling at her.

Rhis felt her cheeks burn. "Oh. Last night—I think everything was overwhelming," she said.

"Everything, or everyone? Or maybe just one?" Dandiar retorted in a good-humored voice. "Never mind, I won't tease you. It's to be expected."

Iardith swept out onto the terrace just then, followed by no fewer than five boys. Rhis thought privately that if it was 'expected' that the girls would react to Lios the way she had, the boys were just the same, it seemed, about the Perfect Princess.

Dandiar was smiling in a way that made her suspect he'd had the very same thought.

But all he said was, "Have you any questions? Is everything to your satisfaction?"

Rhis said, "More than satisfaction. I like everything I see. A question—well, is there also a library here?"

Dandiar looked a little surprised. "Nothing easier," he said. "If you're finished, I can show you how to get there from here."

They left the table and crossed the terrace. Dandiar pointed down the length of the building. "See the corner room? That's the library. It will be straight down the hall to your left when you go out. You came from the right."

"Down and to the left," Rhis repeated. "I can remember that. Thank you."

"If you do go in there, don't worry about the crowd of scribes. They won't disturb you, and your being there won't disturb them. Lios brought back a lot of books from his travels, and they are busy translating and making copies in our language."

"Other languages," Rhis said wonderingly.

She knew, of course, that people in Nym and Vesarja and the other countries on their subcontinent spoke the same tongue, though with some regional differences in pronunciation, and in idiom. Rhis also knew that over the land-bridge of Meshrec the big continent lay, and there people spoke several different tongues.

"It must be frightening, a little, to hear people speak but to not be able to comprehend them, or get them to comprehend you," she said.

"Oh, if you're quick, and pay attention, you learn," Dandiar responded in a light, careless tone.

Rhis studied him, impressed. Despite his airy manner, she knew that the study of other languages was not easy. He was just half a head taller than she, his eyes on a comfortable level. He had a steady, friendly gaze above a snub nose. "You went overseas as well?" she asked.

He lifted one shoulder. "We all did."

Of course the prince would travel with an entourage, she thought. "What was it like?"

"Very, very different from life here," he said with his quick grin. "Interesting, though. Shall I walk you to the library? I have to get to work."

Just then Rhis caught sight of Shera, who bustled toward them, her curls bouncing as she turned her head from side to side as she tried to take in who was here and who wasn't. "I think my cousin is coming to join me," she said. "Thank you anyway."

Dandiar gave her a little salute, a humorous gesture, and left.

"Well," Shera exclaimed, sinking down onto a chair. "I simply have to tell you about my dances last night. But first, any news? Did you get to talk to Lios yet?"

"No," Rhis said, laughing. "But news—yes." She thought of Vors, and the horse races at which she'd surely get to see Lios, at least, and about the library full of books. "Oh, Shera, I think it's going to be so much fun here. It'll be impossible to go home!"

FIVE

The girls walked out into the garden where they wouldn't be overheard. When they reached a little dell shaded by aromatic trees, Shera expertly hummed the tunes as she demonstrated the new dances. Rhis picked up the moves quickly. Then, encouraged by Shera, Rhis talked in tireless detail about Lios—the way he looked, how he had smiled at her at breakfast, and they speculated happily on what he might think and do.

They also talked a little about Vors. Shera explained that he had introduced himself to her during the dancing, asking a lot of questions about Rhis—about her home, her likes and dislikes.

"I don't know if he fell in love with you straight off at dinner yesterday, but he seemed might-y interested," Shera finished briskly.

Fell in love? Rhis stared at some nodding blossoms. "Well, I don't know how he could, since I didn't even see him, much less speak to him . . ." Then she thought about her own reaction to Lios, and how he hadn't noticed her. Then she shook her head. "No, I can't believe it. I'm not the sort people fall instantly in love with—not with Iardith around, and that beautiful one with the red hair and the dimples in her cheeks. I saw her at breakfast this morning. She's just as pretty as Iardith."

"That's the one who snabbled up the Duke's son," Shera said. "She was pointed out to me last night. She's eighteen, almost nineteen, the duke the same age. Two days' acquaintance, and he wants to marry her! But she's not given him an answer, I was told. Perhaps she's got hopes of Lios as well."

"What else did you hear?" Rhis asked.

Shera shrugged, grinning. "Oh, a whole lot of gossip about this and that person, but I expect it all changes as fast as you hear it, if it's anything like our court at home, when everyone is there. They are all so careful with proper protocol when my mother is on the throne, but as soon as she leaves, they start flirting as much as they can!"

"Doesn't your father mind?" Rhis asked.

"I don't think he ever notices. He's too busy talking with his old cronies, or playing crumback."

Rhis recognized the name of a popular card-and-marker game. Elda, like her mother the Queen of Gensam, did not approve of games, and Rhis's father had no interest in them, so no one in Nym's castle played them. Apparently the Queen's consort, Shera's father, was exempt from the rule—at least when the Queen wasn't around.

Her thoughts were interrupted by laughter.

The girls had wandered onto the grassy part of the garden just below the terrace outside the dining area. High, female voices laughed again, and Rhis looked up at the terrace. Iardith was surrounded by a half-circle of laughing girls. Iardith hunched her shoulders, an ungraceful movement that was quite startling, and she made one hand into a claw as she gestured wildly.

"Um! Oom! Ze ribbon she is tied on my nose!" Iardith declared with a heavy accent. "Nose? Toes? Ooom! Boo! What say I? Say I wrong? Boo!"

Carefully modulated waterfalls of laughter met this, led by the beautiful redhead who had snabbled a duke after only two days.

The thin, dainty Grand Duchess of the Isle of Wilfen said in her fluting drawl, "Seeing that one is scrawny as a nestling, shouldn't that be *coo coo*?"

Rhis grinned at the gales of laughter that comment caused. Did Iardith have a sense of humor, at least? She would never have dared clowning like that, not in this company. Maybe the Perfect Princess was bearable after all.

"A sense of humor goes a long way toward making someone likable," Rhis said, trying to be even-handed. The truth was, she was in a fair way of being jealous of Iardith, but was fighting against it. "Sidal often said that to me, and I think she's right."

Shera's lips pursed. "No need to mention that my sister Elda hasn't one. Not even the tiniest speck of one."

"Well, but she's *dignified*," Rhis said.

"Yes, and as we all know, a prince chooses dignity above all else in his future queen," Shera said, as more laughter, like the sudden chattering of birds, brought their attention back to the terrace.

Iardith gestured imperiously, and her admiring crowd, all older girls, followed her inside.

"Probably looking for Lios. Speaking of flirtations, why don't we walk out to the big garden where they are going to hold the race? We can get a good spot to watch from," Shera suggested.

Rhis had no objections to anything that might get them near Lios, so they made their way slowly around the extensive gardens of Eskanda Palace.

By that time most of the prince's guests had begun gathering as well—those who were not going to compete.

When Rhis saw the fine, glossy-maned horses, she felt a strong twinge of envy. She'd never learned to ride one. They were rare in the mountains, and besides, Elda considered horseback riding vulgar and barbarian. Proper people were drawn decorously in carriages.

Rhis did know how to ride a hill pony, but no one rode those in the flatlands. They weren't as fast as these long-legged, high-stepping animals, but they were sturdy and didn't mind the cold weather. Rhis listened in silence to knowledgeable discussion of the horses' attributes and shortcomings, strongly suspecting that the Nymish hill ponies—were they to suddenly appear here—would just be laughed at.

Before the races began, increasing clouds slowly darkened the sky, whipping up a chilly wind. People ignored the changing weather as they watched expectantly.

Rhis peered at the starting line, where riders and their nervous mounts milled around, or walked back and forth. "What's going on?" she finally asked Shera, who shrugged.

A boy overheard, and said, "Stablehands have to finish laying the course. They're going to ride round the perimeter of the estate."

Shera pursed her lips. Remembering the long ride up to the palace once the girls' carriage had rolled through the gates, Rhis wondered if the perimeter was quite a distance.

"Rough terrain," a girl said. "I can ride, but not like that."

"We ride zo creeping, wiss ze mountains. Om! I watch. No ride."

Rhis gasped, and spun around.

The speaker was a short thin girl with a cloud of wheat-colored hair, walking with her arm linked through that of Prince Lios. She wore a fabulous gown embroidered in bright colors, with bunches of ribbons at arms, waist, and down the front of the gown. She had a round, pleasant face, with slightly protuberant light blue eyes.

Lios stopped, bowed, and said, "Give me a favor, cousin?"

This girl untied one of the ribbons from her sleeves and handed it to Lios. She grinned, a wide, laughing grin, as he bent down for her to tie it round his arm.

"That must be his cousin from the Isle of Ndai," Shera whispered. "I've seen her around, but never to hear or speak to. How fun, to come from such a mysterious place, full of pirates and magic!"

Rhis stared at the girl, who was shorter than Shera, and even skinnier than Rhis. Ice seemed to trickle through her veins when she recognized the accent, and the peculiar speech. Ndai, though relatively close, had been settled by different people, and then had endured a long history of battles with pirates. They had a separate language, Rhis had learned in history lessons. So Iardith hadn't been clowning, she'd been mimicking this princess—making game of her.

"You ambulate, Couzzin. Um! Um! Um, boh, I forget ze word. Conquest zis race!" cried the princess from Ndai.

Rhis stole a look, and sure enough, she saw Iardith and her red-haired friend laughing behind their fans. Over the buzz of general talk, Rhis thought she heard a faint "Um!"

"I'm off!" Lios stated, and strode away through the trees.

The noon bells echoed from the far towers, and then, closer by, someone blew a horn. They all turned their attention to the grassy field that had been chosen for the start and finish. Rhis hugged her arms close, glad of her long sleeves, for the air was getting chillier. She felt cold inside, too, at Iardith's cruelty. She hoped the little Ndaian princess hadn't heard any of it.

The racers appeared, all mounted up, and urged their horses into a long, ragged line. Prince Lios rode in the middle, his hair whipping in the wind as he sat easily astride his large, reddish-brown horse.

When the horn blew, he bent forward slightly and his horse sprang into a gallop. For a moment he was lost in the crowd, but shortly thereafter Rhis saw him again, riding like he'd been born on horseback. He was one of the five at the lead by the time they reached the end of the field, and swept round a corner by a pond.

The crowd of watchers started leaving, some to walk through the palace to witness the race at the halfway point, some to retreat inside as large, cold raindrops began to spatter their faces and clothes. Shera touched Rhis on the shoulder.

"I'm going in," she said, shivering. "I can hear about it afterward. Want some hot chocolate?"

"I'll meet you," Rhis replied. "I'm used to cold, and I want to see the end."

Shera smiled, hunching her shoulders. "Then you can tell me everything. If you don't freeze first." She hurried up a trail toward the palace.

When at last the racers neared the end of the course the rain was coming down in earnest, and Rhis was almost alone, standing on a little rise to watch them come round the last sweep of trail before they reached the field where they had begun. A few others stood about, some under a rain canopy set up by servants.

Rhis preferred staying where she was, so she could see the winner. She was sure that Lios would be first; her heart soared within her at the sight of Lios and his horse leaping so effortlessly over a low hedge, neck and neck with two other riders.

They vanished behind some trees and then, two of the horses reappeared again, their riders bent low. One rider wore bright clothes, her dark braids flapping on her thin back; the other's pale yellow hair was plastered to forehead and neck. Lios lagged a full horse's length behind the two leaders.

Taniva of the High Plains sent a grim look over at Jarvas, who sneered back, then dug his heels into his horse's side. The animal seemed to tighten all over. Rhis winced, knowing it must hurt, but the horse suddenly leaped, sailing over another hedgerow, and Taniva's horse was airborne a moment later.

Jarvas reached the field first—just barely. He slowed his horse gradually as he rode straight for the stable. Taniva followed without looking back.

Lios galloped to the finish line right after, and then more appeared, all riding at the same speed. When they finished, they were laughing and calling mock-insults at one another as they brought their sweaty, blowing mounts round to the small knot of people gathered—the cold wind tugging and snapping their clothes and hair—to watch the stragglers finish up the race. Lios was at the center of the crowd.

Lios joked with his friends. Rhis didn't know any of the people any more than she knew their past experiences. Feeling closed out, she left the garden and trudged back against the wind to the palace.

With her tousled hair redone and warm, dry clothes on, she rejoined the party, which was gathered on the windowed terrace adjacent to the garden. They were all still talking about the race, mostly teasing the losers.

Iardith and her admirers all crowded around Lios, of course, and around pale Jarvas of Damatras, who had won. But Taniva, who had nearly beat Jarvas, wasn't included. She stood at a window alone at the other end of the terrace, staring out at the rain.

As everyone wandered about, talking or helping themselves to the trays of hot snacks the servants brought in, Rhis gathered her courage and made her way to the tall princess in the bright vest, layered skirts, and crimson blouse. Vest, blouse, and the top layer of her skirt were edged with tiny chimes; in her black sash she wore a spectacularly handsome knife with a black and silver hilt. The sheath was studded with brilliant blue gems.

"Very fine riding today, Taniva," she said.

The princess turned her head and studied Rhis for a long moment. She had long, slightly slanted greenish gray eyes, broad cheeks, and a flat nose. Her skin was more pale in color than the lowlanders' and Rhis's, with a yellowish cast. It was a better color, Rhis secretly thought, than Jarvas's pinkish pale. Rhis thought her face striking, like her clothes, which tinkled faintly when she moved.

"I do not know you?" Taniva asked. Her accent was strong.

"I'm Rhis. Of Nym. Southern mountains," Rhis added awkwardly.

Taniva smiled, and her face was transformed. "Ah, *mountains!* Then you too must feel this place a cage. Pest! I wish to go home. But I promised to come. So I stay."

"You don't enjoy it here?" Rhis asked.

"Maybe I do, if . . ." Taniva shook her head. "No. To complain is to whine like a zeem-bug. No one wants them around. You are not afraid to be seen talking to me?" Her lips curled.

"Why should I be? Do you kick people?"

"No. Nor do I stab, with the words," Taniva added.

Now Rhis knew what the princess was talking about. And probably who.

"You're too good with a sword," Rhis said, grinning as she remembered her conversation the night before.

"Have to be—" Just then Taniva gave a stiff nod.

Rhis turned. The blond Jarvas, still surrounded by Iardith's crowd, raked his pale gaze down Taniva. His eyes narrowed when they stopped at Taniva's jeweled knife. He gave a slow nod, unsmiling, over the short red-haired girl's head. Then he turned back to the beautiful Iardith.

"There is an enemy," Taniva said, waving a callus-palmed hand toward Jarvas, then placed it on the blue-hilted knife in her sash. "Our people are enemies. We know it, but we understand one another. That Iardith, now, I do not understand."

Rhis remembered the two or three times her eyes had met Iardith's. Each time the Princess had turned away dismissively. Rhis had assumed it was just because Rhis was a stranger, hadn't been introduced. Now she wondered if it was because she was younger, and plain, from a small kingdom.

"I've never spoken to her," Rhis admitted.

"You have not enough importance," Taniva said. Her tone was too matter-of-fact to be insulting. She was making an observation, and Rhis ducked her chin in acknowledgement, not particularly happy to find her thoughts corroborated. But it was probably right.

Taniva gave the garden view a brooding glower. She had little etiquette. Her face was as expressive as her voice, and she obviously said what she thought.

Rhis tried to think of another subject, something to make the girl smile again, but Taniva turned her head, a quick, wary movement; a moment later Rhis registered the approach of footsteps. Taniva's face cleared, and she even smiled again, a slashing, flashing smile that made her look very handsome to Rhis's eyes. "Ah! It is the little scribe, who knows my land so well."

Rhis whirled around, delighted to see Dandiar, one of whose brows arched just slightly at the word 'little.' Taniva and he were the same height, but it was obvious the princess was used to very tall men.

"I came to tell you that everyone is moving to the dining room." The scribe pointed with his chin over his shoulder.

Taniva hesitated, her dark gaze going from Rhis to the door, and Rhis waved. "Come sit with us. Well, with me. Usually I sit with Shera, my cousin. She likes music, as I do."

"Gensam." Taniva gave an abrupt nod. "More mountains. You ride in your mountains? No pony-games, no?"

Dandiar said, "Nym has no highlands. It's all either up or down. Gems, that they've got. And some infamous old mines, sites of some agreeably bloody wars, if you like that kind of thing."

Taniva grinned fiercely.

Rhis realized that the scribe and the moody princess had established a good understanding, and she spoke on impulse. "Have you duties to attend to?"

Dandiar's face was suddenly blank, his voice very polite. "You are inviting me to go find some?"

Rhis felt her neck go hot. "No! Opposite! I was hoping, well, that you might want to sit with us. You know all about our kingdoms, and you talk so easily with—uh, others—" She realized she was rambling awfully, and thought with an inward wince of Elda's disapproval at her utter lack of grace and poise. Now not just her face burned, but her ears and neck. Ugh!

But Dandiar's quick smile, his swift gesture toward the door, somehow made it all right. He obviously understood, and Rhis thought gratefully that she knew the reason why the handsome Prince Lios had made him his personal scribe.

The three followed the crowd into the dining room as outside rain drummed hard against the windows. They sat on the periphery of the crowd, near the windows, to which Taniva's gaze more than once strayed. But once Shera and another girl, whom she introduced as Carithe, had joined them, the talk got more lively as they described parties in the past that the weather had made into total disasters.

Everyone had something to contribute, even Taniva, who uttered her short, breathy chuckle as she talked about a horse race once that ended up with everyone mired in the mud. Dandiar described a learning picnic organized by the royal tutor for the prince, his cousins, and some visiting boys that ended up with them chasing all their wind-whipped papers all the way across a garden into the king's prize prickly shrubs. The resulting howls could be heard in the Royal Chambers, where a visiting ambassador thought he was hearing the torture of prisoners, and almost caused an international incident.

Taniva snickered. "But then, these princes. They did not chase. You scribes did the work. And the yellings."

Dandiar lifted his hands. "What can I say? The princes did get plenty of laughs out of it. So we earned our pay that day. We were useful *and* entertaining."

Intermittently during the talk and laughter Rhis was aware of some exchanged looks between Carithe and Shera, their eyes crinkling, their mouths striving for somberness. It seemed the two girls had some secret together.

Halvic appeared, friendly as always, with two or three other guests in tow—all new arrivals. When Rhis saw shy smiles and averted eyes, and remembered how she'd felt on her arrival—and at the end of the race that morning—she did her best to welcome the newcomers, and learn their names.

As the newcomers joined the talk, she realized that she was having more fun now than she'd had yet. Maybe the perfect party had less to do with everyone being beautiful and fashionably dressed, and more to do with everybody having a good time, talking and laughing? And of course dancing.

The talk shifted from weather to riding to horses and then to life in the mountains—and back to weather. Everyone had stories to tell about famous winters high up, when snow had blocked them in for what seemed ages. Shera told some very funny stories about tricks her dreamy uncle had pulled on some of the stuffier courtiers, which set them all to laughing; they were soon joined by three or four boys, one of whom kept trying—in a shy way that caused sympathetic pangs in Rhis—to talk to the impervious Taniva.

Shera and one of the new boys, a thin, pale-haired fellow named Glaen, kept exchanging mock compliments that were really insults, keeping everyone within earshot in a fizz of hilarity.

It was getting harder to hear everyone. The conversation began breaking into little groups when a horn tooted for attention, and a herald announced that the singers from the south would not arrive in time for their concert, as a bridge had washed out on the main road a day's ride south. Therefore the usual dancing would take place.

So everyone rose to go in to the great salon adjoining for the impromptu dance. Rhis realized with surprise that her group had somehow become the largest in the room, and judging from the laughter, was having the most fun.

The group found an empty corner with seats enough for everyone. Out on the floor, a number of couples had already lined up for one of the dances.

"Your eyes," Glaen said, "—as beautiful as ice at the bottom of a well—entreat me to invite you to partner me in the promenade."

Shera swept a mock curtsey. "Delightful notion, if only to hear again the entrancing knocking of your knees."

"Beauteous princess! Singeth like the frog o' morning."

"Handsome heir-to-a-barony! Speaketh like unto the cricket o' eve!"

Dandiar neatly sidestepped a slow clump of people, leaving the tall, shy Lord Somebody next to Taniva.

"M-may . . ." the poor fellow murmured.

Taniva was looking about—she obviously didn't think he was talking to her.

"May I . . ."

Dandiar glanced at Rhis, his eyes so obviously verging on laughter she muffled a giggle into her sleeve. Dandiar then flicked a look toward the dancers, and his brows arched in question.

She held out her hand, and Dandiar said just a little louder than necessary, "Taniva, why don't you and Breggan here join us in starting a second line?"

Taniva looked bewildered, then shrugged. "Dancing," she said, as though it was as strange and new an idea as balancing peas on their noses. She seemed to be completely unaware of the grateful smile on poor Breggan's face.

As the four walked out to begin a new line, others followed behind them. Rhis used the opportunity to whisper to her partner, "That was smooth. How I wish I had your poise!"

"Oh, it's trained into us," Dandiar said, with a smile.

"Then maybe that's what my parents ought to have done," Rhis said with a sigh. "Sent me to a scribe school. I could even have learnt other languages."

"Was your education so poor, then?" Dandiar asked as they extended their hands, hers on his, and pointed their right toes forward.

"Yes," Rhis began, but bit back the usual list of complains. She thought of Elda, and Sidal, and added contritely, "No. It's just that I paid little heed to what bored me, and instead I spent my time with what I liked doing. Such as sitting in my

tower with my tiranthe and my ballads—" She remembered then
that princesses were not supposed to like either of those things.

Dandiar didn't appear to notice. As the musicians in the
gallery began the opening promenade, he said, "You wouldn't be
the first one in this room, boy or girl, to have spent more time
avoiding learning than in mastering what the tutors came to
teach."

"Perhaps," she said, "if I'd been the heir, I might have
been more diligent about current politics, trade laws, and
treaties. My little niece is so serious in her studies, but from
babyhood she's heard that she will one day be queen."

"Heirs do grow up hearing about their responsibilities,"
Dandiar acknowledged. Another quick look, one of mild
question.

"My sister-by-marriage seldom corrects her daughter,"
Rhis said, thinking back further. "Doesn't have to, because she's
so very perfect. But once she did, saying that Shera's lightest
statement might affect lives unseen."

"You didn't think you might need the same knowledge in
the future?" Dandiar asked.

Rhis thought back about all those reminders of her duty
in making a good marriage. "I guess I never thought at all, past
what I would have liked to happen," she admitted.

Dandiar grinned. "Who our age ever does, unless forced
to?" He added, "How old are you, anyway?"

"Sixteen," she admitted. She was tempted for a moment
to claim an older age, but resisted.

"Just what I guessed," he said.

"And you?" she asked, relieved that she'd stayed with
the truth.

"Twenty." He grinned.

Rhis grinned back, a little surprised. She suspected that she and Shera were among the youngest guests—and that that didn't add to their veneer of sophistication. Couldn't be helped.

With an inward sigh she dismissed the thought. She swept her skirts away from his feet as she twirled under his arm, and then stepped across to wait for his bow. Dandiar, she realized, was quite good at dancing. She was about to compliment him, when she remembered what she'd said earlier about his poise, and his response, which had not been pleased, it had been polite.

She realized suddenly, and uncomfortably, that she never would have said such a thing to, well, Prince Lios, for example. Had she been guilty of condescension? Yes. She would never compliment another princess on her training. Eugh! *Worse* than Elda! Even worse than Iardith's deliberate snubs because it had been unthinking.

The dance ended then, and Dandiar bowed, and she curtseyed, and he gave her his quick smile before moving off, his gaze going this way and that. Checking the room, seeing that all went smoothly for his master, she knew. He obviously felt no animosity toward her—probably didn't even remember what they'd talked about two breaths after the conversation, for she, too, was part of his duties.

Rhis watched him go, her thoughts impossibly tangled.

SIX

"Carithe has the most wonderful idea," Shera said, laughing behind her fan. "We're going to get up a play!"

"A play?"

"She found out that the players who were supposed to come have been delayed by this awful rain, and so we're going to do one ourselves, and surprise the others.

"When?"

"Oh, not until after the masquerade. No one can talk about anything else. After that they'll be bored, and looking for the next thing, and we'll be it. Anyway, you know more about plays than anyone, and so you could help us pick the best. Will you join us?"

"Of course," Rhis said. "Though I've read all the plays Sidal has brought back from her travels, that doesn't mean I'd be a good performer."

"You at least have a pretty singing voice."

"Yours is better," Rhis said.

Shera shrugged. "I'm not all that good, I just seem to keep harmony. As for the rest of us, I don't know how good any of us will be, but one thing for certain, it ought to be quite fun, if we choose the right play. Vors said he'd join in if you would, and we've got several others."

Vors himself appeared a moment later, just ahead of Halvic, and the girls moved out onto the floor for the next dance.

The waltos—the new dance from foreign lands—swiftly became Rhis's favorite, and apparently many others felt the same. Couples circled round and round the floor, stepping and gliding. Rhis turned to admire a couple who danced straight down the middle, whirling expertly, then realized that the pretty golden braid-loops on the girl belonged to that princess from Ndai.

She felt a tug on her arm. Vors pulled her into the dance, and they galloped with enthusiasm, until the last echo of the melody died away and Rhis was breathless with laughter.

"Want another turn?" Vors asked.

"I need something to drink." Rhis flicked open her fan and tried to cool her face.

"Now that was a romp," Vors said. "Did you see how many were staring at us? At you, I should say. They all think I'm the luckiest fellow on the floor!"

"I was too dizzy to see anything," Rhis admitted, gulping in air. She flushed with delight at his compliment. "But it was fun."

"You're a nacky dancer," Vors said. "Best I've seen!"

Rhis sketched a curtsey in thanks, but as Vors walked away to get them something to drink, the glow of pleasure at the idea of 'everyone' watching in admiration faded. Vors's compliment bothered her; after a moment she realized it reminded her of her mistake with Dandiar. Or was it a mistake?

"Here you go." Vors handed her a crystal glass.

"Thanks." She frowned at the punch. Vors had just given her a compliment, and he'd done it with admiration—with exaggeration, too, she had to admit. It was obvious at a single glance that not 'everyone' was watching. But wasn't that the kind of thing you did when flirting? Exaggerated compliments and admiration were definitely a part of flirting. She hadn't been flirting with Dandiar, though, so—

"I wish," Vors said, breaking into her thoughts, "you'd promise me all your dances. But if not, at least the first dance of the masquerade, or I shall die of disappointment. Surely you would not be so cruel?"

There it was again, that flirting tone.

Rhis knew she was supposed to say something flirty back. Like what? Some kind of pretend cruelty, or an exaggerated compliment of her own? Nothing came to her mind, and she mumbled, feeling awkward, "Oh, the masquerade first dance is easy enough—but as for all the others, I do so like to dance with as many people as I can."

"Well, that's to your credit," Vors replied, and he took her hand with the fan still gripped in it, and bowed over it, pressing a light kiss on her wrist. "You're kind to all—and so I told them." He shrugged one shoulder, tipping his head backward.

Rhis said, confused, "Told who? What?"

"Oh, some of the others. You know. Some thought it odd—something maybe that's done in the high mountains, where—that is. Your chatting with the barbarian princess, and dancing with the scribe." He looked at the chandelier, at the marble floor, at people sitting nearby, but not at her, while he tried to avoid telling her—she realized slowly—that people had talked about her. And not in a good way. "But I told them all that's just your way."

She turned to Vors, more confused than before. His blue eyes were steady, his whole face smiling—as if he expected her gratitude. He was proud of having defended her!

Except why should he defend her? Was dancing with a scribe, one who was obviously the prince's friend, a breach of etiquette?

"Taniva is interesting. And Dandiar's a good dancer," she said, trying to get at the truth without making things even more awkward.

Vors shrugged, obviously not interested. "So are any number of us, but you showed a nicety of manners in dancing with a scribe, and so I will maintain even at sword point." There it was—flirting again.

Rhis drank her punch, set the cup down, and then waved her fan again, glad to be busy while her thoughts stumbled between too many subjects. Vors was obviously waiting for some kind of answer. Gratitude, that was what he wanted, or praise, for his tone made it clear he'd done something for her. But what, exactly?

It was impossible to think—and then she didn't have to, for tall, thin, pale-haired Glaen appeared, muscling along another tall boy who hung back, looking uncomfortable. Rhis recognized him as the shy one who'd danced with Taniva.

"C'mon, Vors," Glaen said, jerking his chin over his shoulder. "Let someone else in." Glaen almost shoved the tall, blushing boy into Rhis's arms as he said, "How about a trot round the room with ol' Breggo here? He doesn't blab much, but he's a go on the floor."

Rhis promptly held out her hand, at least as relieved to get away from the awkward conversation with Vors as she was to help out shy Breggan. He bowed over her hand. As they moved away, Rhis caught sight of a very annoyed glance from Vors.

Was he *jealous?* Rhis felt her insides swoop. Imagine anyone being jealous over her! She mentally considered her image in the mirror, and wondered how anyone could find her so beautiful as to fall instantly in love from across a room. But then she thought about some of the twoing couples mentioned in

Shera's gossip. They seemed ordinary, much like she was—so who could say what made people fall in love?

And anyway, wasn't it supposed to be both ways? She liked Vors, but she wasn't in love with him. He didn't make her feel the least bit of invisible-boulders-on-the-head when she looked at him, and she wasn't longing for him to speak to her. And though his compliments were very nice indeed, the real truth was, somehow she didn't find him very interesting beyond that. She didn't really *know* him.

She hoped, suddenly, that he wasn't really in love with her, that he was only flirting, because one thing she did know: she was not going to feign an interest in any fellow just because he showed an interest in her. Especially when all they talked about were her interests, so he could compliment them, and then she had to thank him, and then he'd brag a little about what he'd been doing but then right away compliment her again, round and round. Limp limp limp.

The music had begun, and her feet had carried her into the dance. She remembered abruptly where she was, and she hoped she hadn't been rude. Breggan wasn't even looking at her; his gaze was somewhere over to the left, and when they'd finished a twirl, there was Taniva.

She repressed an urge to giggle, and kept her attention on the music and her steps.

"Did I make a mistake in dancing with Dandiar?" Rhis asked later, when the two girls were sitting in their nightdresses on Rhis's bed.

"What?" Shera asked, blinking.

"Dandiar. Scribe. Promenade. Vo—someone hinted that, well, others disapproved."

Shera shook her head. "Several of the scribes have been dancing, riding, so forth. I've seen Dandiar dancing with everyone—even Iardith."

"Oh, well, that settles it!" Rhis lifted her hands. "If *she* does it, then it must be the fashion!"

Shera laughed. "Only once, that I've seen, and she looked mighty miffed. So I don't think scribes have become the fashion yet! Lios handed her off to him during the taltan, at the partner exchange part, then went off to get something to drink."

Rhis cast a mock sigh. "Poor Iardith!"

Shera snickered, then hunched a little as thunder crashed outside. The rain increased to a roar. "As for dancing with the scribe, why not? The ones we see mixing about are surely born into families of minor rank. Vors is very rank-conscious."

"Yes." Rhis winced.

"Does it bother you, my comment about Vors?" Shera looked contrite.

"Well, no, it bothers me that I've been guilty of the same snobbery." And Rhis told Shera what had happened.

Shera listened in silence, then shook her head, her curls bouncing. "I think you are being too scrupulous, is what I think. The fact is, you *are* a princess, and he *is* just a scribe. Rank is rank. People expect certain kinds of behavior. Downright rudeness, now, would be inappropriate—but there are some who don't even hold to that."

"Like Iardith, making game of that princess with the accent. Somehow you don't expect that from someone older. It seems crueler, somehow."

"Oh, yes," Shera said, rolling her eyes. "Didn't I tell you that Iardith is mean? As for that princess, I talked to her a little. Name is, um . . ." Shera pursed her lips. "Yuzhoo. No, Yuzhyu. Yoozh-h-h . . . yuh! It's hard to say it right! No wonder she has trouble with our language! Anyway, Lios introduced her to

Carithe, and she wants to be in the play. I didn't know what to say! She seems very nice, but oh, she speaks our language so badly! One can't help but laugh at some of her mistakes. I don't know what I ought to do, because if we give her a part, I can just see Iardith and Hanssa and their friends laughing at us all. Ought I to tell her the play is full?"

Rhis thought about the princess's merry face, then shook her head. "Give her a small part. We can always coach her to say her words perfectly. Memorizing is so much easier than conversation."

"Ah. True. And perhaps I can find a play that has a foreign person in it . . ."

Shera went on, trying different ideas, but Rhis didn't listen. Her mind had gone right back to the previous conversation. Shera hadn't really sounded interested—she was comfortable with her ideas about rank being rank.

Is it because my mother was not even remotely wellborn? Rhis thought. Sidal also treated people with respect that had nothing to do with rank, and everything to do with individual merit. Yes, that was her mother's term. *Merit.* You weren't given merit along with a crown and velvet clothes, if you were born a princess. You had to earn it, same way anybody else did.

Rhis stared at the window, against which runnels of rain streamed down, gold-lit from the lamps.

Shera had stopped talking—and she wasn't even humming. She was looking at Rhis with a puzzled, narrow-eyed study.

Rhis tumbled into quick speech. "One thing for certain. Dandiar is more fun to talk to than Vors, lord or not."

"Still thinking about that?" Shera gave Rhis a funny sort of a half smile. "I'm hope you weren't upset with my comment about Vors," she added.

Rhis gazed at her. "This is the second time you've said that—or something like it. You know something."

Shera shrugged. Too quickly.

"You are! You're hinting about something! Come out with it."

"I'm not sure," Shera said in a slow voice—not one of conviction, but the sort of tone a person uses who is determined to at least sound like she's being fair. "It could be he's truly in love with you—and I wouldn't be surprised, for any fellow with taste—"

"Skip the flowery talk," Rhis said.

"He's been asking about Nym. I really noticed it during the dance tonight. He was asking me if the royal family really is as wealthy as rumor has it. More about the diamond mines. Who owns them. If you have any other brothers and sisters. Things like that. The other night he just asked about you—but tonight he wanted to know all about what wealth you have."

Rhis felt her insides swoop again, but this time it was a nasty feeling, like slipping on a rock near the edge of a cliff. "He thinks I'm rich," she said. "That is, he knows I'm rich. He wants a rich princess," she added, her middle feeling the chill of winter, "So *that's* why all those compliments and things. The— the flirting. Is that it, flirting is really just fake compliments and smiles and, well, lies? Because he's not interested in me, but my inheritance."

Shera looked hurt. "I'm sorry."

Rhis hugged her arms tight against her. "It's much better to know. *Much* better. Though it still hurts." She drew in a breath, trying to steady her feelings. "Now. Tell me more about the play." And this time she made herself listen.

"Well, we haven't decided yet. We're all to try to find one we like, and meet the day after the Masquerade to pick among our favorites."

Rhis was glad she knew where the library was. "I know what I'll look for," she said. "Something romantic, not tragical, and not a war-play, because I don't know anything about sword-fighting."

"That's what all the boys will be seeking out," Shera predicted. "We need to find one that has good parts for girls." Thunder crashed again, and she ducked her head as the windows rattled. "I'm going to bed and bury myself under the covers," she announced. "I hate thunder!" On those words, she flitted out the door to her own room.

Rhis lay awake for a while longer, thinking. She rather liked thunder. It reminded her of the sudden storms at home.

Besides, thunder suited her mood. So Vors had been flirting for a purpose that had nothing to do with her, despite all those compliments.

I would be in love with Lios even if he wasn't a prince, she thought firmly. She imagined his tall, handsome form in— well, a scribe's clothes, and he looked just as tall and handsome.

So there.

She flung herself over, pulled the pillow round her head, and tried to go to sleep.

The next morning she was late to breakfast because her maid needed to fit her masquerade gown to her. Rhis was delighted to discover that she was going as Eranda Sky-Born, a fabled princess from another world who had come, as a formidable mage, to right any wrongs she saw.

Rhis didn't believe for one moment that Eranda—if she were even real—had been tall and skinny with plain brown locks, but she was more than happy with her gown, which was made of floating drapes with tiny beads winking here and there among the folds. It was a very old-fashioned style, and Rhis liked herself in it.

After the fitting, she skipped down to breakfast, sitting with Carithe, Shera, Glaen, Breggo, and a growing group of friends, everyone talking at once.

Lios appeared at the door. Rhis happened to look up, and when she saw him glance their way, she flushed.

But just past her shoulder silk rustled and Iardith walked by, her expensive scent drifting on the air. The red-haired Hanssa minced beside her, gemmed gown whispering.

With supreme confidence the two walked up to Lios, slid their arms expertly through his, and led him firmly to their own exclusive table—a small one, deliberately chosen to keep down the number who could sit there.

Then Iardith stopped short.

Shera stopped talking, and watched in the same direction Rhis watched.

At the exclusive table, two of the three empty seats had been taken by Dandiar and one of the newest arrivals, a shy girl named Thirash, from one of the islands.

Iardith stepped away from Lios, whom Hanssa walked with to the waterfall.

Dandiar was talking to Thirash, wiggling his finger like sword fighting.

"That's my seat," Iardith said, clear enough to be heard by the watchers.

Dandiar and Thirash glanced up, clearly startled. "I—I did not know—it was empty—" Thirash said.

"It's my place," Iardith repeated.

"That's all right, we'll move." Dandiar picked up his plate.

Flushing, Thirash picked up hers, and they shifted to a table on the other side of the waterfall as Hanssa brought Lios smoothly back around.

Iardith joined them, and they sat down in the three empty chairs.

"Oom! It is the herded," came a high voice just behind Rhis. "Herded? Grouped? Om! Too much pipples."

Rhis turned her head, to find Yuzhyu standing nearby, holding her plate. The princess's brows wrinkled in perplexity as she looked at Lios's table—now full. Two or three people passed her by, but no one spoke.

Lios's head was turned away—Iardith was talking to him—so he didn't see his cousin.

Rhis said, "Would you like to sit here?" She scooted her chair closer to Shera's, to make space. "We can bring another chair."

The princess blinked, looked at Rhis. For a moment Rhis felt an anxious gaze searching her face, and then Yuzhyu gave a small, rather tentative smile.

"You speak to I, mmm?"

Rhis spotted an empty seat at the next table, and pulled it over.

Yuzhyu sat down with quaint dignity, and broke her biscuit.

Rhis cadged her mind for a suitable topic. "Isn't your land full of mountains too?"

Yuzhyu looked up quickly, her lips moving.

"Mountains?" Rhis repeated, shaping her hands into a peak.

"We have mountains, too," Shera said, speaking a little louder than usual.

The expressive blond brows cleared over those round blue eyes. "Ah! Yiss! Um, we do, yiss. You too? I yam Yuzhyu."

"Rhis." Rhis touched her bodice. "Nym, where I live, is nothing but mountains." She made herself slow her speech just slightly, and was rewarded by close attention, and almost immediate comprehension in the face next to her. "If we had a flat place, we would probably build sideways." Again, she mimed a building going to the side.

Yuzhyu repeated "Sideways—" Looked at her hands, and then she laughed. Her whole face crinkled in mirth, and her laugh was a lovely sound that reminded Rhis of a lark.

"Yiss! Us too. Windows, um, om, up!" Yuzhyu gestured toward the sky, still chuckling. "Door, down!"

Rhis laughed with her. Shera turned back to Carithe, who wanted to talk about the play, leaving Rhis with the princess from Ndai.

For the remainder of her breakfast they struggled through a conversation about mountains, and riding. Rhis wished Taniva was there to talk about riding, for she knew so little she was afraid she was boring, and in truth, it was difficult to make conversation, though obviously Yuzhyu was trying her very best. Then, some of the princess's word choices were so funny that Rhis worked hard not to laugh, but she was quaking inwardly with repressed giggles when at last Yuzhyu finished, stood up, and said, "I fine me tutor. Practice ze talk!" She touched her lips. Then a funny little nod, and a friendly look. "Zank you, Reez."

She walked away, casting one troubled glance toward Lios and Iardith's table. The black-haired princess leaned with her chin on her fingers, a delicate pose, completely monopolizing the prince's attention.

Rhis sighed. She decided to find the library, which turned out to be a vast room lined all the way around with books. Shelves and shelves of books, the top row reaching just above her head. At the far end of the room, scribes were busy at work, just as she'd been told. She tiptoed along the wall, scanning the gold-etched titles on the bindings of the books. Some of them were histories; quite a number of the older ones referred to people and places of which she'd never heard.

She kept walking, hoping she'd discover the plays, when she was startled by a voice.

"May I help you find something, my lady?"

A girl her own age, dressed in scribe garb, stood politely just behind her elbow.

"I'm looking for plays," Rhis said.

"Across that way." The girl pointed to the opposite side of the room.

Rhis murmured a word of thanks as she noticed for the first time that the table was covered with sheets of creamy paper, book paper, and ink and good pens. Immediately in front of her lay a sheet neatly written over, and next to it a book with an unfamiliar script.

"Will Prince Lios be reading these books once you translate them?" she asked.

The girl smiled a little. "He's already read them, my lady. It was he who chose them. We're translating them for people here—now and in future."

How many languages did he speak? Rhis wondered. But she didn't ask. It felt too much like gossip, and all the scribes were looking at her. Waiting in polite patience to get back to their task.

"Thank you," she said, and moved round the table to where the plays were located.

There again she was daunted by the vast number, so she picked three at random, and carried them out, intending to find a comfortable spot and read.

She walked through the main gathering room, where everyone seemed in a subdued mood. Not that many had come downstairs. The people sat in small groups, most of them talking quietly, some eating, some not, as the rain thrummed against the long bank of windows. No one was on the terrace, not even Taniva.

Where was Taniva? Rhis didn't think the highland princess the sort to hole up in her room. Then she remembered something about sword fighting, and wondered if the more restless members of the company were all somewhere bashing and clashing steel together.

A quiet laugh drew her attention. Two scribes sat with two girls Rhis had not yet met. One of the scribes was Dandiar, the other a fellow with long pale hair who seemed to be telling a story.

Rhis passed them by, exchanged a quick smile with Dandiar, then continued on to her room, where she could curl up on her bed. She read until Shera banged on her door and demanded she get ready for dinner.

Shera and Carithe bustled off to a corner, whispering and giggling. Mindful of Lios's rule about dinner, Rhis sat down at a table with three new people. She soon discovered that the girl and boy with hair the color of mahogany were cousins. They had made friends recently with the other fellow, who had a head full of bright red curls. This boy sat at Rhis's left.

Though they welcomed Rhis with a friendly enough manner, it was soon evident that this was going to be a boring meal. All they talked about was horses. Raising, trading, types, costs, saddles, and racing. Rhis pretended to listen, keeping her attention on her plate. She did not want to be seen searching around for Lios, and she was glad not to have to see Vors.

"Eugh, there she goes," the dark-haired boy muttered.

Four quick looks as Iardith crossed the room, her arm linked through Lios'. Rhis looked at that shining cape of black hair drifting against the princess's skirts, and sighed. If she wore hers loose like that, it would tangle into unsightly knots and straggles in no time.

Iardith sat down with Lios at one of the waterfall tables, and then—with perfect poise—beckoned to two of her particular crowd. Obviously she didn't have to bother with the rule about mixing around.

But just as Rhis was fighting against a sharp pang of envy at the Perfect Princess's self-possession, the horse-mad girl said, "I wouldn't be her for all the beauty in the world."

Rhis looked across the table, startled. The horse-mad girl was short, plump, and except for her rich mahogany curls like a cloud round her head, not beautiful. She wrinkled her nose at Iardith and Lios.

"Why?" Rhis asked.

The girl looked up, startled, and then blushed deeply.

"There you go again, Moret," her cousin muttered, rolling his eyes.

"But it's true," Moret replied, crossing her arms. And to Rhis, "You don't know the king of Arpalon, do you?"

Rhis shook her head. She suspected it was one of those questions no one expects an answer to, but she said, hoping for more information, "My father has a quarrel on with him, so I know nothing about Arpalon."

"*Everyone* has a quarrel on with the king of Arpalon," Moret said in a low, grim voice. "Or rather, he keeps the quarrels going. He's had my mother exiled to our estate for nearly ten years. I really didn't think I was going to get to come here at all."

"You aren't here," the cousin said, grinning. "You're visiting me."

Moret laughed, patted his hand, and then said to Rhis, "Iardith might be the sourest pickle of a princess who ever walked this floor, but that's because the court of Arpalon is pure vinegar. Her father made it very, *very* clear that if she doesn't come back with a royal crown, she can't come back at all."

SEVEN

The next morning dawned clear and pretty. Rhis, staring happily out her window at the bright blue sky, said to Shera, "Oh, I just have to take a walk."

"Now?" Shera asked, looking surprised.

"Yes." Rhis opened the window wide and breathed in the scent of flowers. "In Nym, sunshine is rare enough that we don't waste it. Not that we can grow even half the flowers I've just glimpsed here. I've never smelled that before, those pretty scents. No wonder people write poetry about flowers! Go on—I don't mind skipping breakfast. I'll join you in the library when I'm done."

Shera said, "The garden is beautiful here." But she said it in the voice of compromise, not of conviction: Rhis suspected that the blooms she herself found so charming were common in Gensam. Then Shera smiled. "I have to admit that I prefer plays and boys, even that Glaen and his insults, to flowers—which I will get plenty of when I have to return home."

So the girls parted, Shera to join the gathering for breakfast, and Rhis for her solitary walk. She wandered the paths without paying any attention to direction, moving as slowly as the bees that drifted from blossom to blossom. The breeze was warm, and carried such delicious scents. She kept bending to sniff at various flowers, trying to identify which smells went with which blossoms.

She'd worked her way halfway round the palace when voices interrupted her solitary walk, and three scribes walked through an arch with roses twined over it, just as she was approaching from the other direction.

They all saw one another at the same time. The three scribes, one of whom was Dandiar, bowed in salute, and Rhis smiled and sketched a curtsey in return. Dandiar exchanged some quick-spoken words with the other two scribes, and then stopped for Rhis to join him as the others continued on.

"You look like you have a question," Dandiar said.

"Well, I do," Rhis said. "But I didn't know my face showed it!"

Dandiar smiled. "Actually, I had a question, truth to tell." He looked up, his light brown eyes reminding Rhis of the color of honey. His gaze was watchful as he said in an easy, off-hand tone, "It seems we scribes are not to be excluded from the masquerade. Our reward for working extra duty, you might say."

"I'm delighted to hear that," Rhis said truthfully. Then she realized that Dandiar did not look particularly delighted. "Do you not wish to attend?"

"It's a bit of a duty," Dandiar acknowledged. "But there are ways to make duty turn to pleasure. I suppose you already asked or promised someone for the promenade?"

Rhis opened her mouth to deny, remembered Vors, and sighed. "I was asked. And I accepted."

She didn't feel it was appropriate to say more, but Dandiar, she had learned, was very observant.

"Regrets?" he asked.

She shrugged, knowing it would be impolite to express her disappointment. She'd actually managed to forget about

Vors. "Oh, well. Though I'd rather have danced it with you," she finished truthfully.

"I'm honored." Dandiar gave her a bow, smiling. "So, I asked my question. What was yours?"

"I would like to know the names of all these flowers," Rhis said. "Not that I'll probably remember past tomorrow—or anyway, past a week when I get home again, because we can't grow anything like these in Nym."

Dandiar gave a nod, then bent to whisk a weed away from a new plant. "Too cold and wet in Nym, right?"

"Yes. Here's another thing I'm wondering. Why is it that the prettiest flowers don't have the prettiest scents? The nicest scents seem to belong to the smallest blossoms. Or the plainest. And that wonderful one over there, with the blue and lavender petals, which I think the prettiest plant in the garden, smells like moldering grass. Phah!"

Dandiar paused to flick a withered blossom off a tall stalk of pale pink queenspease. "I don't know, but I suspect it's because the big, bright ones don't have to compete so hard for the attention of the bees and butterflies. The little ones put out the powerful aromas to get their share of attention. A lot like people," he added.

"It makes sense," Rhis said. "As for people, I think I remember an old ballad about that. Oh, what was it . . ." She clapped her hands together, trying to jar it loose from her memory. "Foo! It's so old—my sister taught it to me when I was about six—the one about the short, fat princess who gets courted by every fellow in the world, so she changes gowns with her pretty maid, to see who is true, and who just wants a crown, and then the maid falls in love with a prince, and—"

Dandiar said in a quick voice, "I know a better one." And he quoted off a poem, a dialogue between a cat and a dog about who was the most beautiful animal. His voice went high and squeaky on the cat's part, low and growly on the dog's, which caused Rhis to laugh.

When he was done he did not wait for Rhis to comment, but said in a thoughtful voice, "What I've always wondered is, why do we find flowers beautiful when they aren't the least useful to us? We don't eat them, we don't need pollen, and yet no garden is complete without blooms."

Rhis said, "Before I started sniffing for scents, I was trying to decide whether the beauty was all in the colors, or in the shapes. Amazing, how many shapes the flowers have, at least I think so. Some like bells, some like stars, some like puffs. How do we find beauty in them all?"

"Hm," Dandiar said, hands on hips. "I never thought of that before." He looked around with a proprietary air. "No, I haven't. Hum! Good question. Here. These lilies, plain white. It's their shape that makes them beautiful—that pure curve, the simplicity."

"But those angel-puffs, it's that delicate color, like the sky just before the sun comes up. Not quite pink, not quite yellow, nor pale gold. It's a warm shade," Rhis exclaimed. "Yet they look just like my bath-sponge otherwise."

"Blue starliss is both handsome in shape, with those petals drooping so symmetrically, and the color," Dandiar said, crossing his arms as he looked about.

Rhis also glanced around. Then up. She realized that the fading of the colors was because the sky had clouded up again. "I don't recognize that poem about the dog and cat," Rhis said. "Do you know who wrote it? If the poet is in one of the collections in the library—"

He shook his head. "No, he's not." He gave her a lopsided smile, a blend of humor and wince. "I wouldn't ever claim to be a poet."

"You mean to say *you* composed that poem?"

He shrugged. "If you read good poetry, it's nothing to be proud of. Oh, it's funny enough, but the truth is, it's full of trite phrases just to make out the rhymes, and when I read real poetry, mine don't compare well."

Rhis nodded in sympathy. "I know that feeling. Before the invitation came, I was writing a ballad and—" She remembered how she'd gotten stuck trying to describe her handsome prince, and blushed, even though Dandiar could not know what her ballad had been about. "Well, in short, writing one is a lot harder than it seems, and your efforts are much more successful than mine."

Dandiar looked away, then down at the blossom he'd been shredding in his fingers, as if amazed to discover it there. "Rhis?" he said tentatively.

"Rhis!"

Shera pelted up the garden paths, skirts bunched in her fists. When she saw Dandiar she stopped, her face crimson.

"What's wrong?" Rhis asked. "Go ahead."

Shera flung her hands out wide. "I don't know—I don't know what to do—all I could think is, maybe the more the better. At least, Rhis, can you come with me? Maybe if several of us are there . . ."

"What happened?"

Shera cast another troubled glance at Dandiar, who said, "Feel free to speak. I usually hear all the rumors anyway." He smiled. "Or would you rather I go away?"

"Oh, I don't know what to think. I'm so angry my mind is like a hive of wasps. It's that Iardith," Shera said with loathing. "She *swept* into the library, where those of us doing the play were all presenting our latest choices, and said—" Here Shera stuck her nose into the air. "'You *little girls* really *ought* to know your literature if you are venturing out as *wits*. The only *appropriate* play is *The Golden Throne*.' 'Little girls,'" Shera repeated very sourly. She cast a glance at Dandiar, and with an obvious struggle, suppressed some fairly heated comments, other than a muttered, "Carithe is almost eighteen."

Rhis bit her lip, thinking rapidly about plays. "*The Golden Throne* was written in compliment to Queen Briath's family some time back, so it might seem like the proper choice," she finally admitted.

Shera sighed. "That's what Iardith said—" She paused, staring in surprise at Dandiar.

Dandiar pinched his nose and groaned. "That pompous and boring play has been dragged out every time someone at court wants something," he said. "Let me tell you a secret: The royal family is sick of it. Very sick of it. Lios will want to run and hide if he has to sit through one more of those long speeches."

Rhis laughed. "I wasn't going to say that, but it really is pretty awful. Of course a good performer might make it more bearable."

"Oh, it's written competently, but it's so full of blandishments it's like making a meal of cakes and nothing else. Honey cakes. Sticky-sweet honey cakes," Dandiar added, seeing Shera's continued puzzlement.

At that last, Shera's brow cleared, then she said, "Euw. I see!"

"So you've read it, I gather," Dandiar said to Rhis.

She said, "I've read lots of plays. And histories. Not much else to do in Nym, to tell the truth."

"You said you avoided learning."

Rhis laughed. "About trade laws and taxes and who the king of Arpalon is squabbling with now, and why. I like plays." She turned to Shera. "So what is the problem? You need people for a vote?" Rhis asked.

Shera tossed her ringlets back. "No, we all agreed to it, for it did sound like the right thing, but then the room was full of her own friends, and before I quite knew what was happening, Hanssa said, *Oh, but you will be the best Queen Arilde*, and Iardith was smirking and pretending to be modest, but before anyone else could speak, she said, real quick, *Who better to play his great-great-great grandfather than Lios? And you, Hanssa, can be Princess Gaela* . . . And right like that she was giving out all the parts," Shera finished, her voice uneven, her eyes filled with tears of rage. "Though she did condescend to give me a tiny role as the chambermaid who finds the hidden crown, it's all spoilt."

Rhis sighed. "I don't know what I can do. By now she's given out all the roles."

"That wasn't the worst," Shera said, heaving a shuddering sigh. "She looked around, and when everyone was talking, she said to that little princess with the difficult name and the gold hair—"

"Yuzhyu," Rhis said.

"Lios's cousin—that's the one," Shera said, nodding. "And I think Iardith is mad because Lios shows her so much attention. Anyway when the others were talking, Iardith said to her in this spun-sugar voice, *I'm sorry, my dear, but plays have to be spoken by people who can actually be understood.* Yuzhyu didn't say anything, but you should have seen her eyes. So I ran out to find you."

Rhis scarcely heard the last words. An idea had occurred to her. She rubbed her hands. "Oh! I have the nackiest notion! Come on!"

"May I come watch?" Dandiar asked.

Rhis glanced over her shoulder in surprise. "Of course!" She laughed. "Besides, you really ought to be there, because you gave me the idea."

"I did?" Dandiar asked, looking about as if he expected to find his idea written on the air.

Rhis didn't answer. She sped up the walk to the palace, the other two on either side.

They arrived at the library, which was crowded with what seemed to be half of Lios's guests, all circled around Iardith, who was reading out one of the play's long poems in what (Rhis was forced to acknowledge) was a beautifully trained voice. Next to her, in the next best chair, sat the supercilious Grand Duchess of the Isle of Wilfen.

Rhis looked past the Grand Duchess (who ignored Rhis) and spotted Carithe in the corner, looking dismal, a couple of the other younger girls near her. Yuzhyu was not even there. Neither was Lios.

Iardith lifted her beautiful eyes from the page at the interruption, her attitude one of patient expectation. But when she recognized the newcomers as Rhis, accompanied by Shera and the scribe, she went right back to reading.

Rhis forced herself to wait patiently until the poem (a very long, formal court poem, likening the long-ago Queen Arilde to a series of gemstones each more beautiful and more precious than the last) was through, and the admirers had applauded and acclaimed Iardith, who smiled as she closed the book.

Rhis felt her heart thump against her ribs, and stepped forward. "It's pretty, and Iardith reads very, very well, but that poem is so old-fashioned it's kind of, well, boring."

A murmur of protest went up—but not very loud, Rhis noticed. Had others privately thought it kind of dull as well? Heartened, she went on. She would never betray a secret, but wasn't there a way around that? "Any of us who have read it know that the rest of the play is the same, and remember, we have to get it all by heart, and that means practicing it over and over."

"It's a compliment to the royal family," Vors said, turning to the Grand Duchess to see if she agreed.

"But did anyone ask Lios if he likes it?" Rhis asked, thoroughly disgusted with Vors. "Or even better, what his favorite might be?"

Sudden whispers.

Iardith said, "Perhaps I ought to inquire."

"Why don't you?" Rhis asked, smiling.

Iardith smiled back, but her eyes were cold and wary. She did not speak, only inclined her head graciously, and left at her customary unhurried, graceful pace.

As soon as she was gone, Rhis said, "You know, I had an idea. If Lios doesn't mind, we might have some fun with it."

"Like?" one of the ducal heirs asked, looking skeptical.

"Well, we could reverse the roles. We girls would play the boy parts. And the boys would play the girls."

A gasp. People exchanged wondering, delighted looks. Except the Grand Duchess, who just stared past Rhis, her lips curled in distaste.

"Including costumes," Rhis added.

On the periphery she saw Dandiar clap his hand over his mouth, his face red with his effort not to laugh out loud.

"Oh, what fun!" Hanssa exclaimed.

"Only if I get to play a prin-cess," Sefan, a big, brawny young ducal heir, exclaimed in a squeaky voice. Sefan sashayed across the room, pretending to wave a fan.

Everyone laughed! Except the Grand Duchess, who rose, and walked deliberately out of the room in such a manner it was plain she expected everyone to follow.

But the others, for once—even Vors—were too busy talking, exchanging ideas and laughing.

Rhis waved her hands for attention. For a time the voices rose, each one exchanging ideas with friends, until one by one, focus returned to her. The faces around her now looked expectant. "Here, where's the play?" she asked. "We have to cast it for best effect. The biggest fellow has to be the daintiest princess, and so on."

Again the voices rose. While they were talking again, Rhis motioned Dandiar over.

He came obediently, his expression curious. "Do you want to me to perform?"

"Do you want to be in it?" Rhis asked. "But I was going to ask you to find Yuzhyu, because I mean to make sure she's in it if she wants to be."

Dandiar gave a short nod. "On my way."

He started out, almost colliding with several people, who glanced at him and then ignored him without moving out of his way. He went very still for a moment, then threaded his way through the crowd and disappeared out the door.

"All right, Thanelan will have to be Princess Gaela. And who's the shortest of the girls?" one of the ducal heirs called out.

Voices clamored, everyone with ideas.

Rhis held up her hand, since no one could hear anyone else. When they were quiet, she said, "Let's perform for one another here first. Whoever is the funniest gets the part."

Pause. Looks. More laughter.

Then one of the dukes said, "Wait, we cannot decide without Iardith."

"Oh, yes! Iardith," several other boys repeated, with varying degrees of admiration.

"Beautiful voice," Hanssa said. And with a challenging glance at Rhis, she added, "The prettiest voice of any here."

Rhis was not about to challenge that. "Well, of course we can wait for Iardith to return—"

"Iardith is here," came Iardith's voice from behind. Her face was smooth and unreadable. "Lios begs to be excused. He says his part is best acted as appreciative audience, and not as awkward performer. And he says one play is like another, but he prefers one that makes him laugh."

"Then the idea is perfect," Vors exclaimed. "Now that we've turned it all about." He looked around—for approval, Rhis guessed. "I myself would be happy to regale the audience with my fine approximation of this chambermaid here. How else am I going to get close to a crown?" He gave Rhis the same smile he'd always given her, but all she could think was, *Did your parents tell you to bring back a rich princess—any rich princess? Or Grand Duchess?*

He got a laugh, and then the voices rose again. Iardith crossed the room, and everyone gave way before her. Her male admirers all tried to be heard at once as they told her what parts they had—which one she ought to take—who was going to do what. She laughed a little and said, "Please! One at a time."

Iardith's perfect mouth pressed once into a thin line as someone outlined the plan, then she smiled up at Rhis. "Do you think it entertaining to play the buffoon? To confess, I am not certain that I can!"

An outcry against her ever seeming buffoonish met this statement.

Rhis sensed something not quite friendly in Iardith's tone. "I just thought it would be fun."

"And fun it will be," Shera said, coming forward to stand beside Rhis. Her cheeks were red, her shoulders tight, but she looked about with an air of challenge. "I have always wanted to pretend to be a bard, and for once I shall!"

More noise. In the middle of it, Dandiar returned, not just with Yuzhyu, but with Jarvas, who ignored everyone except Iardith.

The princess from Arpalon lifted her chin, her gaze narrowed. Jarvas leaned against the wall near the door, his expression one of derision. He also looked tense. As did Iardith, Rhis realized.

"Ho! Shall we drag ol' Breggo in and make him act the part of this silly countess here?"

Laughter went up. "You won't get Breggo on any stage unless you tie him up, and that's to play a regular role," Glaen exclaimed, dashing a drift of his pale blond hair out of his eyes. Then he drawled in a high squeak, "Besides, he cannot dew the countess as b-r-r-illiantly as I, dew yew not think sew?"

More laughter—except from Jarvas, whose mouth turned sardonic. He had those pale-colored eyes, the color of ice in winter. There was no humor in his expression, just disdain.

Iardith flushed. When the laughter had died down, she turned in a circle so her skirts flared slightly and then dropped into graceful folds. That brought everyone's attention back to her, and she smiled. "I fear your talents for this sort of thing far exceed mine, and so my part is to acknowledge superiority and withdraw."

Her tone was just a little too sweet. Some smiles faltered, and people looked around as if to see what their companions would do or say. Rhis began to wonder if all those handsome, popular leaders weren't secretly as uncertain inside as she was. Something to think about.

Then Shera went up to Glaen, and began to sing one of the ballads in a fake deep voice. The ballad went on about 'her' glorious eyes, her dainty step in the dance, and her pure singing voice—and once again everyone laughed, as Glaen swanked about, pretending to be a fluttery countess.

Iardith disappeared—but for once no one noticed.

EIGHT

Keris had just finished dressing Rhis's hair for the masquerade when a knock came at the door.

A scribe handed Rhis a sealed note, and then disappeared.

In surprise, she opened it, to see a neatly written note:

> *Rhis: My anticipation of happiness centered on dancing the promenade with you tonight, but I have since received a personal request. Lios has asked me especially to escort one of his own relatives. I knew you would understand that honor due to one's host must take priority, and I hope we can dance together many times during the evening, for I remain your most ardent admirer—*
>
> *Vors*

Rhis tossed the note down and shrugged. Honor? More like flattery, but she was more relieved than disappointed. If Dandiar hadn't already asked someone else, she could ask him, and best of all, she would not be thought as a flatterer, since he had no rank. He was so interesting, and fun, and wouldn't flirt just because she came from a rich family. She'd enjoy dancing with him—and then later, some time, she'd get her heart's desire: a dance with Lios.

At last!

She turned around and around, examining herself in her mirror. Her palms were sweaty, her heartbeat fast. How long until those stupid bells rang, announcing the masquerade?

The truth was, she didn't care about any of those ducal heirs, or lords, or even the three princes. All Rhis could think about was how she would have Lios's attention, his proximity, finally.

She knew she was in love with him. What would he think of her? Rhis stared at her reflection. With her eyes mostly hidden behind the little mask, she looked like a stranger, especially in the unfamiliar lines of her pale blue gown. Her plain brown hair was all swooped up on her head with blue ribbons and gemstones here and there. Tiny mois-gems twinkled among the many folds of the filmy fabric of her gown.

"You're charming," Shera said.

Rhis turned around. Shera's gown was very different— tight in the waist, with a low scoop neck that made the best of her lovely figure. Puffy sleeves and a broad skirt, all of it in various shades of rose, with cream and touches of gold, exactly suited her complexion and rich, curly red-toned long ringlets bouncing around her charming shoulders.

"Not as much as you," Rhis said truthfully. "I'm afraid I'm a beanpole, and I'll always be a beanpole."

"So? Everyone likes beans," Shera said.

"Beans. They are not romantic, no matter what you say," Rhis declared. "Don't make game of me now. My stomach is all butterflies."

Shera put her head to one side. "But it's the truth. Beans aren't like flowers, maybe, but they are good, and wholesome,

and welcome at every meal. Some flowers," she added, her voice
sharpening, "look pretty, but are poison."

Of course Rhis knew what she meant—and more
important, who—but the bells rang then, and there was no more
time for talk.

The girls walked down together, joining more as they
progressed down the hallways. A sharp crack of laughter from
ahead brought Rhis out of her worries about herself. She
recognized immediately in that laugh more nerves than humor,
and as she looked more closely at the faces around her, she saw
all the signs of apprehension and even tension that she felt—
quick gestures, darting gazes, titters rather than real laughter, the
shimmering of fans plied just a little too fast.

So everyone else had expectations? Probably not the
same ones, Rhis thought. Or did every single girl love Lios too?
She sighed inwardly, thinking that Iardith wouldn't be worrying
about sweaty palms and stepping on her partner's feet.

But then Rhis remembered what Moret had said about
Iardith, and her perspective swooped once more. Maybe Iardith
did, in fact, worry. She had perhaps greater stakes than anyone
there. Rhis knew that her own romantic wish that Lios would fall
in love with her in return was just that—romance—but if he
didn't, she would go home feeling disappointment but no
disaster. More important, her parents would welcome her home
with pleasure whether or not anyone fell in love with her. Same
with Shera, she was certain. One might have a sour governess
and the other a sister-by-marriage waiting at home to scold her
back into proper behavior—but that was the worst of it.

Then she saw Iardith—or what had to be Iardith. No one
could have dared to wear that spectacular white gown, pure in
color as fresh snow; one tiny spill, one false step, and it would
turn grubby. Iardith's black hair was bound with pearls and
diamonds; the only color in her costume was a great amber stone

in a fabulous setting round her neck, which brought out the rich glints of her eyes behind their dainty white-feathered mask.

Her slim hand rested lightly on the arm of a tall figure with light hair that contrasted with the pure black of his costume. Costume? It looked more like a military uniform than a costume, right down to the high black cavalry boots. Rhis recognized Jarvas's pale hair in neat looped braids, his distinct stride.

Audible gasps of breath surrounded the two as they glided inside the ballroom, Rhis and Shera and a crowd of others filed in unnoticed behind them. Iardith and Jarvas made a striking contrast. Awareness rippled through the room in widening circles, just like when one drops a stone into water.

Jarvas did not turn his head, but Iardith scanned in quick motions—in anyone else, Rhis would have thought her manner furtive. She was seeking Lios, of course. The formal throne at the other end was still empty.

Rhis was impressed by the grand ballroom's white and rose marble, and the contrasting bluish marble flooring. The musicians played in a gallery high above, just under the ceiling, around the edge of which were sculpted and gilt interwoven garlands of fantastical flowers. The gently domed ceiling had been painted a deep blue with an unfamiliar constellation glowing softly in the light of the thousands of honey-smelling beeswax candles.

What a splendid ballroom! And it wasn't even in the capital. This ballroom belonged just to the prince, yet it was many times grander than anything in Nym.

She sighed, wondering how she could possibly be interesting to someone for whom this setting was familiar. No wonder Lios had never come near her!

"Rhis! Excuse me. Eranda Sky-Born," came a familiar voice, ending with suppressed laughter.

Dandiar! Here was one friend, at least.

Dandiar was dressed in costume as well—a very old fashioned long tunic of deep, forest green, embroidered with silver and a blue so dark it was almost black. It fitted his slim form quite well, making him look somehow taller. His wide-set light brown eyes behind his mask were observant as always, quirked slightly with question.

Rhis glanced at his partner, and then recognized the frizzy cloud of curls belonging to Yuzhyu.

"What a beautiful costume! Who are you?" Rhis asked, admiring the Ndaian princess's short crimson velvet jacket, the lacy shirt beneath, and the full trousers below. A golden sash round her waist, and shoes with slightly curled up toes added a delightfully exotic touch. Yuzhyu was too small and thin to look good in a ball dress, but this outfit was just right.

"Me, I be Todozh Yimba, ze Pirate-fighting Queen from me—um, om, days-before—no, om—"

"History?" Rhis suggested tentatively.

Yuzhyu snapped her fingers. "History. Zat's it!"

"A ship-captain queen? What fun! You must tell me her story."

"Oom, I do zat!"

Shera, Glaen, and several others appeared then, and there was general chatter. Shera and Carithe exclaimed with delight over Yuzhyu's costume, and insisted on hearing about the pirate queen.

While that was going on, Dandiar motioned to Rhis and they drew a little aside. "I knew I could count on you to take her in," he murmured. "She's Lios's cousin, you know. He feels an obligation to see that she enjoys herself, but tonight he can't devote most of his time to her."

"Of course she can stay with us," Rhis whispered back. "Are you strictly on duty, even though you're in costume?"

Dandiar shrugged. "Can't be helped."

Rhis bit her lip. "I was going to mention that I no longer have a first partner, but if you have someone else, or duty—"

"Well, no, the first dance isn't assigned," Dandiar said with a quick grin. And he bowed. "Your obedient servant to command."

Rhis smothered her laughter, as pleasurable expectation made her heart feel light as a cloud.

"But speaking of duty, I'd better get some of it done now," Dandiar whispered. "I'll be back on the strike of the promenade."

He flicked his fingers to his heart in salute, and then dodged neatly between two strolling couples in their grand masks, and vanished.

Rhis discovered that the group had grown to include what seemed to be half of Lios's guests. She recognized Moret and several of the people who liked horse-racing. There was Taniva, demonstrating some kind of sword-fighting technique to the shy Breggan. Taniva looked spectacular in an outfit of black and crimson and green, with real gold all over, in tiny round dangles, chiming with an exotic *ching!* every move she made. The crimson and green were mostly embroidery, great winged shapes in stylized fashion on the front and back of her vest, which covered a black silk shirt with wide sleeves, and petticoat-trousers tucked into riding boots. Gold was also braided into her dark hair; several of the more martial of the male guests were clustered round her, trying to talk one another down as they made dueling gestures.

"Zat is pulchritude body-cover, om, no?" a voice murmured next to Rhis.

She felt a flutter of laughter inside at Yuzhyu's word choices. But she only nodded. "I love those golden metal things. They make such a pretty sound," she said.

"We have." Yuzhyu nodded. "Oom. Vest? Pest? Time of the pestibule?"

"Festivals?" Rhis guessed.

The golden-haired princess looked relieved. "Yiss! Zat is word."

Rhis sighed. "We don't have any interesting costumes in Nym. We used to wear clan colors, but we don't any more, because we had too many clan wars."

"Oh. Is bad." Yuzhyu nodded, her lips pursed. "Us. Yiss. Same. Not clams. Clams? Clans? Families, not make ze battle. Mages. Magic-wars, ship-makers, pirates."

"I'd like to hear more about your kingdom," Rhis said.

Yuzhyu grinned. "Me! I tell bad. I find book for you—"

The brassy peal of horns rang out then, cutting through the voices like a knife through bread.

It was time for the promenade—the dancing was about to begin!

Before Rhis had time to prepare, Lios had appeared almost at her elbow. She glanced up, despite the blush heating her face and neck. She could see the exact shade of his dark eyes, which reminded her of the richest dark chocolate. Oh, how handsome he was! She sniffed, smelling the herbal scent on his magnificent costume: he wore a long blue robe embroidered with gold and silver, with a sash round his narrow middle.

He nodded pleasantly to Rhis, then said to Yuzhyu, "Ready, Cousin?"

"Yiss, ready-ready-ready," Yuzhyu sang out happily.

Lios crooked his arm, and Yuzhyu chuckled, a merry sound, as she took it. "I like that outfit you have on."

"I yourss. You old krandfadder-kink, yiss?" And again the merry chuckle. "I come back?" she asked over her shoulder to Rhis.

Rhis smiled in answer at Yuzhyu, who disappeared with Lios into the crowd. Of course they had to lead the line. But not far behind them, there was Vors, leading out the Grand Duchess of Wilfen, who was sister to the heir. Wilfen, like Nym, had veins of gemstones; the Grand Duchess wore so many on her costume that she sparkled at every move.

Behind came a whisper, just a little too loud, from one of the boys, "Pity Vors."

"Maybe she bribed him," came an answer, and the boys moved away, laughing.

Rhis grimaced. So Iardith's great friend wasn't quite as popular as Rhis had assumed.

Dandiar appeared at Rhis's side. "Your royal highness?"

"I'm a mage, remember?" Rhis corrected, laughing. She knew her laugh sounded silly, but she couldn't help it. "And you are—who?"

"I'm a poet from three hundred years back." Dandiar made a very elaborate bow, then stepped to her right side.

Anticipation fizzed inside of Rhis like bubbles in a stream. Lios was tall and imposing on the other side of the ballroom, at the head of the line. Supposedly no one else was to go in rank, but as usual Iardith calmly pushed her way through until she stood directly behind Lios. With a sauntering step, Jarvas stopped at her side.

Iardith talked across poor, short Yuzhyu. Lios responded with polite gestures. Jarvas stood with his arms crossed.

The musicians played their third and last warning chord. Rhis turned back to her partner, and felt a quick, self-conscious pang when she saw that familiar quirk of humor in Dandiar's wide-set eyes. Brown eyes, like Lios had, but light in shade, the color of honey-mead in sunlight. Amazing, Rhis thought, how many shades of brown there were, and most all of them attractive.

She remembered her silly ballad, and all those gemstone eyes she had been trying to foist onto her Perfect Prince, and her neck and face felt hot.

Dandiar didn't say anything embarrassing. The music started, they both lifted their outer hands, and Rhis placed hers right atop his left in the correct mode. She wondered suddenly who his poet was. Three hundred years back? Who was famous then? A tug at memory—

"I like what you did with that play," he said, scattering her ruminations.

"It was your idea, really," she replied. "It was that song you wrote. Singing it in that squeaky voice. It made me laugh."

"So with laughter you managed to level the competition. A remarkable weapon," Dandiar replied.

"But it isn't a weapon," she protested. "No one was laughing at anyone."

"No. I did not express myself adroitly. Laughter used in competition is particularly cruel, but you effected the opposite, enabling them to be willing to laugh at themselves. It forced the social competition to cease. At least for a little while. I wondered—did you intend that?"

Rhis's thoughts tumbled between delight, pride, and a little uncertainty. She wished she could say *Yes! I did!* except it wouldn't be true. So she shrugged, her face hot again. "Well, no, all I remembered was your squeaky voice, and how funny it was, and I thought if I could get an idea going that made everyone laugh in the same way, they might go for my idea."

They could not talk; she had to twirl under his arm and then bow to the fellow on her right—Glaen, and who grinned at her with his usual good humor—before circling round him and then back.

"By the way, I appreciate your taking Yuzhyu into your group. She knows that her conversation is difficult, poor soul," Dandiar said.

"Well, I don't really have a group, but Yuzhyu is certainly welcome. Truth is, I like her conversation," Rhis admitted. "She makes me laugh inside. Not at her. It's the words she chooses. Of course when I think of me being sent to some land—well, I wish I'd do half so well." She thought of something, and asked in what she hoped was an offhand voice, as she looked across the room at the couples circling gracefully around one another, "I suppose there's some kind of unofficial betrothal? With Lios, I mean. Not announced?"

"No, nothing like that. Yuzhyu is the heir to her kingdom. She has had to stay home. But she made Lios's life in the Isle of Ndai pleasant. She and her cousins. When he returned for the last time—now the heir—she was invited here to broaden her experience before she has to go home for good. This is her one chance to travel."

"Oh." Rhis heard the laughter in Dandiar's voice—which really was a pleasant voice. She wondered if he sang serious as well as silly songs. "Well. I do like her," she finished, feeling adrift.

"Tell me something. Is there anyone you don't like?"

His tone had changed.

Rhis gave him a looked midway between question and surprise; his expression was hard to interpret. "Well—" She didn't want to say anything about Iardith, about whom her feelings were more mixed than negative. "It's things I dislike, more than people," she said slowly, reaching for the right words.

Dip, swap, turn under his arm. She liked his scent. It was more astringent than Lios's, but just as nice. Would he find her own lavender scent as nice?

She gave her head a shake and said, "Cruelty."
Remembering Vors, she added with even more feeling,
"Falseness. I really dislike that."

"Falsity? As in . . .?" Dandiar prompted.

"As in pretending something one isn't." Rhis
remembered that awful last line on Vors' note—about being her
most ardent admirer. It implied he was her only admirer, and he
wasn't even an admirer! "I hate that," she finished in a sharp
voice.

Dandiar gave her a comical smile as they dipped and
turned again. This time she exchanged bows and turns with the
next fellow down, one of the ducal heirs who was usually with
Iardith's crowd.

Rhis scarcely paid him any attention. She saw that
questioning look in Dandiar's eyes, and waited impatiently until
they were together again.

Dandiar said, "False courtship, or false guises?"

Rhis grinned. "I don't mean masquerades. Or plays.
Those are fun, and everyone knows they are false faces, so to
speak. But to say a lot of things about admiration, and to flirt, to
a person's face, but behind her back ask a lot of questions about
wealth and so forth—well, I hate that."

"Isn't that a part of position, though?" Dandiar asked.

"Position?"

"Royalty can't marry entirely to suit oneself. There's the
kingdom to think of, and sometimes a desperately empty
treasury, and a wealthy spouse can bring about needed reforms.
For others, a marriage might be necessitated by a treaty—the
joining of two powerful families in order to prevent war."

Rhis peered past his shoulder as the dance required them
to turn. The lines of brilliantly dressed dancers dipped, whirled,
and swayed. "I know," she said. "My brother married to benefit
both kingdoms. Well, and so did Elda. But neither of them told

lies to get the other to like them. Or at least, I don't actually know that—"

She paused. Dandiar handed her expertly under his arm and they whirled back to back and then faced one another again.

He said, "Go on."

"I guess they might not have told me everything. About their courtship, I mean. But neither of them is the least romantic, and even my sister Sidal says that they understood one another from the start. And neither is the type to tell even the smallest fib, even the 'I like your gown' kind, if they think the gown really ugly. Both would think it their *duty* to tell you your gown is ugly."

Rhis peeked past Dandiar as they did hands-across and twirled again. Lios was still almost directly opposite, dancing gracefully next to the little golden-haired princess from Ndai.

"No romance at all?" Dandiar asked.

Rhis grinned at the teasing tone of his voice, her attention back on him. She laughed, secretly admiring the way his velvet, plain as it was, moved so flatteringly across his back, and outlined his arms. He had well-shaped arms. "None," she said, and aware of having gotten distracted, she forced her mind back onto the subject. "It was Elda who drilled both Shera and me with her favorite maxim, that a crown prince looks for dignity and dedication to duty above all in a wife. And she believes it to be true. But I wonder if it's really true."

"For some, I suspect." Dandiar grinned. "But others probably look for other things 'above all.'"

Rhis returned his grin. "If there's no real feeling of romance, then I'd so much rather that the pretty words of romance be left out. I'd respect a person who said, 'Rhis, I need to marry wealth, and you are wealthy.' The pretence of, of, liking, or romance, is what I hate—it's too sickening when someone glops on about flowers and hearts and how beautiful I am and how smart, and so on, but not really meaning it. I guess that's because, well, if they lie to me when we are strangers, when does the lying stop?"

"Some are not permitted the luxury of plain speaking," Dandiar said in a low voice. And, quickly, he quoted,

> *"They all see the mask upon my face,*
> *Some hear my voice despite disguise,*
> *Who shall sense somber spirit 'neath its merry façade?"*

Rhis laughed silently in recognition.

> *"Clouds mask the stars,*
> *Then pass for those who are patient,*
> *Leaving eternal sky, constant as my spirit—"*

she quoted in triumph. For a moment her mind was no longer in Eskanda's ballroom but back in her tower, looking at a very worn, green-covered book—

"Will you not look up,
And see them?" Dandiar finished.

"Dandiar the poet-king!" she exclaimed. "Traveled the world, his sister was the heir, she was killed in a sea-battle, and so he became king! *That's* who you are!"

Dandiar grinned. "Great joke, isn't it? I mean the name." He gave a little laugh. A self-conscious one, the first she'd ever heard. "I couldn't resist, because of the shared name. Does it sound high and mighty?"

Rhis said in surprise, "No—of course not. Everyone here is pretending to be someone famous—" The dance ended then, everyone bowed or curtseyed to their partners, and Dandiar excused himself and moved on.

Rhis plied her fan, peering past it to locate Lios. When would it be her turn? Her insides behind her fine bodice were full of butterflies of anticipation. The ordered couples dissolved into knots of three and four or more, but most faces were turned toward him. Expectant females smiled, some of them with nervous gestures, or giggles that Rhis could hear across the room: so everyone else remembered that Lios was going to dance with every girl at this masquerade.

The party will be over in a few days, she realized. *We'll be going home. How many were sent here, male and female both, under orders like Iardith's father gave her?*

Vors appeared next to her then, and she made herself smile, and hold out her hand. At least the second dance was lively, with frequent changes of partner. As he carried right on with his campaign of compliments, she didn't have to do much but smile and flutter her fan as she danced.

Her next was with Glaen, a much preferable partner— even if he kept craning his neck to see who Shera was with.

After another pair of dances, with Sefan and Halvic, she realized that the dances calling for diamonds of four couples were being alternated with the waltos and other single-partner dances. When she paused between dances to rest, catch her breath, and drink some of the spiced punch, Rhis observed Lios working his way through the females a little faster by doing the fours-dances, which meant he could dance with two girls in the same dance.

She also noticed that there were quite a few scribes dancing. All boys, and a few who had to be young men well into their twenties. Dandiar was busy with a different partner every time she glimpsed him. Rhis realized then what she hadn't before, that girls far outnumbered boys at Lios's great party. Lios had gotten most of his male scribes to dress up and join the party, so that everyone who wanted a partner had the opportunity.

As the evening wore on, she too danced every dance—each time one ended, she would turn around, and there was another partner waiting. At first all partners she knew, but then boys she hadn't met yet, including several of the scribes. Most of them were a lot of fun. She actually managed to forget Lios for long periods of time because she was enjoying herself so much.

Especially during the fours dances, when there was plenty of joking and laughter. And yes, even flirting, but somehow it was all right with Breggan and some of the others. Their compliments didn't feel like a . . . campaign.

During one lively eights dance Glaen and Shera were again partners, and their continuous fire of insults kept everyone in the group laughing—even the shy Breggan, who had managed to get Taniva as his partner. Rhis was with one of the scribes for the second time. She snickered so hard she had a stitch in her side, and she felt damp and overly warm in her layered costume when it ended.

"Oh," she said, fanning herself. "I think I need—"

Something to drink never made it past her dry lips. She turned around, and Lios was there, holding out his hand in invitation. "Will you dance with me?"

NINE

Rhis sensed her friends stepping out of the way, and she held out her own hand, damp and hot as it was.

Ought she to wipe it down her gown? Except that would look so, well, grubby. Iardith would never do such a thing! And anyway the musicians were now playing the introduction to a waltos. So she just lightly touched his fingers, and when he clasped her hand to hold it, she realized his hand was also warm and damp.

Lightning sparked through her. She was getting one of the couple dances, not a fours dance! Pride—trepidation—apprehension—delight—a cloudburst of emotions followed the lightning, almost making her dizzy.

Counterpoint to that was the movement of the dance itself. Round, and round, step-two-three, step-two-three. Lios was very good at it.

Breathe, she commanded herself. This was her chance, probably her only chance. She was finally alone with Lios, or as alone as she was ever going to be.

She peeked up. His dark eyes under their long lashes flicked continuously from side to side as he watched everywhere, steering them through the whirling couples. She was intensely conscious of his hand gripping hers, damp as it was, and the other resting correctly against her waist at the side. It was only a dance, she wasn't really in his arms, but still she felt as shy—as stunned—as she had her very first evening.

Talk, she commanded herself. *Don't be a bore!* Graceful conversation. So what ought she to say?

Her mother's admonitory verse flitted through her mind, quick as one of those invisible butterflies of flame:

> *"Fall in love with heart, not head,*
> *   to trouble you're led.*
> *Fall in love with heart and mind,*
> *   then true love you'll find."*

She looked up, to meet a polite smile.

Just polite. Not ardent, or lingering. Polite.

Lios was very tall—much taller than she was used to— and as she tipped her head back to see him more clearly she inadvertently found herself staring up his nose. She felt laughter bubble inside, and she must have smiled, because he smiled down at her, this time a real smile.

"Who is your favorite poet?" she asked, the first question she could think of. "Someone in our language, or do you find one of the foreign ones better?"

"Poet?" Lios repeated, and blinked once. He smiled again, this time a quick, self-deprecating smile, before he returned to his scanning. "Poetry isn't much in my line, I'm afraid. Do you like it?"

Well, how was one to answer that? His voice was deep, and attractive, but the words were not the least romantic.

"Well, yes," Rhis said.

"Tell me about your favorites," Lios asked. His voice was so pleasant.

"I don't want to be boring," Rhis replied.

Just then Lios's breath whooshed past her ear, and his grasp tightened, spinning them into a quick circle. Rhis felt herself pressed against the glorious brocade of his costume—he was being one of his most famous ancestors, no doubt—and then a pair of unheeding couples spun past, almost colliding.

Appreciation for Lios's skill mixed with a distinct awareness of the fact that Lios was much more damp than she was. In fact, that clean herbal scent she'd sniffed earlier had given over to the scent of damp fabric and plain, honest sweat. Then he let her loose again, a gesture that somehow underscored that he'd pulled her close not out of a sudden, mad passion, but to keep her from being knocked down by those couples galloping by, twirling as fast as they could.

He whooshed out his breath again. *He will dance with every one of you*, Dandiar had said that first night. Until now, Rhis hadn't realized what that meant. As the evening had gotten later, she'd sat out for one, then two; sometimes friends had joined her. But Lios had been on his feet the entire night.

She glanced up again—her neck cricking—and saw him watching the other couples. For that moment his polite smile had faded, leaving him looking distinctly damp and tired.

"Do you want to sit down?" she asked.

Lios glanced down at her, his eyes startled for a moment. At first his perfectly arched dark brows indicated surprise, and then drew down into worry. "Am I stepping amiss?" he asked.

"Well, no," Rhis said. "Not at all. You're good—very good—but I was just thinking, there are a lot of us females, and if you have to dance with every single one—well, maybe at least one of us ought to be merciful and give you one chance to sit down."

Lios grinned, a big grin with beautiful, even white teeth, and a flush under his brown skin. "That's all right. It's—you know—a part of the duty, you might say. No worse than a long day in the saddle."

Rhis tried to smother a laugh, but was unsuccessful. Being likened to a long day's ride was not at all romantic, but on the other hand, it was funny, and if she couldn't have romance, wasn't a good laugh a decent enough trade?

"So you like riding?" she asked.

Another of those quick glances, slight worry quirking his brows. "Well, it's also, you know, part of the duties, in a manner of speaking."

"True," she said, feeling that this conversation was like laboring uphill back in Nym. Determinedly she added another boulder to her back, and toiled on. "What things do you like that *aren't* part of duty?"

Another quick grip, tight spin, and a collision averted. Rhis just glimpsed snowy white and black from beyond the curve of Lios's shoulder. Iardith. Not trying to collide—she would never embarrass herself that way—but trying to listen?

"Oh, I don't know, I enjoy everything I do. I, you know, keep busy." Lios blinked down at her, and must have seen something in her expression that she hadn't known was there, because he added in a low voice, "Gaming. I like gaming. Not big stakes. It's the chance, not the money. Horseracing too. When there's time, d'you see."

"Well, I would think you didn't have much time, what with duty, and all those translations in other languages. All that reading," she added.

He looked over to the side, his expression odd. Half laughing, half—worried? And who was he looking at?

Rhis turned her head and just glimpsed Dandiar, dancing with Hanssa. Dandiar grinned at them both, and then vanished.

"I think everyone is on the floor this round," Lios added. "Crowded."

"So do you want some punch?" Rhis asked. "I know I could use some."

"You don't mind?" he asked, and this time his relief was unmistakable.

She shrugged, thinking: *I still have your company*, but somehow it wasn't important any more. He was still handsome Lios, he was just as handsome up close as he'd been across the room, and he was nice—but somehow that boulder-on-the-head feeling was gone. In fact, she could say she was no longer in love. If that boulder-on-the-head feeling really was 'being in love.'

He guided them in a long, slow spiral toward the edge of the floor, and they ended up at the refreshment table. Again, everyone there gave way, and Rhis and Lios did not have to wait for a cup of the spiced punch.

He gulped down one in the time it took her to take a sip, then reached for another. He'd drunk half of that before they were surrounded by people who did not give way.

Iardith's white gown was at Rhis's right.

"Your blue and his silver look quite well on the floor," Iardith said to Rhis, smiling.

"Thank you," Rhis began.

One of Iardith's ducal heirs was talking to Lios.

"Your gown is the most beaut—"

"Will you just set this down there for me?" Iardith asked, handing Rhis a cup.

Rhis turned aside to set the cup down, wondering why Iardith couldn't herself, but of course there was that fabulous white gown. Which still looked as fresh as ever.

When Rhis straightened around again, the perfect white shoulder had turned, and suddenly Iardith was standing between Lios and Rhis, leaving Rhis staring at the shining black waterfall of hair, and the back of the wonderful white gown.

Iardith was busy talking to Lios, so quick and so smooth there would be no interrupting her. " . . . and we thought that a picnic would be a splendid idea, in the afternoon, of course, after everyone has a chance to rest . . ."

Rhis sighed, finished off her punch, and set down her cup down next to Iardith's. No one noticed as she made her way back through the crowd to her friends.

How late was it? Suddenly the millions of candles were too bright, her feet hurt from the marble floor, and she was tired of feeling hot and sticky from so many people pressed around her. The dance ended, and the musicians immediately began another. Rhis did not even turn around to see who Lios chose next.

"There you are, Rhis! C'mon, Breggo wants desperately to be in that diamond with Taniva and old Thenstras, there," Glaen said, emerging from the crowd and beckoning.

Glaen's pale hair hung in damp strings across his brow, and there was a splotch of punch on the side of his costume, but he grinned just as engagingly as ever, pulling Rhis forward.

Poor shy, tall Breggan gave her a distinct look of relief, and Rhis felt some of her malaise of spirit fall away as the dance began. If she'd been in a mood to laugh, it might have amused her, the way Breggan glared at the red-haired Thenstras, the short, burly, and very self-confident son of a wealthy and powerful baroness, whom Shera had pointed out their second day. Thenstras talked nothing but fighting, in a voice better suited to the field, and there was no mistaking the interest Taniva took in his talk.

As the four danced, Breggan glared, Rhis watched, and Taniva and the baroness's heir exchanged knowledgeable talk on the benefits of different types of swords for infantry versus those for mounted fighting.

Frequently Thenstras made Taniva laugh. It was a wonderful sound, and she looked like a warrior princess with her head thrown back and her wide, toothy grin.

But every laugh seemed to make Breggan more miserable, until finally Rhis whispered, under cover of her hand as she passed by Breggan, "I happen to know that he's twoing with someone at home."

Breggan's face went crimson, but his glance seemed more grateful than strained.

The dance ended a moment later—and Rhis soon saw that Lios and Shera were next. They danced in the middle of the floor, Shera chattering away with a bright smile. Of course Iardith was nearby—for once not with Jarvas, who watched, frowning, from the other side of the room. Iardith paid no heed to her partner, but kept her attention on Lios and Shera.

Shera seemed completely oblivious to Iardith, or Jarvas, or anyone else but her partner. Rhis admired her poise, not really thinking past that until she caught sight of Glaen dancing nearby, his forehead tense as he jerked his head to twitch his long, wispy hair out of his eyes.

Glaen, the joker, the one who never ever said anything serious, who sought Shera out just to exchange insults that kept everyone in earshot laughing, looked—well, he looked dismal. *Forlorn.*

But a moment later he was laughing again, his back to the royal couple in the center of the ballroom, and then Rhis found herself surrounded by a group who wanted to make up a round for the circle dance.

Glaen's look was still on her mind when the blue light coming in the high windows drained the gold from the candlelight, and the shine from the rich fabrics of everyone's clothes. Gradually the ballroom began to look dull, and everyone's clothes, once so rich and glittering, now seemed wrinkled and wilted. In twos and threes, the guests began to drift toward the doors.

Rhis had come to the masquerade with the idea of staying until the end, in case something magical happened with Lios. She had entertained in her secret mind visions of him coming back to her, and the two of them finishing out the night dancing—the way that Jarvas tried to maneuver Iardith into doing. Lios introducing her as his chosen as the sun came up, and they were surrounded by astonished, admiring eyes—

Feh.

Rhis blinked bleary eyes as Jarvas and Iardith stood in the middle of the floor, she with hands on hips, he talking, one hand making a quick, almost violent motion.

"That's one fellow who will never even do his duty," she muttered, and then was taken by a sudden, vast yawn.

"What's that?" Shera murmured.

Rhis blinked tiredly. "Oh. I didn't know I'd spoken aloud. Jarvas. Won't ever do his duty. Dance with the rest of us, d'you see? Lios did his duty."

Shera brushed a damp curl off her forehead. "Well, Jarvas would probably see as his only duty leading war-parties for Damatras's glory."

She yawned fiercely as they trailed other tired guests through the doors and down the halls. When they reached their rooms, Shera followed Rhis into hers.

"So what did you think of him?" Shera asked.

"Who, Jarvas? Oh! Lios?" Rhis asked.

Shera sighed, and rolled her eyes. "Who else? You've only been looking forward to tonight—last night—since we first arrived."

Rhis began to unfasten her hair, her fingers working steadily as her mind sorted through her emotions. "He's nice. And handsome as handsome can be," she said slowly. "But . . .

whatever I was feeling, it wasn't love. I think it was probably just—"

"Attraction. And silly girls our age—and silly boys, too—mistake attraction for love every day. Twice a day." Shera waved a hand. "I've heard that only a hundred times. A day. From my governess. When I first began to attend court."

Rhis grimaced. Why was Shera's voice so sharp?

"Well, my heart wants to be in love, but it's with his looks, and his voice, and the way he rides, and so forth. But our minds—" Rhis shrugged. "I don't know. Somehow all the, the tingle is gone. In me, I mean. He certainly never felt any toward me, he barely *saw* me. He's handsome, and kind, but being with him—well, I could imagine kissing him, but not talking to him, and if I can't talk to him, I find I don't really want to kiss him, either. Not any more." She was so tired she didn't even blush at the word *kiss*. "Does that make any sense?"

Shera was, after all, more experienced. She'd been twoing with someone for eight months and seventeen days before she left for this palace party, while Rhis's only experience had been a practice kiss or two with the cook's nephew, who'd taught her some ballads. Rhis had learned two things: one, ballad-kissing was more exciting than kissing the cook's nephew behind the flour barrels, and two, don't lift your chin at the last moment, because his nose might bump into your upper lip and that *hurt*.

"Of course it makes sense," Shera said in a flat voice, her gaze on her gripped fingers. "The fire of attraction comes and goes, just like lightning." She smiled a crooked sort of smile. "Our governesses don't tell us that when they prate of duty, but the ballads tell us."

"Some ballads do," Rhis acknowledged, eying Shera's odd expression, which brought her mind back to Glaen, and that unguarded stricken look. Glaen without his own mask. "I just didn't know what it meant. So how about you?" She sensed that something was very wrong. "Um, not just Lios, but what did you think of, well, the whole masquerade?"

"It was—interesting," Shera said, looking out the window.

Rhis felt as if someone had poured cold water inside her head. Shera's shoulders were hunched, she gripped her forearms across her front, and the corners of her smile turned down, not up. That was not the Shera she knew. Shera loved to laugh!

"Interesting?" Rhis asked.

To her surprise Shera's eyes began to gleam in the candlelight, gleam and gather light. Just as Rhis's confused, tired mind realized that that liquid glimmer along Shera's eyelids was tears, Shera got up, turned her back, and started out.

"We're tired," came her unsteady voice. "Good night."

TEN

Rhis woke up to the sound of a pair of birds squabbling musically right outside her window. She got up, her limbs feeling heavy but her head light, and knew she had not been asleep very long at all.

She glanced outside. A bird's nest was wedged neatly into some of the golden stone carving just above the arched window, little beaks just visible beyond the twigs and bits of duff forming the edge of the nest. A parent bird plunged its beak down toward the babies, giving them food.

A quick shadow flitted across the other side of the window. What had to be the other parent bird darted at a third bird, larger, with bright red and yellow feathers. Again and again it darted, warbling a loud, excited fall of notes, until the strange bird flew off, skimming over the treetops.

Rhis drew her knees up, put her chin on them, and watched the birds for a time. The one in the nest darted out of sight, then returned with more food. The other bird then took off, and it, too, returned with food. They took turns; the one not feeding defended the nest.

Birds, nest, mates. No, don't think about that now.

Rhis felt a kind of tired pleasure weighing on her mind, a little like a comfy quilt in winter. There was a lot of winter on

Nym's heights. In Damatras too, apparently. She'd heard people complaining how this was the worst spring they'd ever seen, but Rhis found the weather quite pleasant.

So thinking, she realized that what she saw outside was sunshine—and so she scrambled up, deciding that she could always sleep later. A bath, and breakfast, and a walk outside were what she needed now.

Especially as she did not really want to be alone with her thoughts, at least not yet. Somewhere under that comfortable blanket of tiredness was hurt, she knew. It had been made obvious last night that her dreams about Lios were just that, dreams, that she had probably shared, without knowing it, with more than half the girls present at this great party.

And why shouldn't they? Rhis thought as she slid into the bath. Short girls, tall girls, skinny, plump, some with talents at this, others good at that. Each is the heroine of her own ballad, Rhis thought as she used her favorite lavender-scented soap on her hair. How many had wished that Lios would abandon all the dances after hers, and devote himself to her alone? And make that dawn announcement, *This is the one I've chosen—*

How many times did he hear *What poets do you like?*

Rhis groaned, and ducked under the water, wishing she could rinse away her regrets as well as she could rinse away the stickiness from her night of dancing.

Well, she thought as she emerged, *at least if I was silly, I was just one of many, and he probably never remembered my babble past the time we parted. I was part of his duty last night, same as a long day in the saddle.*

She got dressed. Paused at Shera's door, hesitated, then knocked very softly.

No answer.

Remembering the tears of the night before, she tiptoed away, and wandered down through the palace—which seemed rather empty. Surely Shera had not suffered the same disappointment? Rhis shook her head. Shera had talked about Lios jokingly, not longingly. No, it couldn't be Lios.

Glaen?

She remembered that look on Glaen's face. And Shera's tears. What about Rastian, back home in Gensam—he of the eight months and seventeen days?

The sounds of voices, and the occasional clash and clang of steel broke into Rhis's circle of unanswerable questions. She wandered down a hall she'd never explored until she found a big room with a bank of east windows letting in morning light.

In the middle of the room several pairs, mostly boys but not all, were busy sword fighting. Others gathered round, watching. One of these was a familiar figure—medium height for a fellow, compact build, well-defined shoulders, long brown hair neatly tied back: Dandiar.

He stood with two other scribes, both holding papers. Dandiar stood with his hands clasped behind him as he talked with the other two in low voices.

Rhis headed that way.

Now the voices were clearer.

" . . . and the invitations ought to go out before nightfall, because there seems to be another storm due in."

"Any more bridges down?" the female scribe asked.

"Two," Dandiar said, waving a hand. "We've sent—ho! *Nice* defense, there, Tam. Laernad, keep that blade up, or you're going to have them coming at your neck every time."

On Dandiar's other side, one of the boys Rhis didn't know added, "Try using your back foot, Tam."

Out on the floor, two of those heirs to powerful Vesarjan duchies flicked up swords in acknowledgement.

Rhis's gaze went to Dandiar's hands. She'd never noticed before, but the visible palm was callused. She remembered the way his arms shaped the fine velvet robe he'd worn the night of the masquerade. So Lios made his scribes learn to fight? The other two scribes, one male, one female, still clutching their piles of papers, watched the practice. Did the girl also do sword fighting?

Dandiar spotted Rhis. "You're up betimes," he said with a welcoming smile.

"As are the rest of you," Rhis said.

A sudden, loud clash and a "Hah!" brought everyone's attention to the far end, where Jarvas, with a slight smile on his long, hard face, stood with his sword point resting lightly before one booted foot, other hand on his hip. His partner—one of the bigger, more brawny ducal heirs—wrung his hand as he stooped to pick up his dropped sword.

"Plays for keeps, looks like," one of the scribes observed.

Dandiar shrugged one shoulder, his brows slightly up. "Well, we can finish our discussion after the immediate duties are done," he said.

The girl scribe waved her papers, the boy sketched a wry salute, and they departed.

"Doesn't Lios let you people sleep?" Rhis asked. "At least you and your fellow male scribes. I noticed you were all on duty last night."

"Part of the job," Dandiar said. Then he grinned. "But we get to live in a palace, so there are advantages as well as drawbacks."

"The same could be said for princes and princesses," Rhis joked.

Once again Dandiar's brows soared. Rhis had never really noticed, but his light brown eyebrows were very expressive above his wide-set eyes. Of course with that snub nose and the broad forehead that made his face seem round, he wasn't handsome in the manner of Lios, but neither was he ugly. He was, if you had to say anything, *interesting*.

"Problem?"

His voice broke her thoughts.

Rhis realized she'd been staring, and her face heated up. "No," she said, looking down at her toes. "Lack of sleep. I'm awake, but my mind isn't. It still seems to think it's upstairs, under the quilt, asleep."

"Well, that state could describe most of us," Dandiar admitted. "I had to rewrite a letter three times this morning, just for stupid errors."

"You ought not to be working at all," she said, without thinking.

"Ready to take over the care and feeding of Lios's scribes?"

In other words, she thought, was she ready to marry Lios and take over his palace?

This time her face went fiery red, and she winced.

"Beg pardon," Dandiar said. "My attempts at jokes are about as clumsy as my letter-writing today."

"Well, if you were twitting me for sighing over Lios, I suppose I deserved it."

"You didn't deserve any hurt. I'm the one who deserves a sting," he retorted, looking at her with that narrow, searching gaze she'd seen once or twice before.

She looked away, her skin tingling as if butterflies made of flame scorched her with their wings. "Your costume was well-chosen," he added. "Did I tell you that? I meant to. You looked good in it."

Well-chosen. Not the words of court flattery, perhaps, but they felt the more real for all that. Again she tingled, like she was made of light. She said, "So did you. In yours." And blushed, turning away to watch the toiling fencers. Most of them seemed tired, and red-faced, all except Jarvas, whose blade flashed and clanged with phenomenal speed and strength.

"Was your dance with Lios disappointing?" he asked. "I noticed that you didn't finish it—unlike all the others."

"It was fine," Rhis said, and forced a smile. "He was hot and thirsty, anyone could see it. And I don't blame him. I mean, to him, I'm just another girl here." She hadn't meant to, but somehow she couldn't keep herself from rushing on. "If I were to make any guesses, Iardith is the one—and she'll look just splendid, gracing that ballroom, and all the other rooms too," she added, trying to be fair.

"There's a great deal more to being a queen than looking ornamental," Dandiar commented. He clasped his hands behind him again and rocked back on his heels and then forward again. "So Lios has been pursuing her? Or is it the other way around?"

Rhis opened her mouth to say that Lios seemed to be pursuing her, but then she thought back, and realized that every time she had seen them together, it was usually after Iardith had walked up and calmly taken her place next to him as if it was her right.

"Do people always defer to her? I mean, is it Iardith, or does that happen with everybody who is really gorgeous?" she asked, not seeing Dandiar any more, but Iardith's cool confidence, her seemingly unshakable conviction that she and she alone belonged at Lios's side.

Then she realized she was wit-wandering again, and shook her head. Blinked. Looked at Dandiar, to discover an unreadable expression.

"What do you think?" he asked.

"Lios doesn't pursue anyone. Not that I've seen, anyway. But then I've only seen him across rooms, and spoken to him once," she said. "He seems good-natured, and talks to whoever talks to him. Iardith is the pursuer, but," she added, "he hasn't exactly hinted her away, so I suspect that everyone else has assumed that he wants her beside him."

"How do you know that he hasn't tried hinting, but that she won't take no for an answer?" Dandiar replied.

Rhis remembered the gossip the horse-mad cousins had dropped about the King of Arpalon, and she grimaced. "Maybe she can't take no for an answer," she said. "Just as well I am no longer sighing!"

"Are you really glad? Would you like more time with Lios?"

People wandered around them to the sword rack to choose more weapons, and began new bouts, or commented on old. No one paid them the least heed. They were alone in the middle of a crowded room.

Alone to Rhis, too, who looked around without really seeing the combatants, or the observers. Was Dandiar serious? Of course she had seen that he had a special place with the new crown prince of Vesarja—and maybe he had enough influence to get her a private interview.

Did she want one?

"Not really," Rhis said. And then, quickly, "He's very nice, and I do appreciate this wonderful party. We have nothing like this palace, or these kinds of gatherings in Nym, and I'll remember it all my life—"

Dandiar waved a hand in a quick circle, and Rhis knew her compliments sounded more like excuses—both equally empty. She grinned, feeling foolish. "You *know* what I mean."

Dandiar bowed. "Could you doubt it, your highness?" He grinned, a strange sort of grin. "You've probably observed that he does talk to me. Rather a lot. You did make an impression. This morning he told me that five girls tried to get him alone in a cozy nook on one of the unlit balconies, three proposed to him, offering things their parents had coached them to offer as alliance bribes. One wanted to get him drinking wine, who knows why. And one—Taniva—commented that he moved as if his feet hurt. But only one asked him if he was thirsty, and he tried to make me guess, but I knew it had to be you."

"That's me, short on romance, but long on being practical," Rhis said, feeling an urge to giggle. She realized her emotions were going unsteady again, and she shook her head. "And it's not even my duty! Oh, I don't know what I mean. I think I need breakfast."

"Well, I know what I need, and that's to get to work." He executed a practiced bow, and then walked rapidly away.

Rhis stayed where she was, feeling oddly bereft. She liked talking to Dandiar. He was so easy to talk to—and everyone else, she realized, thought so, too.

Except Iardith, perhaps, because she didn't talk to scribes.

Rhis watched Jarvas tirelessly dispose of three partners before she realized that she hadn't seen how he did it, nor could she name the last combatant. Her mind kept twittering around in circles, just like the birds outside her window, except there was no food, no baby birds to benefit, just questions and more questions.

So she went in search of breakfast. There she found many of her friends, most of them looking as groggy as she felt. Vors was not there, she was relieved to see. Neither were Shera—or Glaen.

Carithe said, fighting a yawn, "There you are, Rhis! I wonder if Shera will wake up at all today. I have a suggestion. Let's begin rehearsals tomorrow. I'm too tired today."

"I am too," Rhis said. "I don't even want to think about entertaining. I just want to sit."

"And let people entertain us," Moret said. "Well, I've got some good news, as it happens. Just heard as I was coming downstairs. The singers have at last arrived, and their concert will be tonight."

Various people expressed pleasure—though not with any conviction. They all sounded too tired. Rhis decided she only had to stay awake until the concert was over, and then she could go early to sleep. If they arranged dancing that night, she was going to skip it.

Shera appeared not long after. "Oh, there you are. I must have slept too long," she said in a bright voice, but her eyes were pink around the rims, and her nose suspiciously pink as well.

So they all sat in the dining room talking about the masquerade. The talk quickly devolved into a guessing game about who had come as what famous person in history—and who had been the other half of their love story. Shera distracted Rhis with her frequent giggles, and the restless way she kept looking up at everyone who entered or left.

Rhis listened with scattered attention. Ordinarily she liked this kind of talk, but her wandering wits kept pursuing stray memories of the night before, and when she found her eyes closing once, she decided to get up and take that walk she'd promised herself.

No one else wanted to get up. They were all too tired.

"Are you crazy, Rhis?" Carithe asked.

"It's sunny," Rhis said, pointing at the windows. Somehow the sun had already slipped west. Her mind persisted in thinking the time late morning, but it was actually late afternoon. "We in Nym don't ever waste a sunny day, as it might be six months before we get another."

The others all laughed, and she exited on that happy sound.

Out in the garden, she realized that 'sunny' might have been the real joke, and not her six months. Though there had been blue visible in the sky, most of the rest of it was fast covering with clouds.

A coldish breeze kicked up, sending all the blossoms nodding and bowing, just like the guests at a masquerade, she thought hazily, as she wandered down a path. Occasional big splatters of rain smacked her face and the backs of her hands, but they felt good. The fresh air, the cool drops, all woke her up, and she began to walk more briskly.

A good walk, she decided, was exactly what she needed. And so she turned off the path and crossed a long grassy field toward the trees that bordered the lake. She'd go and watch the raindrops falling on the water. She loved seeing the sky reflected in the lake, and the wind-ruffled water, and long-necked birds gliding over the surface, wings just touching and sending rings rippling outward.

Maybe she could try to write a ballad about that, she thought as she started down the gentle slope toward the lakeside; her fingers twitched, and she realized she hadn't touched a tiranthe for days and days. Well, soon enough she'd be leaving, and she'd have plenty of time to play.

Lush trees formed green canopies overhead, warding the rain; the pleasant smell of wet grass and trees and ferns made her breathe deeply.

She began to round a bank of ferns, faltering when she heard voices.

Voices? Here?

She put out a hand and thrust aside a ferny branch. Two figures sat on a flat rock just above the plashing lake water. Two heads close together, one brown, the other golden.

Then she recognized them: Dandiar and Yuzhyu.

As Rhis watched in blank amazement, Dandiar took both Yuzhyu's hands, and pressed hers between his palms, and leaned forward to kiss her cheek.

Her low, infectious chuckle sounded above the patter and spat of rain on the leaves overhead, then she looked up, and went still, her mouth an O of surprise.

Dandiar's head turned. Quick, sharp.

For a long, agonizing moment Rhis stared down into his stricken brown eyes, and then she turned away, and stumbled up the hill.

"Rhis!"

Why should she stop? Why should she feel as if she'd been betrayed, and not the two who obviously wanted privacy?

She couldn't answer anything—or anyone.

She swept up her skirts and ran.

ELEVEN

Shera sat very straight and stiff next to Rhis, her face rigid, her eyes wide open, her focus on the stage, but every so often a silent sob shook her frame.

She tried to control them. Rhis could feel the effort Shera made. She could also feel Glaen's gaze, two rows behind them. At the other end of the first row sat Yuzhyu, her round face troubled, her attention on her lap. No one, as usual, paid any attention to her, but Rhis avoided her because she did not know what to say.

A kiss? Dandiar?

It's none of my business.

She would have assumed that Dandiar was the tutor the Ndaian princess had mentioned. What could be more natural? He spoke several languages, and he was a favorite with Lios. But kissing? Even cheek-kisses—

None of her business! Except the image of those two heads together would not leave her alone, it made her feel sick inside. She was ashamed of herself for that reaction. What two people did while obviously wanting privacy was none of her business. And she couldn't understand where the feeling had come from. But it was there.

Rhis turned her head just slightly, and strained her eyes to peer at Lios, who seemed to be the only one relaxed that evening. He lounged back in his chair, seated between two of the older countesses, both known for being betrothed. For once Iardith had not claimed her 'rightful' place at his side.

When had that occurred? And why?

Iardith was sitting four people down from Rhis, almost as rigid in posture as poor Shera. And next to her was Jarvas. Rhis could see his large, strong hand clenched on his knee. And just in front of them sat Taniva, who glanced back once, her brow low, her mouth grim, as she exchanged warlike glares with Jarvas.

Then there was Vors, three people down on Shera's side, and Rhis glimpsed *his* unhappy gaze, for just after dinner he'd come up and taken her arm, saying with a proprietary air, "Here I am, if you were looking for me. Let's go find a good seat."

Rhis had felt her rare temper flare.

"No, I wasn't," she snapped, and then immediately regretted it. But it was too late, for her mouth seemed to belong to someone else, for she heard herself add, "But I'll leave you with a little hint: Lelsei Sanlas is three times as wealthy as I am. Why don't you sit with her instead?"

And she'd left him standing there, his mouth ajar.

Was *anyone* listening to the singers?

Her thoughts swooped heart-ward with a kind of hilarious despair. She knew she ought to be listening. Indeed, she was, for at least some portion of her mind registered that the singers were exquisitely good, and further, they were singing ballads—her favorite kind of music. They sang in counterpoint, in difficult chordal changes that altered the mood of each song, but she could not get her mind to concentrate on that music!

Don't think about a scribe and a princess . . .

No. She wouldn't think about Dandiar and Yuzhyu. What was the use? And anyway, she seemed to be surrounded by unhappy people no matter where she looked. Had the masquerade turned out to be some sort of disaster, or were all the grim moods just resulting from tiredness? She just hoped that she, and everyone else involved in the play, could get a real night of sleep, or their "entertainment" was going to be a disaster before they even began to rehearse.

The only person missing was Dandiar. She'd noticed that right away. Not that she had the least desire to talk to him. But none of the scribes were about, so either they had other duties, or Lios had let them get some sleep at last.

A song ended. Clapping startled Rhis, and she joined hastily, locking her jaw against a yawn until her face ached and her eyes stung.

She blinked, sneaked a peek sideways—tears bounced off Shera's bodice, like glimmering gems, and splashed onto her lap.

Rhis bit her lip. No doubt the singers were glorious, but oh, would this evening ever end?

It did, and the audience began to rise, some furtively stretching cramped muscles, some shaking out skirts or tunics, pushing hair back, sending sidelong glances here and there. The mood in the room, despite the echo of sweet music lingering, was both strange and strained.

Shera slid her arm through Rhis's, her grip tight enough for Rhis to feel the trembling through Shera's frame. In silence they worked their way toward the door. Rhis felt a pang behind her eyes, the ache of tiredness, of lack of food—for she had not been able to eat—of too many emotions and no resolution.

"Reez—"

Rhis turned her head, gazing into wide blue-green eyes surrounded by bright corn-colored hair. Yuzhyu bit her lips, frowned as though trying to find words. Unheeding, Shera pushed on by, pulling Rhis, who followed without resisting.

What can she say? Rhis thought. Oh, of course. She probably wants to make sure I won't tell anyone. Anger flared through her, righteous anger. As if she would!

Shera stifled a sob.

A touch on Rhis' other side. Quick look—

"Vors."

His face went crimson. "Rhis, didn't you remember you promised to sit next to me at the concert? As for—as for what else you said, I beg your pardon if I said anything to lead you to believe—"

Rhis shook her head. Shera had paused, but Rhis could sense her looking the other way, occasionally dashing her cheek against her shoulder.

Rhis forced a smile. "Never mind, Vors. I apologize, too. We're all tired. Nobody is in a good temper. Let's both forget it, shall we?"

She stepped forward, Shera speeding her steps, and *at last* they were out the door.

Rhis peered anxiously down the hallway. It was full of tired-looking guests, most of them heading toward the sleeping chambers.

She and Shera were quiet all the way upstairs. When they reached their rooms, Rhis hesitated, wondering what to say, but Shera mumbled without looking up, "Good night."

So Rhis went alone into her room.

And though she did not intend to, and could not have said why, she cried herself to sleep.

And woke to the sound of thunder.

Morning. Morning? The light coming through the window was eerie. Rhis got up to look out. Huge dark clouds rolled inexorably overhead, the edges greenish with threat. A break somewhere to the east caused the early morning sun to reflect light weirdly under the clouds, making them seem darker.

But as Rhis watched the yellow glare vanished, swallowed by the forming storm. Again thunder rumbled, and Rhis opened her window, breathing deeply.

She smelled that wonderful scent of wet grass, and rain-drenched blossoms, but underneath it was a peculiar metallic taste.

Lightning arced over the sky, a violent purple, followed immediately by a thunderclap so loud she was almost deafened. She saw the sudden deluge before she heard it; as the thunder died away the hiss of rain abruptly became a roar. Rain sheeted down, a gray curtain.

Like home, she thought. Where I'll be going in a couple days.

Now the lightning was blue-violet, and a sudden gust of wind nearly ripped the casement from her hand.

Rhis swung the window shut with a worried glance up at the bird nest. There they were, snug in their carving-refuge. Lightning gleamed briefly in one bright round bird eye; the rain sheeted well beyond the stone carving without reaching the nest.

Rhis turned away.

What now? Breakfast. And the promised gathering in the library to begin on the play. But would it still be fun with so many people glaring at one another? She grimaced. What had seemed so good an idea before the masquerade seemed thoroughly dreary now.

She'd just finished dressing, and Keris had taken away her nightdress, when she heard a soft knock. She went to the door she shared with Shera, but the knock came again—from behind.

She realized it was the door onto the hallway.

Puzzled—her heart beginning to beat rapidly—she crossed the room and laid her hand on the latch. Then she said, "Who's there?"

She was not certain who she expected—or what she'd do if it were *any* of the males—but then she heard a familiar voice.

"Yuzhyu. May I march wissim?"

Wissim? Within. Laughter fluttered inside Rhis, but only for a moment. She remembered what she'd seen the day before, and winced, then smoothed her expression as best she could before opening the door.

"Come in," she said.

Keris appeared at the servant's door. "Would you care for refreshments, your highness?"

Rhis looked at Yuzhyu, whose lips moved, then she gave her head a quick shake.

"No thank you," Rhis said.

The door closed soundlessly, and then Rhis was alone with her guest.

"Want to sit down?" Rhis asked, feeling horribly awkward.

Yuzhyu ignored the question. Her small hands were pressed together, her fingers twisting, as she enunciated carefully, "I explain. I am alone in Vesarja. Dandiar, he iss kind. Like brosser. Me like sister."

She stopped, and smiled, her brows quirked with hope.

Rhis realized the poor thing had probably worked out her speech and memorized it. Why? "It doesn't matter," she said slowly. "It's none of my concern. And I won't tell anyone what I saw, if that is your worry."

Yuzhyu's wide gaze went diffuse, and Rhis saw her lips move as she translated to herself.

But before she could frame a reply the side-door opened, and Shera stood there, looking surprised. Yuzhyu backed up, her expression one of blank dismay.

"We were just about to go down to breakfast," Rhis said hastily. "Yuzhyu stopped by here on the way."

Lightning caused all three to look at the windows. Thunder smashed overhead, making the windows rattle, and the downpour intensified to an impossible din.

Shera said loudly, "I guess we can all go together, then?"

Rhis agreed, still feeling uncomfortable and awkward. Her relief gave way to a kind of chagrin as Shera chattered about the rain, and thunder, all the way down the hall. All of her remarks were addressed to poor Yuzhyu, who obviously did not understand the half. Rhis came in only for the occasional bright, false smile, and slowly she came to realize that Shera was just as glad that a third had appeared, preventing any kind of real talk.

Hurt and annoyance were her first reactions, but as they walked into the breakfast room and Rhis fought to control her almost overpowering urge to look around to see who was there, she realized that Shera was acting guilty.

Yuzhyu touched Rhis on the hand, smiled, and then sped away, her embroidered skirts swinging. Rhis turned her back; she did not want to see who Yuzhyu was joining. Lios or Dandiar, it was none of her concern.

Instead, she spotted Taniva standing with Moret and her cousin, plus some of the other riders. They were all ranged along the window, looking out.

The rain had turned to hail. Rhis hoped the garden would not be spoiled. The grass outside the terrace looked like a small lake with tiny white hailstones floating in it. Rain dappled the gray surface. Then lightning flared, the light mirroring back into the sky.

"No picnics today," Moret commented in a wry voice, with a meaningful glance at her cousin.

"Well, that was settled last night," he returned in a low voice.

"I know what you heard." Moret made a face. "I just don't believe it."

The rain outside was loud, and the thunder rolled almost continuously. Did the cousins think they were not overheard? Rhis was unsure whether to move or not, for if she did, she'd draw attention to herself.

"Oh, he was definite. As definite as he can be. At least, she thought so. She looked as sick as a fish out of water . . ."

Thunder blasted again. The tall cousin bent to hear something Moret said. As both backs were turned, she eased away, wondering who the 'he' was. Moret's sour tone made her think of Iardith. Lios, maybe?

Rhis sighed. What had happened to everybody? *Next time someone invites me to a masquerade, I ought to run and hide in a cave*, she thought as she got something to eat.

Only where to sit? Shera was over there, Glaen at her side. The two of them were conversing in low, fierce voices. Shera's back was stiff, her arms tense. No one sat near them; it was obvious they wanted to be alone.

From behind came Lios' familiar voice, easy, friendly as always—and with it, Dandiar's quick laugh, followed by the chatter of a growing crowd.

Rhis's cheeks burned. She was surprised at how her entire body was poised to turn, to search the crowd until she caught Dandiar's eye, to exchange the smile she had somehow become accustomed to. Looked forward to.

No. She would not, not, *not* turn around.

With relief she saw Taniva just sitting down in the far corner, and went to join her. Taniva gave her a preoccupied little smile, but said nothing. That was all right with Rhis.

Taniva's back was to the wall. Rhis vaguely remembered someone or other saying that that always betrayed the person with military training. They never sat with their backs to a room—they had to see everything. Well, Rhis was just as glad she had no military training. She wanted her back to the room. She didn't want to see anyone.

But she couldn't keep from noticing how Taniva's narrowed gaze searched the room continuously. There was a grim set to her jaw, as if she were brooding over something. But Rhis didn't ask, and Taniva did not offer any talk.

By the time they had finished, Rhis realized she'd heard no more thunder.

The violent part of the storm was over. The light had changed to a kind of silvery gray, and the rain was now a steady, gentle mist.

Taniva murmured, "I think I check something. I am suspecting something bad, like the rock on the edge of the cliff."

Without waiting for an answer, she got up and left.

Rhis followed more slowly, without looking to either side.

Almost immediately she found Glaen before her. "Rhis. May I talk to you?"

Rhis stared at the tight strain across his forehead under the drifting hair, the shadows of tension around his mouth. All the humor that characterized him was gone from his face.

She opened her hands, not sure what to say. Glaen took that as an invitation, and motioned for her to follow. They walked up a staircase she'd never explored before, and he ducked his head into a room, looked both ways, pulled back and beckoned. "Empty."

Rhis followed him into a little parlor, pleasingly furnished with an embroidered couch and two tables, with potted ferns set before the window.

"Part of being a worthless flirt," Glaen said as Rhis sat down on the couch, "is always knowing where there are little rooms where one can be alone." He leaned against one of the tables, arms crossed, his fingers tapping against his arms.

"You want to talk to me about flirting?" Rhis asked, confused.

"No. I know about flirting. I want to talk about Shera." And as Rhis made a gesture, he added, quickly. "Nothing that is confidential. Perhaps I ought to say that I wish to ask your advice."

The soft gray light coming in behind Glaen made him into a silhouette. Rhis shifted sideways so she could better see his face.

"I've done something really stupid," he went on. "Really stupid, and I don't know how to get out of it." He looked out the window, then back at Rhis. "You might as well know the worst. I called her a heartless flirt."

Rhis sat up as if someone had poked her, instantly annoyed. "Shera?"

"I know. I know." He clawed both hands through his hair, his fingers tense. "It wasn't Shera—she wasn't flirting, she was just having fun. It was I who was flirting. I've been flirting with every girl I've ever seen, ever since I discovered how much fun it was. In fact you might say I flirted not just with girls, but with everything." He cast a look back at Rhis. "Including work. Last year on my twentieth birthday my parents gave me my last warning, which I ignored like the previous ones, and on New Year's Day I discovered that they meant what they said, and they made my sister their heir. She's barely fifteen—six years younger! But she already knew three times what I did about the barony."

Rhis did not know what to say, so she said nothing.

"Don't worry about hurting my feelings. You can't say— or think—anything worse than I thought myself. It was salutary, and so I threw myself into learning shipbuilding, which had been meant for my sister, or my younger brother. And I have been. I like it. My sister never did. That's not the problem. Here's the problem. No one believes I'm serious. *I* didn't believe I was serious until this year, and it takes a lot longer to convince others when you've been a fool for years. Meanwhile along comes this party. I am invited here, and my parents send me, saying at least I can meet my peers while I'm wasting time. My sister—the new heir—is too young, and anyway she hasn't time to waste. No one knows I'm not the heir, by the bye." His wry tone, usually so full of humor, hinted at unhealed hurt. "I come, thinking I'll play hard. A lot of these fellows—Laernad, Dris, Breggo, Tam— came to play hard, because they work hard at home. Some of the others are here to play because they're going to spend their lives playing, and they either have the wealth to do it, or will marry it. Everyone thinks I'm one of the latter. Shera probably does too, because anyone from the south will have told her that I am worthless, don't mean anything I say—" He waved a hand in a circle.

Rhis said tentatively, "But Shera didn't come looking for a husband. She came to have fun."

Glaen turned around. "Right. I know all about Rastian. She never hid anything from me. And right from the start it *was* just fun. She's so quick with a joke, so much fun in a mock verbal battle. It was I who found ways to get her alone for more banter, more laughter, nothing serious, not until the other night when I saw her bantering with Lios, and I called her a flirt, and worse, tried to kiss her."

"Uh oh," Rhis said. "It made her mad?"

"Worse. It hit us both like that storm this morning." He clapped his hands. "Dazzle! I know better than to think dazzle is eternal, because it usually isn't, but dazzle on top of laughter, and companionship, and—" He sighed. "Well, after that, she *did* get mad. And flung that Rastian in my teeth. And I called her a heartless flirt and stomped off."

"Oh." Rhis now understood the crying.

"And this morning I tried to talk to her—explain—apologize—and she wasn't having any. Flung that 'heartless flirt' lightning-bolt right back at me, and added, it takes one to know one. So she dusted off, and here I am. What do I do now?" He turned away, a quick movement, and faced the window.

"I don't know," Rhis said. "Let me think. Is that all right? I have even less experience than—well, anyone here."

Glaen sighed. His thin fingers trembled as he wiped aside his eternally drifting hair. "I guess it's foolish to imagine you'd set all to rights with a few suggestions, like you did the other day, when Iardith almost hammered Carithe's and Shera's play. At least you aren't telling me I'm worse than mud-slime."

"Nobody is mud-slime. Unless they want to be," Rhis said, getting up. "And I don't believe you want to be. I never thought it before, and I don't now." She sensed he might be regretting what he'd said, and she didn't want him feeling any worse than he obviously did already. "Let me think. And if you want to talk again, well, I'm here."

"Thanks," he said, his back still turned.

Rhis let herself out of the room, and started down the hall. But when she reached the turning, just ahead walked a familiar figure—a male of medium height, long brown hair neatly tied back. A familiar figure dressed in the plain clothes of a scribe.

Bang! Her heart thumped hard. Glad of her soft slippers and the deep carpet, she experienced a sudden, intense urge to be outside, to see how the garden had fared, whirled around and sped downstairs.

Who cared about getting wet? No one in Nym—not if they ever wished to go outside at all, she thought, as she slipped out one of the arched access ways, and hastened along the flagged path toward the garden.

Why didn't she want to face Dandiar? Too many thoughts all yammering for her attention. Shera—Glaen—Lios—Iardith—Yuzhyu—even Taniva, and her odd attitude at breakfast.

Dandiar. Why did it upset her so, to find him kissing Yuzhyu's cheek? Whether that 'brother and sister' talk was true or not, Rhis could understand why Yuzhyu had come to see her about it—she didn't want gossip. The thought that Dandiar was prowling this empty hall, maybe looking for her in order to get reassurance about Rhis not blabbing it around, made her tense with disgust. No, more than disgust, with anger.

Why? She blinked rain from her eyelashes, rambling faster down the pathway as her thoughts galloped along. Dandiar. How much fun he was! And interesting. She liked him better than anyone else. Oh, he wasn't handsome like Lios or that grim, tough Jarvas, or powerful and wealthy, like half-a-dozen others easily named, but he was so very much . . . *himself.* She'd never met anyone like him. She'd felt, without even knowing it, that she could talk to him forever, that she would search every corner of her mind for something interesting to say, just to see that sudden smile with the shadowy quirk at the corners of his mouth, and the way his eyebrows rose in a sort of rueful humor, like a silent sharing of a private joke, just between Dandiar and Rhis. She liked the way he'd looked so appreciatively at her the night of the masquerade, admiration making his gaze linger. Nobody else's admiration made her feel outlined in light.

For a moment she imagined bringing him home to Nym, to meet her mother and father. Her mother, who was not the least interested in rank, would like him at once. Silly! The kiss with Yuzhyu presented itself insistently to her inner eye, and the fact that if it wasn't serious, then it had to be flirting. Had he been flirting with Rhis as well?

Was I flirting, and I didn't even know it? But it wasn't at all like the flirting she saw around her, the fans, the sidled looks, the compliments and giggles and going off to be alone. Of course, flirting could take a lot of forms—she'd just learned that with Glaen. Even mock insult fights could be flirting.

A quick step interrupted her thoughts. She looked up, her mind going absolutely blank when she discovered she was face to face with Dandiar himself.

"I saw you from the window," he said, pointing back over his shoulder.

Rain made him blink, and he wiped a lock of hair from his brow. Had he been running?

He smiled that funny smile she'd seen so many times, and couldn't quite interpret. He was so expressive, and yet she couldn't always tell what he was thinking. "Are you part water-bird?" he asked. "Half the times I've seen you have been out here in the rain."

"I like gardens," she said, the words random. "We don't have any in Nym. Not like this."

His smile disappeared, and that searching gaze replaced it. "Look," he said. "What you saw at the lake. It's not what you think. I don't know what's right, or if I ought to tell you—"

"You don't owe me anything," Rhis said, feeling that sick anger again. "I won't blab to anyone. Never intended to.

And I hate being asked not to," she couldn't help adding, though she felt hot and scratchy all over.

His cheeks reddened, but he'd gone pale around the mouth. "That's not it at all. Well, it is, but I never thought you'd say anything. I couldn't believe you'd want to hurt poor Yuzhyu, who's so blasted lonely here. It was a mistake for me to bring her, I know it now," he went on quickly, his words no longer carefully considered, but tumbling out, almost too quick to comprehend. "Some have a talent for picking up languages, others don't. I do, and I thought she would as well—"

Rhis waved her hands. "Wait. Wait. *You* brought her? I don't understand."

Dandiar grimaced, and looked down at his feet. Then up, straight into her eyes. "That's what I'm trying so badly to tell you. Yuzhyu is my cousin."

Her body had turned to snow, but she ignored that, struggling grimly to understand. "You mean she's not a princess after all?"

"Oh, she's the heir to Ndai, all right."

"All right, let me get this straight. She's your cousin. And a princess."

"Yes."

"And you brought her here, so . . . you wanted her to meet Lios?"

"No."

"No? Then why—"

Dandiar looked up at the clouds tumbling across the sky. "This is harder than I expected it would be. I—I thought it would be fun. I certainly liked being a scribe—"

"Wait. Wait." Rhis pressed her fingers against her head. "I wish this day hadn't started so awry. You are cousins with Yuzhyu."

"Yes."

"And you brought her here."

"Yes."

"But not to meet Lios. But it's fun to be a—you mean, you're not a scribe?"

"No."

"Then—who are you?"

Dandiar said gently, "Can't you guess?"

"How should I—" Rhis began, but then the puzzle pieces began falling into place. Princess as a cousin—not a scribe—

He was watching very closely indeed, for he said, "Go on." As if she'd spoken.

But she only looked up, unable to hide the sick feeling that replaced the confusion. "No."

"Yes," he said, and let out his breath in a short huff. "Here's the truth. I'm Lios. Lios Menelaes Dandiar Arvanosas if you want the whole name, as set out in treaty before I was even born."

TWELVE

"Impossible."

But as she said it, her mind raced from memory to memory, beginning with that kiss. A kiss on the cheek, with the clasping of hands, a gesture that really was *like a brosser*—or a cousin—like a member of a family, and not like a lover. Sidal had kissed Rhis just that way, the night before Rhis departed on her journey. Her mother had held her hands.

Back, back. The facility with languages—and the fact that Lios (the false Lios) hadn't spoken with Yuzhyu in her home language, when supposedly he knew so many. Dandiar's graceful bow, so practiced, with just that hint of humor; his callused hands, his trained eye in all the things you expected of a prince. Dandiar's freedom of movement, how he knew everyone, how much he knew of songs and history and books, like those many tomes being translated in the library that *the prince had already read in their many languages*—

Dandiar the Poet-King. *The joke*—

Rhis looked up.

"Go on," he said, again as if she had spoken.

"The joke." She wasn't solving a puzzle. There was no puzzle. There was only a masquerade, a false face, put on to fool his unsuspecting guests. A joke. Not on his name, but on his rank, so in essence, the joke was really on everyone who didn't know.

Her memory had now winged back to her first morning, and Lios—the pretend Lios—standing at the rail, laughing.

Laughing at the blindsided guests. Laughing at her, perhaps? For staring at the false Lios with lovestruck longing?

Rain streamed down both their faces now, unheeded. She dashed the water from her stinging eyes as she exclaimed, "Why?"

"I had to know what was real—" he started.

"How? When *you* weren't real? You were *lying*."

"I never lied. I just didn't tell all the truth—"

"Yes, you did," she declared, her chin trembling, her knees going watery. "When you said you were 'just a scribe.' As for the rest of what you said, maybe not the individual words, but in intent."

Dandiar looked down, his mouth pressed in a thin white line. "I did work as a scribe before I was officially made the heir, though it's true I was also a prince, and I knew that my work as scribe was part of my training."

Rhis went on, her voice trembling, "It was a lie in intent. Because it was real enough for all of us. But that is of no importance, of course. I remember very well how you and your false Lios—what is he, anyway?"

"Andos. Sword master's son."

"I don't care," she cried, though she knew it was unfair. But growing anger dismissed any such quibble. *She* was unfair? She hadn't even begun enumerating just how many unfairnesses had been perpetrated from the moment she'd arrived. "I. Don't. Care," she repeated, fighting to control her voice, which squeaked and shook. "I remember you two standing at the rail my very first day, how you were laughing away. Laughing over those who pursued Andos the sword master's son, thinking him

Lios the prince, and gloat over their futile efforts? Did you bother finding out why they did it, or was the joke much too funny for that?"

Lios Arvanosas, new Crown Prince of Vesarja, looked down at the rain dappling his open palms. "At first. But only partly—"

"You're so very clever, aren't you?" Rhis swept on, now furious. Her entire body trembled. "Running everything just like a play, and we're all the puppets. So you can pick and choose? What were your standards for picking a good queen? Beauty? Brains?" Her voice caught on a sob, and she gulped angrily, fighting for control. "*Truth*?"

Lios Menelaes Dandiar Arvanosas no longer spoke, just stood there, his mouth pressed in that thin line, his eyes wide and steady, his face blanched of color despite the streaming rain.

"Then you only had to snap your fingers, and what, tell whoever you finally picked that you were just fooling, but she won the prize? And she'd, what, be *grateful* that she won the prize?" Another sob of rage, and grief, whooped from deep inside Rhis's chest. "Well, I don't think it's clever. I think it's horrible, and disgusting, and mean, and the worst kind of lying, and I hate you, I hate you all, and I—I—I'm going *home*."

It took all her effort to get the last two words out, but she managed, then she whirled around and fled, crying hard now, hot tears mixing with the cool rain, almost blinding her. She stumbled once or twice, and blundered into a rose trellis, but she no longer cared about hands, or gown, or mud. She wanted only to get away, to be alone.

But she was not going to get her chance.

She had just reached the covered path leading to the west terrace when she almost ran into a little group.

"There you are, Rhis!"

Rhis stopped short, smoothing her hands over her face.

Carithe laughed. "You really do like being outside, don't you? We came to find out when we ought to begin practice with the play. Shera said you were the one to ask, so—" She shrugged, looking up at the two young men on either side. "We're asking."

Rhis opened her mouth to snarl, *Ask Lios*, but she stopped. With Carithe and the fellows was Terash, the shy islander, and a couple others that Rhis recognized having been once part of the crowd around Iardith and Lios.

Should she tell them? How would they feel? Humiliated, of course—as much as she felt. No, she was going to keep that secret, not for *his* sake, but for theirs.

If he wanted to tell anyone, he could do that on his own.

"How about later?" Rhis said. "I—I have kind of a headache."

"Well, of course, running about in that rain," Carithe exclaimed. "Go, order a hot posset, and rest! We can always begin later. Truth is, I think everyone is still tired, or something, because they're all out of sorts."

"Yes," Rhis agreed with false cordiality. "Indeed."

She felt the puzzled looks that followed her, but she would not turn around, or explain. She slipped inside, and almost fell into Vors's arms.

"There you are, Rhis," he said. "I've been hoping to get a chance to speak with you alone. Do you know you are the only person who is never alone here? I—"

"I want to be alone now," she said.

Vors's jaw dropped.

"Oh, it's not because of you." She gave a shuddery sigh. "Not at all. I—I got myself into trouble, and I—"

"Who?" Vors looked affronted, and clapped his hand to his side—though he wasn't wearing any sword. He looked a little silly for just a moment, then scowled and said in a deep voice, "Just point the villain out. I'll thrash him until he begs pardon. Or would you like me to challenge the rotter to a duel—"

Rhis snorted a laugh, surprised she *could* laugh. But it was an unsteady laugh, and tears were not far behind it.

"No. No. Nothing like that. Never mind, Vors. Anyway, it would never work, us courting," she babbled.

"Is there someone else?" he asked, his anger fading into a kind of wooden expression.

"Yes. Someone else." She thought about—no! "Someone—someone at home," she added in a sharp voice—as if he had questioned her, which he hadn't. But she realized that she was beginning to lie. "Look, Vors, I really must get out of this wet gown."

Vors bowed. "May I still count myself your friend?"

"I'd be honored," she said, but she knew as soon as she said it that they weren't going to be friends. Never had been. With a friend she would never use that formal tone—but it was the least she could say to salve whatever chagrin he might be feeling.

He stepped aside, and she picked up her soggy skirts and began to run.

She'd made it as far as the first stairway when she nearly collided with another figure. This time is was Glaen.

"Have you seen her?" he asked.

Rhis just shook her head.

Glaen rubbed his thin hands up his face and through his wild, drifting hair, the tendons standing out.

She resisted the impulse to linger, to offer comfort. What comfort could she really give? She sped on, pausing at corners to peer round lest someone else be lying in wait.

When she reached her rooms, it was to find Shera's door open, and a chaos beyond. Rhis stopped in the doorway, staring in amazement. Both Keris and Shera's maid were busy sorting, shaking out, and folding fabric, which lay everywhere.

In the middle of it Shera stood, her beautiful ruddy ringlets messy, her face blotched, her eyes and nose pink. She looked up.

"I'm leaving," she said, her tone half-defiant.

"I'll go with you," Rhis replied.

"I mean to home."

"I'll go too. Well, to the border of Gensam, anyway. Then I'll go home to Nym."

Shera stared. "What? You don't want to stay?" Her brows lowered. "Why are you all sopping wet? Rhis, has Glaen gotten you into his toils as well?"

"No. Of course not. Nobody has got me into any toils that I didn't walk into. I just want to go home."

Keris smiled at the other maid. Those smiles were calm, and adult, and Rhis knew that once they were away from their princesses, they would be talking.

That was a disagreeable thought, wondering just how many people, unseen as well as seen, were talking all through the palace. What kinds of stories were circulating.

Rhis felt dizzy as her perspective altered. In truth, she'd forgotten about the servants, who saw most everything, and heard more. How many of them knew about Lios and Dandiar? All those scribes had known, she realized. And that morning he'd been not talking, but issuing orders—

Forget him.

None of it would matter as soon as she and Shera had gotten through the palace gates and were rolling eastward toward home.

Rhis backed away and wandered into her room. 'Her' room. Hah. She went to the window and looked up at the birds in their nest. They belonged here more than she did, and probably no one but she knew that they were there.

Rhis heard a step behind her. "Something happened, didn't it?"

Rhis turned away from the window as Shera shut the door between their rooms.

Shera's eyes looked greenish in contrast to their pink lids. Her round button mouth puckered. "Have I been selfish as well as a heartless flirt? What has hurt you? Or should I say 'who?'"

"You are not a heartless flirt," Rhis declared, sidestepping the latter questions.

Shera sank down onto a footstool. "I am a heartless flirt. Worse. I'm fickle, and untrustworthy, and s-s-silly." She gulped.

"Uh oh," Rhis breathed.

Shera said, "Rastian is at home, trusting me. I know he is. I promised—so easily—I'd come here to have fun, and meet people, and be diplomatic, because you never know who you're going to end up on the other side of the treaty table from. I've seen that plenty of times, and I haven't even been at Court long. And then, and then, well—" She waved her hands in the air.

"It's Glaen, isn't it?" Rhis asked gently. "You don't have to answer."

"Oh, it'll be all over soon anyway. Everything always is, around here. And when I think how much I enjoyed hearing the latest gossip! Well, I guess it's my turn to provide the entertainment over chocolate and cakes. Yes, I somehow managed to fall in love, or in something, over that selfish, worthless, smart-mouth of a Glaen, and all in a very few days, when I've known Rastian all my life, and half of that time we've always known we would marry each other."

"You mean, arranged?"

Shera shook her head, and a long curl drooped over her eyebrow. She flung it back. "My father insisted that there'd be no arranged marriage for me, since I was not the heir, and my Mama agreed to it. So I was always able to pick for myself— though of late I've begun to realize that their worries about me were because my brother is probably never going to marry, and so the next heir will have to come from me. But I've liked Rastian all my life. He was the first boy I ever noticed, the first—the only—one I've ever kissed, and everyone likes our twoing, his family and mine." She covered her face with her hands.

"Well, we're going home, Shera. No harm done," Rhis murmured.

Shera flung her hands down. "Then you don't *know*. You couldn't, or you wouldn't *say* that. I can't just go back and *no harm done*. How can I face Rastian when I keep thinking about Glaen? *Surely* it's not just attraction, because I've been around much more attractive fellows, and while I know what it feels like, I never ever wanted to kiss them. And now—" She looked miserable. "How can I go home and try to kiss Rastian, and all the while I'll be thinking of that worthless Glaen?" She got to her feet and whirled around. "But I *have* to go home. Maybe I'll invent a crime, and get them to lock me in a tower somewhere. Or I'll ask Papa if I can go to his summer house on the mountain, and live there as a hermit, and grow roses."

Rhis remembered her mother's words: *Flirt all you like, but know you cannot marry until you are at least twenty. That might be a comfort.* For the very first time, Rhis allowed the possibility that those words might have some truth to them. Poor Shera!

A knock on the door caused the girls to go still.

Another knock. Louder, more insistent.

Rhis trod to the door, and called, "Who is it?"

"It is I, Taniva," came the strong accent of the Princess of High Plains.

Rhis pulled the door open, and Taniva strode in, her layered skirts swinging. Rhis was slightly distracted by the dashing outfit the Plains princess wore; high riding boots with wool tops and a fringe dangling down, the gold-edged layers of skirt, black, red, black, tight vest, and green silk blouse with long, dashing sleeves. Her hair had been braided and looped up; Rhis recognized the outfit as one she'd seen when Taniva was riding in the horse race.

Taniva ignored Shera, and turned to face Rhis, hands on her hips. She opened her mouth, then her striking black brows quirked in a comical frown. "You are wet. This has a reason?"

"Nothing that matters now. Is something wrong?"

"Yes," Taniva said. "I had suspicion yesterday. I challenge Jarvas, but he evades me. I watch this morning. They do not appear, do not appear, and so I am going about to check. Not loud. I go to stables, pretend to wish to look at his horses. They are both missing."

Shera looked from one to the other. "Who? Who is missing?"

Taniva paid her no attention.

Rhis said, "Jarvas? He's missing?"

Taniva nodded once, and crossed her arms, a martial movement that brought Jarvas very much to mind.

"And—" Rhis prompted.

"Pah. You did not know? I thought you saw everything! Jarvas has carried off Iardith."

"Carried—" Rhis tried to make sense of the words, and couldn't. "You mean . . . abducted?"

Taniva jerked her chin up. "Gone."

THIRTEEN

"Gone?" Rhis repeated. "Jarvas? And Iardith?"

"Yes. Yes. Yes," Taniva said, jerking her chin up and down each time.

"Gone." Rhis drew in a breath. "I'm sorry, but I'm very wet, and cold, and I think I'm dizzy."

She plumped down onto a hassock.

Taniva scowled at the door leading to Shera's rooms, which had opened. Shera's maid whisked back and forth inside the room. How much had she heard? Taniva strode over in two long steps and slammed the door, then she stood with her back to it.

"If I am home, I know what to do: I ride and bring her back. But here, I do not know what to do. If I go to Lios, will I start trouble? Rhis! You always know what to say, I see this in the few days we are here. So I ask you. What shall we do?"

Shera let out a long sigh. "If the King of Arpalon finds out, he'll have a perfect excuse for war. Not that that is our affair."

"Is. Mine. War against Damatras will mean Arpalon's army marches through my lands," Taniva stated. "I do not care who wants what. When armies march, their trail leaves broken land. Especially if Damatras tries to meet them outside his border, as any smart king will do. It will be in High Plains he does it."

"Jarvas's father is smart," Shera added in a sour voice. "At least, when it comes to fighting. Anything else is arguable, from what I overheard at my mother's court."

Taniva gave her a look of mild appraisal. "You speak right, you."

Before she could go on someone new banged on the door.

"Reez! Reez!"

"That's Yuzhyu," Rhis said, looking at the other two. They just stared back at her, so she went to the door herself. "Yes?"

"I must see you. Trouble! Zat pest from Arpalon—"

Rhis opened the door.

Yuzhyu almost tumbled in, her frizzy blond hair wild. "Ah!" She pointed at Taniva. "I am in stable. I want to ride. Before ze boomer-in-sky. I hear him. He see me once. I zink. He zink I not . . . om! Um! Conceive? Follow?"

"Understand?"

Yuzhyu nodded in relief. "Jarvas zink I not understand so much. But I do. I know he want zat princess. Iss angry wid my—my cousin . . ." Yuzhyu looked away, and Rhis knew she was referring to Iardith's determined courtship of the false Lios.

Before Rhis could draw another breath, Yuzhyu pulled from her clothing not one but two long, wicked looking knives. For a moment she held them along her forearm, blades out, then with a complicated whirl she flipped the knives up, caught their handles, and held them points out.

Taniva whistled, her approval unmistakable.

"He like trouble," Yuzhyu said. "Make trouble for my cousin." She moved her hands in a quick blur, and the blades vanished in her clothing again. "I zee you come here. I sit and zink. Do I tell my cousin? Or do I follow Jarvas, make him come back wiss princess? No, I first zee why you are here." On the word 'cousin' Yuzhyu sent a questioning look Rhis's way.

Rhis shook her head.

Yuzhyu's expressive brows arched in relief.

"I do not want war," Taniva said. "I have said nothing to anyone yet, except here." An emphatic thumb toward the floor of Rhis's room.

All three of the others looked at Rhis.

And Rhis stared back, wondering why they expected her to decide.

Should they all troop off and find Lios? No. Not the pretend Lios.

She slid her hands over her face. War—Dandiar—Lios—

The whirling thoughts, each carrying its own load of emotions, seemed to turn her brain into stone.

Then something Yuzhyu had said recurred, and she said, "*We* can go after them, and bring Iardith back."

Taniva's dark brows lifted, and she whistled soundlessly. "Yes. Then there is no war."

Yuzhyu nodded slowly. "And no skittle? Scattle?"

"Scandal," Shera said dryly. "Get her back? How? We don't have armies. We don't even have guides!"

"I guide." Taniva smacked herself in the front. "This, I know what to do. How to tell Lios, how to avoid war when I am in another land, that I do not know. I act in my land. Here I listen only."

Yuzhyu concentrated on Taniva, her mouth moving, but at the end she gave an emphatic nod of agreement.

Shera sighed, long and shuddering. "It—well, it makes sense. If it wasn't us. I mean, if no one finds out about the abduction, then there can't be any war, right? Only how can *we* save her?"

"It is for you to talk," Taniva said to Rhis "You talk good. You get her out without war."

Shera sighed again. "I'd offer to come, but I don't know that I could do anything."

Rhis said, "You know all the local politics, and I sure don't. I never needed it before!"

All four looked at one another.

Rhis shook her head. An abduction? War? None of it yet seemed real.

Her inner eye offered her a memory of Dandiar's face, but she thrust it away in anger. His masquerade was real enough, and so was the anger and hurt she felt.

Even so, she did not want there to be a war. And if she could prevent it, why not do so? And, oh, if she could make some kind of . . . grand gesture, show that Dandiar—

Show him what?

"If we ride fast, we catch up," Taniva said. She gave a grim smile. "Jarvas will not find it so fast, traveling with female who does not want to travel. Maybe this Arpalon pest makes the journey heavy for Jarvas. We catch up, Rhis talk Jarvas out of it. If he acts like fool, we steal princess back. I know how to do that." She grinned, a challenging grin, and smacked her hand against the jeweled blade hilt at her waist. "It's a game for us, in High Plains. We ride back with her, pretend we are all making a long journey together. No war."

"Ride fast?" Shera repeated faintly. "How *long* a fast ride?"

"Week." Taniva shrugged. "Maybe two."

Rhis and Shera exchanged grimaces. Two *weeks?* They'd never ridden longer than an afternoon. If that.

"But it must be now." Yuzhyu pointed up at the sky. "Rain going." Her expression changed. "I get horses." She whirled around. "You can ride?"

"Ponies," Rhis admitted.

"On bridle paths," Shera said slowly.

Yuzhyu grinned. "Is enough. You learn on ride."

Taniva said, "I will go with you, give commands to my people. They say nothing to anyone here. No one will know." She turned around. "You two come to stable with your things. I will be ready."

And the two princesses disappeared.

"Two *weeks?*" Shera squeaked.

Rhis thought about Dandiar—no. "If they can do it, I can do it," she said firmly. Adding in a lower voice, "Two weeks away sounds fine to me."

"They might be able to disappear without causing comment, but what about us?" Shera said.

"Well, I happen to have declared that I'm leaving today," Rhis said, feeling that horrible heat in her face again.

But Shera, it seemed, was too preoccupied to notice. "I did as well. It's really our maids, then. What do we tell them? I know mine will send messages back to my mother."

"Then don't tell her anything," Rhis said. "She's already packing—have her unpack, except for a riding journey. She needn't know any more than that."

Shera stood up, then plopped down again. "What do I need?"

Rhis rubbed her thumb against her lip. She remembered a few of her childhood journeys, before Elda had declared that it was time to become a young lady. "Riding clothes. A waterproofed cloak, if you have one. Money, if you have it. We'll probably find cleaning frames, or maybe we'll use streams, but this much I remember: you can't overburden horses with a lot of stuff."

Shera stared down at her hands, then nodded. "Yes. That makes sense. All right, then, two riding outfits, one to wear, and one to keep as a spare . . ."

She went out, muttering.

Rhis opened the door to the little side room that served as her wardrobe. There she found Keris busy. The woman saw Rhis, curtseyed, then, as Rhis didn't speak, went back to her work.

Rhis realized that Keris was sewing beads back onto her masquerade gown. When had she torn it? A pang of guilt squeezed her heart. She sighed.

Keris had been selected by Rhis's own mother. Where did trust begin?

It has to begin here, Rhis thought.

"Keris, there's trouble," she said.

Keris looked up, her face kind, but aware. And not surprised.

"How much did you hear?" Rhis asked, pointing back to her room.

"Very little from you and your guests," Keris said. "But I am afraid that Princess Iardith's maids are hysterical. His highness's own people are keeping them sequestered—and protected."

"Then Lios knows," Rhis murmured—and Dandiar's image came to mind. Lios's image. Odd, how the right face flickered before her inner eye, but the names were still backward. *That handsome fellow has his own name. Andos.*

Rhis shook her head. "We're going to bring her back. But I don't want anyone to know. Including Shera's maid, if you can. The idea is to prevent war, not cause it. I do have my sister's ring, in case there's danger, so we ought to be all right."

A crease appeared in Keris's brow, but she merely bowed her head.

Rhis looked away, fighting that detestable blush that always betrayed her. "This morning I, ah, made it clear to, ah, the prince of Vesarja that I was going home. I'm not sure what to say now. I don't really want to say anything, I just want to go, get Iardith, and think."

"I can put it about that you decided to take a little trip instead," Keris offered. "Some time for reflection."

Rhis said hesitantly, "Shera is going to come. I don't think she is telling anyone. She doesn't want trouble at home."

"Leave it to me," Keris said. "I know your mother would be pleased that you're trying to take action to help another. And as you say, you have Princess Sidal's ring. I will get your things together."

Rhis sighed with relief, her face warming at the compliment.

And each turned to her task. Rhis was glad to get out of her wet clothes at last, and into her riding outfit. While Keris was busy packing a satchel, Rhis stuffed a goodly portion of her jewels into a pocket in her tunic. She did not know how the other three would fare for money, but Rhis knew that gems were easily replaced in Nym, and they would have to get food somehow.

Shera reappeared just about the time Rhis was done. Each hefted up a fairly heavy satchel; by the time she reached the end of the hallway, Rhis was sorry that she'd included her tiranthe. What had seemed a scarce selection of essentials while the satchel was lying on the dressing table now seemed like a year's worth.

"Ugh," Shera muttered, shifting hers to her other shoulder. "If we have to carry these the entire way, I'm not going to make it."

"Horses," Rhis said.

"Then the horses get the weight—including us."

Rhis grimaced. She said nothing more. Her insides had tied into knots of apprehension, lest someone see her. Someone like Dandiar. Er, Lios.

But the hallways were empty; either something had been planned to draw the guests, or everyone was still tired from the masquerade.

Whatever the reason, she and Shera made it down to the stables without seeing anyone they knew, and there they found the other two waiting.

Rhis was surprised to see three young women—one of them a girl, on closer look—waiting with Taniva, all of them armed not just with swords and knives but with bows and spears. These latter they carried in the crooks of their arms, pointing at a slant forward, horsehair decorations below the blades streaming. These three each also led a couple of riderless horses on long ropes. Satchels and travel gear had been strapped to their backs.

Taniva saw everyone mounted up. Rhis got a shaggy horse with yellow hair. Shera's was a roan beast who showed teeth at Rhis's, sidling and rolling its eyes.

Rhis looked around with apprehension, but the few stablehands in sight were busy elsewhere. No one seemed particularly interested in Taniva's prospective riding party.

In silence they rode out into the misting rain. The silence stretched as they cantered easily down the stone-paved road, first south through the gates, and then west, to catch up with the north road. Rhis discovered that riding a horse wasn't all that different than riding a pony, except the animal was much taller.

Rhis pulled her waterproof cloak around her like a tent. This cloak had been a gift from Sidal, the magic spells that kept the water running down it performed by her. Shera also had a magic-protected cloak. Neither of the others did; Taniva's hooded jacket was made of long white yeath-fur, naturally water-repellent, and hideously expensive anywhere but in the highlands, where the yeath shed their coats every spring, scratching the strands off in clumps against bristly shrubs. It then had to be picked off by hand.

Yuzhyu wore a layered cape of wool that seemed to keep her warm, if not as dry as the others. Her yellow hair was damp, but her face, glowing pink from the cool wind, was expressive of good-natured enjoyment.

The sight of Taniva's silent guards, who had put their spears into rests hanging from their saddles, made her mind range back to what Keris had said. Then she considered what Keris had not said.

Rhis knew there were two worlds in any given castle, palace, or home big enough to function as a little kingdom inside itself. There were the servers and the served. If people had lots of money and power, they could be served and do nothing.

Rhis had also learned that there were two kinds of loyalty: there was paid loyalty, and personal loyalty. When young Ama, the upstairs maid, had been so sick, Rhis had done all her room chores herself. Why not? She'd learned how to braid her hair and dress herself when she was small, because her mother had insisted. And she knew how to make a bed and sweep a floor and pass dirty clothes through the cleaning frame, fold them, and stow them in the chests. So she'd done it, just as her older sister Sidal had done it, but afterward she'd realized that Ama the steward had a different attitude toward her than she did toward Elda, who expected her servants to work every day, just like she did. She often said that if you did your duty, you had no time to be sick—but then she never seemed to get sick.

When Rhis had talked about it with Sidal, her sister had said, "Paid loyalty stops at the chores the person is hired to do, just as if I were hired to guard a caravan down the mountain. I would do that, and only that, unless I found the leaders to be worth my personal loyalty. Then I might choose to see them safely home past the agreed-on place, or give them some other help that was not in the contract, like watching their little ones during a rest stop. It's my personal choice. Friendship works that way. You don't have paid friends—and never forget that, if you do end up living in a court somewhere. There is no such thing as paid *friends*. Paid *companions*, whose job it would be to nod and smile and pretend you're the center of their lives, courts are full of those."

The other girls were all silent, obviously lost in their own thoughts. *I don't know Keris*, Rhis thought. *She doesn't really know me. But if she has personal loyalty, it would be to my mother.*

That left Shera's maid, who might be reporting on Shera out of personal loyalty to the Queen of Gensam. She didn't have any loyalty to Shera, or she wouldn't be sending reports back. Or did she, and the reports were written to please the queen—to hide worrisome things, and report only the good things?

Rhis didn't feel she could ask Shera those questions. She couldn't even resolve them in her own situation. What worried her was what Lios might find out—if he did, and what would happen. Keris had promised that she would 'take care of everything.' Rhis did not know what that really meant.

It means I should not worry about it, Rhis thought. *Since I can't do anything about that any more. I chose to see this chore through.* She sighed. She was tired, despite the night of sleep, and desperately hungry, for she still had not eaten, though the sun was well west.

So she turned her attention to her companions. Yuzhyu had brought no one along, just like Shera (whose head was bowed, and occasional sniffs issued forth from under her hood) and Rhis. Taniva had the three servants with her. Even the girl was armed and very fierce looking.

These three set up camp once Taniva had chosen a good spot beside a stream, where the horses had sweet grass to crop. They were swift and efficient; in a shorter time than Rhis expected they had two tents set up, and a savory-smelling meal cooking: mostly boiled grain, with spices added in, shallots one found farther down stream, and sprinkled over it a very sharp cheese that they'd brought from home and preserved carefully.

The portions were small but Rhis discovered the grain was filling. The dishes were carved out of wood, very flat—easy to pack, Rhis discovered, watching them clean up.

No one spoke much that first night. They were all far too tired, even Taniva, who sat brooding near the fire, which reflected in her eyes. The sleeping arrangements were crowded—Taniva and the servants in with her (one of the women was always on guard duty) and the other three princesses in the tent that had been the servants'. They slept rolled up in their cloaks and capes, with clothes from their packs as pillows. Nobody had night clothes.

Rhis was determined not to complain. *Adventure*, she kept telling herself. She avoided the other term in the old saying: she did not want to think about tragedy.

FOURTEEN

Rhis woke to the sound of laughter, followed by chatter in a language she had never heard before.

Her face, hair, and mouth were gritty, her legs horribly sore, and the rest of her body felt as wrinkled as her clothes looked when she forced herself to get outside the tent, stand up, and shake out her cloak.

Taniva was already up, hair brushed and braided. She was helping with the cooking. The good smells chased away some of Rhis's wrinkly mood. "I heard laughter," she said.

Taniva's grin widened. "They say, my people." She indicated her three guards. "They not want to be in Lios's guard. When they find out that princess is missing."

Rhis folded her cloak. "Oh, I hadn't thought of that." She remembered Lios's guards. They were vague memories, silent—mostly men but not all—who stayed out of the way of the guests.

"What I wonder," Shera said in a very disgruntled tone as she crawled out of the tent, her curls wild, "is how Jarvas managed to get Iardith away without anyone knowing. He can't have any magic—not that I ever heard—and the way she was making a dead set at Lios, you'd think they'd hear her kicking and screaming clear in the capital when they tried to wrench her from his side."

"No magic made by Damatrans," Taniva stated definitely. "They hate mages."

Yuzhyu looked up from brushing off her clothes, her eyes narrowed in a way Rhis had never seen before. Very intent.

"They must be tough if they don't fear busy-body mages nosing in anyway, and making trouble," Shera observed, adding a soft "Ouch! Eugh!" in an undervoice as she fingered the tangles out of her hair. "*Why* did I think a hairbrush was too much trouble?"

"You can share mine," Rhis said. "Maybe the Damatrans have magical protections. Many lands do, if the kings don't want powerful mages around, even with the laws against magicians in government, and the vows they make."

Taniva said, "That is what we are told, on the High Plains. Damatras has some kind of protection. *Verrrry* powerful. They fear no mage. They fear no one!" She grinned, making a swift motion like a sword slashing.

"Well, about Lios," Rhis began.

Yuzhyu paused in the act of braiding her hair, question puckering her brow over her big blue eyes.

Rhis didn't finish her sentence. Was what she'd heard a secret or not? It was a despicable secret, if so—but it wasn't hers.

"About Lios?" Shera asked, shaking her cloak with a snap. "Eugh. Dirt got into *everything*. How is that possible? I was so careful when I lay down."

Yuzhyu said, "Lios is cousin to me."

Shera said crossly, "We knew that." Then she crossed her arms. It was evident that already she hated this venture. But she seemed determined not to be the first to complain.

"I don't suppose," Rhis said as politely as possible, "there is a chance of washing up a little?"

Taniva pointed with good cheer at the stream, then sat on a mossy rock, her bowl on her lap.

Rhis gritted her teeth. She knew the water was cold from drinking it the night before. But she marched to the stream-side, crouched on a rock, dipped her hands into the water. The first splash of cold water on her face made her gasp, and she almost missed the squawk, "What?" from the campsite.

Yuzhyu told them about Dandiar's masquerade, she thought, and finished with her washing.

When she reached the camp, her face and hands tingling, it was to find Yuzhyu eating her breakfast, her expression unhappy. Taniva was laughing. Shera stood in the middle of the camp, her eyes wide, her mouth open. "I can't believe it, I can't!" As soon as Rhis appeared at the top of the trail, she turned on her. "Did *you* know that Dandiar the scribe was really Prince Lios?"

"Found out yesterday," Rhis said.

Shera clapped her hands. "I have to admit, it gave me a bad moment, until I thought over everything I'd said in front of Dandiar. You know, about Lios. But I scarcely was ever even around Dandiar, because I thought—well, anyway, the important thing is, how *romantic!*"

"Ugh," Rhis exclaimed. She absently accepted a bowl of warmed-over boiled grain with more cheese crumbled over it. She found a flat rock to sit on as Taniva's guards silently dismantled the tents, rolled and packed them on the waiting horses.

"Eat up," Taniva said, slapping her leg. "Then we ride. Ha! It's very funny, that about Lios. Why he do it? Makes me think of war ruse, back in history."

"War ruse?" Rhis asked, to shift the subject from Lios.

"King traded clothes with his man. Traveled with servants on treaty mission. Heard all he should not have. Servant heard all they wanted him to hear. At meeting, out he comes with truth instead of lies they told servant!" She slapped her leg again.

"So," Rhis said. "Meeting all of us at his party needed a ruse of war?"

Taniva paused, staring skyward at birds streaking from treetop to treetop. She held her hand out stiffly above her knee as if frozen by a stone spell.

Yuzhyu cradled her bowl in her lap, mute and unhappy.

Taniva's dark brows contracted. "Did not think of that. Hah!" She slapped her leg yet again, then rose from the rock she'd been sitting on. "I wash bowls—you eat fast. We must ride. When we did not come back, maybe they think we are also taken. Hah! Hah!" Her laugh was somehow both jolly and fierce.

The idea of Lios's guards riding after them made Rhis hurry her breakfast down far faster than she would have liked. It was still sitting in what felt like a solid lump inside her when they resumed the northern trail, every trace of their campsite having been thoroughly eradicated to the two guard women's satisfaction.

This second day on the trail the riding order changed. The two women rode far in the back, and the younger one ahead, out of sight. Later Rhis realized that they were expecting trouble, and so having guards far ahead and far behind lessened the chance of the princesses being taken by surprise.

At first Rhis and Shera rode next to one another.

"My butt hurts," was the first thing Shera said, in a sulky voice. "I hate this. I don't know why I did it. Yes I do. I had to get away from Glaen. And, oh, I think I wanted, and still want, to do something to make them all—" She waved a hand in a circle.

"Stun them," Rhis said.

"Yes."

"Make them sorry."

"Yes!"

"You realize we're probably going to end up doing something really stupid," Rhis said regretfully. "I mean, you and I barely know how to ride a horse. How are *we* going to rescue someone?"

"I don't know," Shera admitted. "I thought I'd just copy whatever Taniva does when the time comes. She certainly knows what to do. As for everything else." She slewed around in her saddle. "Exactly how did you find out about Lios and that scribe—I mean, the scribe and the—what *is* Lios, anyway? Er, the false Lios?"

"His name is Andos, and he's the sword master's son. Dan—Lios told me himself," Rhis said.

Shera's eyes widened. "He did? And you did not come straight to tell me?"

"No. I was too angry. And when I got to our rooms, you were already upset."

Shera frowned between her horse's ears. "Then that has to have been yesterday."

"Yes."

"And you're angry? *Why* did he tell you?" Shera's eyes narrowed.

"Because I saw—something. By accident. He came to explain, and, well, it just popped out."

"I'd love to know what you're not telling me," Shera said, still with that unnerving stare.

"Not my business to tell," Rhis retorted.

Shera flickered her fingers like a fan waving. "What I really want to know is, why are you angry? Did you say something awful and the wrong one heard it?"

"No. It's lying, don't you see? Judging us, like, like, I don't know, some sort of spy, and laughing about it, and gloating—"

"Did you ever see them laughing and gloating? I didn't spend much time with either of them, but neither seemed the gloaty type."

"The first morning. They were alone by the rail on the terrace, laughing away. Probably at the rest of us."

"You don't know that, though, right? I mean, they could have been laughing over some mistake one of them made, or Lios trying to wear Dandiar's clothes—or the other way around—oh, you know what I mean."

"He said it was all a joke," Rhis muttered.

Shera was silent as the horses stepped onto a narrow trail above a rocky gorge. Below water fell with a roar. The trail was slippery, the horses stepping carefully single file. Shera slewed around again to glare at Rhis. "I don't want to make you mad, but sometimes I wonder if you're more like Elda than you think."

Rhis flushed. "I am not!"

"Well, you sure can get all superior," Shera said. "I mean, about this. Usually you're the nicest girl I ever met, better than anyone in Gensam, and I *mean* that—"

"Skip that," Rhis said crossly. "This what?"

Shera waved her hands—the horse stumbled, one hoof slipping in mossy muck, and she clutched hastily at her saddle, her curls swinging forward and catching in the reins. "Ur-r-r," she growled. "I do hate this. Riding, I mean. 'This' before was Prince Lios, the real one. Can't you see how romantic it is, he wants to be appreciated for his own self? And when I think of Iardith so very busy chasing after a sword master's son, I could fall off this horse laughing. I might fall off anyway," she said, and straightened around as her horse slipped again.

Rhis did not answer as the animals plodded upward. She was suddenly aware of Yuzhyu riding silently behind her. Rhis could not guess how much the Ndaian princess heard or understood. Now she was afraid to turn around. Besides, she had to think about that nasty comment about Elda. She didn't think she was being superior, but that didn't mean others might not see her that way. Elda certainly didn't see herself as superior, she saw herself as truthful and duty-minded.

These disagreeable thoughts chased round in her mind without ever coming to rest as the horses climbed ever upward into a spectacular mountainside. Nym mostly had a variety of evergreens growing, but here there were all kinds of trees, and wild roses climbing over rocks, and a hundred other types of plants that Rhis had never seen before.

Taniva kept urging them on, despite Shera's increasingly plaintive requests for rest. Yuzhyu never spoke at all, and Rhis stayed quiet. Her first reaction was relief when they stopped on a grassy plateau with a rocky fall at one side, obscuring the valley below.

The guard women built a fire under the shelter of the outcropping. Rhis sat passively, glad to be off that horse as she watched the two working. The oldest woman stepped out to check for telltale smoke rising, then put one hand to her back and another to her neck. Rhis grimaced, realizing they had to feel as tired as the girls. More, if they'd traded off patrolling outside the tents the night before.

So she made herself get up and offer to help with the cooking. Taniva translated, got a brief answer, and handed Rhis a flat board and some root vegetables plus more of the shallots from the day before, somewhat withered after a day in a saddlebag, but still aromatic when she began chopping with slow care. She worked with the board on her knees, unused to these wicked sharp knives as well as chopping. Not that it was hard work.

Shera eyed her, then silently picked up the saddlebags from where they'd been piled when the High Plains guards took care of the horses first thing. As the younger girl and Yuzhyu set up the two tents, Shera dragged the saddlebags to each.

The meal was potatoes and vegetables cooked on a flat pan with pressed olive to make things crisp. More of the cheese was dribbled on, and this time, for dessert, one of them brought out a pomegranate, which they shared seven ways.

Yuzhyu got up and collected the dishes this time; Rhis forced herself to join. In silence they worked at the stream, rubbing the plates clean in the rushing water, using long grass to do the rubbing.

When Rhis had finished the wooden spoons and Yuzhyu stacked the dishes, the latter said in a low voice, "You are hate. My cousin. Yiss?"

Rhis struggled within herself. She'd spent an entire day arguing with Lios Menelaes Dandiar Arvanosas in her mind, each time after determining never to think about him again.

Finally she said, "I hate being lied to. He can explain all he wants about how everything he said was strictly true, but only if you knew the real truth."

Yuzhyu's lips moved as she translated; Rhis carried her spoons back to the guards before Yuzhyu could say anything more.

Shera and Rhis rolled up in their cloaks, wriggling around to find a comfortable position on the bumpy ground to rest their aching bodies. Yuzhyu joined them, silent and somber in the flickering light of the campfire. Four High Plains silhouettes further blocked the light as Taniva and her three guards spread a map between them, talking in low voices until

Taniva jabbed her finger on the heavy paper, traced a trail, and clapped her hands.

The three gave nods, one doused the fire, the other rolled the map, the third started on her patrol by starlight. Soon the camp was quiet.

Rhis fell immediately into exhausted sleep, to be woken what seemed moments later. "Quick, quick," Taniva whispered. "We hide now."

"What?"

The tent vanished from around them, a whoosh of cold air waking Rhis further as Shera snorted and sat up. Beyond her, Yuzhyu was already folding her coat, her summer-sky blue eyes reflecting starlight.

Rhis shoved her things back into the saddlebag and picked it up. Her muscles had tightened unpleasantly into a bunch of knots, making movement painful, but she said nothing as she followed Taniva across the plateau. Her eyes had adjusted. Above, the sky was filled with different stars than she'd seen before bedtime, and in the east a pale smear.

There wasn't real light, only a vague lessening of the intensity of shadows. Rhis's heart pounded as she followed Taniva along a very narrow trail that seemed to lead straight down a cliff face into a uniform blackness the more frightening because she couldn't see the bottom of it.

Presently she heard snorts and thunks and rustles—the horses being saddled by feel. She smelled the horses a few steps later, and mounted in silence.

They rode very slowly down and down, the cliff overhead hiding that faint glow of dawn. But on they went, until the low, soft warble of a nightbird sounded on the soft air. The horse in front of Rhis abruptly stopped, tossing its head. The bird sound had been false, Rhis realized—one of Taniva's guards on the watch somewhere on the road above them.

Rhis also stopped, and Yuzhyu's mount behind her. They stayed in place, still and silent, as distant noises gradually got louder.

Rhis recognized the rhythmic thuds, rattles, and creaks of a riding party on the road uphill. It seemed a long time before the noises diminished to a muffled rumble, and then vanished.

Another wait. In the weak blue light Rhis made out Shera's wide-eyed question, but no one spoke until Taniva came sliding down the trail.

"Ha," she said in a low voice. "It was them."

"Them? Damatrans or Vesarjans?" Shera asked.

"Lios—Dandiar—whichever is the little one with the brown hair." Taniva chortled. "The little one in the lead. He not wear the scribe clothes now. He wears the clothes of the guard, with much weapons." She smacked her side where a sword would go, and her boot top, and the other side of her belt, where she wore her long knife in a sheath, all the while chuckling. "Remounts. Mud splashed to here." She smacked her thighs. "They must be very much tired! They seek us!" She laughed. "But they do not find."

Lios himself was chasing them? Rhis shivered, remembering with an acute pang exactly what her last words to him had been.

"They'll certainly find Jarvas before we do," Shera said.

Rhis nodded, not sure if she was disappointed or relieved.

"No," Taniva said, with another fierce chuckle. "He not know this countryside. He not grow up here. I have good map. They ride the road, but we will take shorter road." She laughed again. "Get ready for a *real* ride—like we do in High Plains!"

FIFTEEN

Rhis never liked to remember the first part of the ride after that. Not that much remained in memory but a weary blur. A *painful* weary blur.

She could never count up how many days it lasted. One day, near the end, when the worst of it was almost over, she woke up before dawn at the same time as the High Plains people did, instead of having to be shaken awake. The day's hard ride had gradually ceased to seem unbearable. Perhaps the tough High Plains princess had seen Shera's silent tears and relented about the terrible pace at last.

That night, instead of feeling the urge to drop into exhausted sleep the moment her dinner-chores were done, Rhis looked forward to staying up. She even brought out the tiranthe that had banged against the back of her left leg for days and days until she almost threw it away.

But she didn't throw it away, and was glad she hadn't. The ride hadn't gotten easier, she realized as she tried to limber up her fingers. It was just that she'd found it easier to endure. As for Shera, Rhis hadn't seen the tears for a couple of days. Rhis admired Shera for how grimly she'd stuck to a task she clearly had begun to dislike right from the beginning.

Another thing: she and Shera had learned some of the camping tasks, so camp was easier and faster every day. By now everyone had tasks that they'd taken as their own. Rhis had decided to learn how unappetizing-looking roots and bits of herb and so forth turned into tasty meals. The guards had gladly taught her to cook—mostly by show, at first, then gradually using more High Plains words as Rhis worked to learn the language. Lessons progressed faster, to the point that Rhis learned to spot certain wild herbs from the trail.

Right now she had a potato stew simmering, full of vegetables, fresh herbs, and some of the hoarded High Plains spices, as she ventured from warm-up into a few simple songs.

Shera appeared, laying a hand on her wrist. "That sounds pretty, and I beg pardon for interrupting," she whispered. "But I think you need to see this."

Rhis had gotten used to Shera's habit of saying 'this' for what could mean any of five to fifty things. It wasn't the word you listened to so much as watching for the gestures she made to tell you what 'this' was supposed to be now. Shera's chin tipped toward the river.

Rhis laid aside her tiranthe and noiselessly followed Shera.

Over the days the two of them had removed all the unnecessary decoration from their riding clothes, until they were pretty much indistinguishable from the High Plains people. Both had learned to braid their hair simply and tightly for riding. There were no maids for the pleasant morning and evening ritual of brushing it out and dressing it elaborately.

Shera paused on the high ridge above a river-bank, and pointed below.

They'd stopped at sunset, as always. Silhouetted in the mellow golden slants of the vanishing sun were four figures on the flat riverbank, moving in cadence. Rhis blocked the last bit of the sun with a hand. Taniva and the guards were twirling and stabbing and lunging and sweeping real weapons round. And—farther up the bank—there was Yuzhyu's bright head as she bounded about, practicing with her knives!

Shera clutched her hands to her front. "What do you think that is about?"

"I don't know, but I am going to ask," Rhis said as they turned away.

When the others returned to the camp, they did not act as if anything was amiss. Taniva sniffed appreciatively at the stew Rhis had made.

Rhis wondered if the others had always gone off like that to do their things with the swords and knives, and she had failed to notice because she'd been so tired and sore.

Still. After she'd dished the food out, and they all sat in a circle eating with hearty appetites, she said, "So what is that with the weapons? Are you planning to assassinate somebody?"

Taniva glanced up in surprise, her spoon halfway to her mouth. "Is drill. We always do. You did not see at Eskanda palace? Yes! I see you there one time."

Rhis said, "All right. So you practice. But I'm asking again, are you planning to attack someone?"

Yuzhyu's abilities with language had improved vastly since they'd left the palace party, where she'd mostly been on the outside of things, looking in. "Not attack," she said. "But defend? If we must."

Rhis considered that, then turned to Taniva. "So you're not thinking about carving up D—Prince Lios."

"Him? Tchah!" Taniva said, stirring her stew vigorously. "It is Jarvas whose blade I hope to cross." She added some pungent insults in her own tongue that made her guards grin, then added, "He and his pest princess are nothing but trouble."

Rhis said, "I wondered about that. Why you'd want to rescue the 'pest.' I mean, I understand about keeping various kings from leading armies across your kingdom, but there are other ways of doing that, aren't there?"

Taniva chuckled. "My father want me to marry Lios. For much-needed alliance. I do not want to marry him. My father has very bad temper. I knew Lios not want me any more than I want him. But if I go, my father cannot say I do not try. Now, when that black-haired pest is grabbed, and by our enemy, I am thinking first that I prove myself a worthy leader. Get her back. And save Lios much trouble, so maybe he makes alliance with us *without* any marriage!" She pointed. "You play this wooden thing with strings?"

"I would be happy to," Rhis said, and did.

Taniva listened, a curiously intent expression on her face.

When Rhis finished her song, Taniva insisted she play more—songs from other lands—and she listened carefully as she took her turn with the washing up.

Rhis felt self-conscious. She'd usually played for herself, or for her family. She knew she wasn't a great player.

But Taniva seemed serious. So Rhis played, wincing at fumbles, hating it when she lost her timing, until she noticed that the others all seemed to appreciate the shimmering sounds of the strings, damped to shift to minor keys by the finger-pedals. At Taniva's gesture the girl guard, Dartha, began a dance to a lively tune, clapping her hands in counterpoint, and stamping her feet. She was an excellent dancer.

The other two got out their vests with the chimes, put away the day they left, and they too joined the dancing, their chimes ringing sweetly in time to the music. Yuzhyu brought out a pair of wooden spoons and tapped out a rhythm on a rock.

When they were done, Taniva said, "You two sing?"

Shera and Rhis exchanged looks. They'd sang harmony on the journey to Eskanda, but not when anyone heard them. But they sang a couple of ballads, watching one another for cues as they harmonized. At the end, when Rhis wrung her fingers and moved to put away the instrument, Yuzhyu, who hadn't spoken to her in days, put the spoons away then said shyly, "Iss good. The music."

Taniva grinned. "Is very good. Heh!" But then she turned away, falling into conversation with Dartha and the older women. Rhis caught a few words. Path. Ride. Horses. Prince.

With an inward jolt, she realized she'd forgotten about Dandiar and his guards, somewhere presumably running parallel to the girls.

Rhis shoved him out of her mind, and determinedly talked about ballads, and where they came from. Yuzhyu listened, no longer moving her lips. As the others began packing against morning and their usual fast departure, Rhis stayed where she was. The way Yuzhyu leaned toward her, showing far more interest in the rambling conversation about songs than it warranted, Rhis sensed that the Ndaian princess wanted to talk to her.

And she knew what about. She also knew that she was still angry with the false Dandiar the Scribe, though defining why wasn't as easy as it had been. So she gave one last strum in the lowest minor chord and set aside her tiranthe. If she was right, she only had to say, "So tell me his reasons."

Yuzhyu did not ask 'who?' or 'what reasons'. She said, "You not want to listen."

"I'm listening now."

"I think very long how to say." Yuzhyu flashed her lovely smile, not seen for days. Then she leaned forward again, and in smoother language than Rhis had ever heard from her, she explained how Lios's mother, Queen Briath, had married the

Ndaian queen's brother. He was also Yuzhyu's uncle. Queen Briath and the Ndaian prince made a treaty alliance with their marriage. But Queen Briath had sent her consort home for good before Lios was even born.

"She hate my uncle. My uncle not like she. Her. When my cousin came for to stay—the treaty said he must—my uncle was so unkind to him. Said he be like his mother. So Lios and my home-cousins all played together. Then life not so bad for him. When he went home, his mother not like memories of Ndai, or how he reminded her of my uncle. She leave my cousin live at Eskanda."

"So Queen Briath doesn't really know Lios?" Rhis asked.

Yuzhyu shrugged her shoulders up and down, a sharp movement. "Not much pipple do. Me. My brosser. Some cousins. We all good friends. We make his stay in Ndai good. And when I come, he promise to make my visit good." She smiled wryly. "He tried."

Yuzhyu continued, "This is why he makes a party to meet girls and no treaty . . . how you say? No treaty mask. Not like his mother, and my uncle, who pretend friendship for treaty when they are courting. But they do not know each other, and when they do?" She made a terrible face. "They do not like the other."

Rhis watched the way Yuzhyu rubbed her knuckles over her knees as she crouched there. It was clear how much she liked her cousin. But. "He said it was a joke," Rhis muttered.

Yuzhyu looked up in the fading light. It was difficult to see her expression. Rhis had seen a wide range of her moods, but the Ndaian had never been sarcastic. So her sardonic tone was a surprise now as she said, "You do not think Iardith chasing Andos a joke?"

Rhis picked up the tiranthe, ducked through the tent flap and slid the instrument into her saddle-bag. Yuzhyu hunkered down nearby, watching. Rhis thought back, then said, "I do. But it makes me feel mean. Because of what I heard about the King of Arpalon, who told his daughter she cannot come home without a queen's future crown."

Shera, lying in her cloak, said, "What are you two talking about?"

"Lios. The real one."

"Urf. I don't want to talk about boys." Shera turned the other way.

Rhis said to Yuzhyu, "I feel a little sorry for Iardith. But only a little. When I remember the way she pushed other girls out of her way, as though she was the only one who mattered, well, yes, then I see the joke."

Yuzhyu grunted, rolled up in her coat, and that was the end of the conversation.

The next day, they reached the border of Damatras, which was a long chasm cut by a river through some jumbled mountains.

The regular road ran along the ridge above the chasm. Taniva pointed out how it meandered among the slopes, gradually rising and falling. "Easier for armies to march. But much slower than old trail," she said as they rode slowly along the edge of the road.

They finally found what she was looking for—and even then almost missed it, a turnoff that looked like a footpath. When they edged up to the roadside above the chasm, they saw that there was not a sheer drop, but a slope leading down to a little bridge that connected to an outcropping, well shaded with ancient trees, on the adjacent hill.

Without explanation one of the older women took off down this little path, raced over the little bridge, and vanished into the shaded old forest growth. Taniva and the other woman followed more slowly, and Rhis, Shera, and Yuzhyu followed them.

The path into the old forest appeared to be an animal trail, but Rhis discovered after a time that this was instead a very old footpath. The horses had to walk, in single file, for most of that day.

Then it was time to go upward again. Mossy marker stones, the carvings in them obscured by time and thick, rambling thorn-bushes, rested beside twists and side paths, matching signs on the map.

Huge dark green trees with thick clusters of hanging leaves obscured the travelers as they continued the long climb up the mountain paths. Slowly, Rhis noted, the lovely leafy trees of the lowlands were giving way to firs, though some of them were different types than those she'd grown up with in Nym. Once a band of clouds moved across the sky, and Rhis listened to the rustling patter of rain in the leaves overhead while only occasionally feeling a drop or two.

They halted just above a wide river full of stones and white water. Beyond a wide bend Rhis could make out part of a vast bridge.

"We wait here," Taniva said.

"Why?" Rhis asked.

"Because they patrol all time. Beyond here, we do not go as us. They know we are here before we see any of them. We change," she said, dismounting.

"Change?" Shera asked, hands on hips. "Back into civilized people, I hope."

Rhis studied her sister-by-marriage, who stood there in grubby riding clothes without a hint of ornament, her face smudged, her hair skinned back into a tight braid. Shera didn't look like a princess any more. She looked more like a weathered, practical courier or caravan rider. Rhis wondered if she herself looked like a cook. *Not a very successful one*, she thought with an inward laugh. *I'm too skinny*.

Taniva smacked her hands together. "We change into players. Music players." She pretended to strum a stringed instrument. "We practice when we stop."

Shera crowed in delight. "A masquerade! Oh, how *fun!*"

"Wait. Wait," Rhis said. "We won't fool anybody who really knows music like court musicians play."

Taniva waggled her hands. "No matter. It gets us in castle gates. You perform. If they like you, you play for king. If not, they say go away next day. Gates close at night. No one goes in or out."

"But—" Rhis faltered as Taniva glanced at her impatiently.

She studied the others, finding similar expressions. They thought she was being too fussy. She struggled for the right words. "I just do not want them suspicious. I mean, if we arrive right behind Jarvas and the Perfect Princess, and they lock gates at night. Doesn't that mean these are people who *really* don't like strangers?"

Yuzhyu poked her chin out in her definitive nod. "Is true."

"That's why we practice. You two sing and play. Yuzhyu plays hand drum. Dartha dances."

"Looking like we do now?" Rhis asked.

Taniva laughed. "Where you think Arnava goes? To get disguises, and find a Damatran hand drum! We get in. You perform while I find pest. Then it is up to you, for they can never see me, as High Plains and Damatras are old enemies," Taniva said. Her lips curled deeply. "And I have been here before." Her smile vanished. "So you have three days. We travel. You practice. We act when we get inside."

Shera turned to Rhis, hands on her hips again. "Taniva has gotten us safely there. So now it's our turn . . ." She looked uncertain.

She said in her brightest voice, "All right."

Taniva laughed. "We are girls. Musicians. What can go wrong?"

In a castle full of enemies? When Rhis had never held a weapon in her life?

"What can go wrong?" Rhis echoed with completely false confidence.

SIXTEEN

The capital of Damatras was a long, narrow walled city, built along a very high ridge above a slow river. The king's castle commanded the view from the center of the city, with its own towers and high walls—higher than the city walls. There were four towers connecting these walls, and a central one that was the highest of all. It made the various towers to the sides look kind of like a crown, all coming to that central point, silvery in the watery sunlight.

All the castle windows were arches, widened from the old-fashioned arrow slits. Rhis wondered if, like in Nym, there were wards against arrows passing through windows—or if the people had sturdy iron-reinforced shutters to be put up in bad times, like many who didn't trust magic, high on Nym's more distant peaks.

Behind the city rose sheer cliffs blasted by powerful magic a couple of centuries ago. Long striated layers of rock glittered in the sun. At one end the mountain sloped away, impossible for any enemy to climb without being seen; the other end was marked by a spectacular series of waterfalls that fed into the great river.

A single bridge of awe-inspiring beauty crossed from the main road to the ridge above the river. There was no other approach to the bridge but the main road—full of armed people riding back and forth as they scanned the market and city traffic.

After Taniva's guards had done a scouting foray—looking for sign of Dandiar and his group—the girls had proceeded in a sedate ride along the main road, Rhis with her tiranthe worn over her back in the style of a traveling harper. They were all dressed alike now, in high-waisted cotton-linen blouses, worn over split skirts of a brown or blue so dark it seemed black. The sleeves were loose in the Damatran style. The clothes were pretty much like what they saw girls and women around them wearing. At night, while Rhis and Shera practiced singing, Shera making up tricky harmonies that actually sounded pretty good—if not (she was the first to admit) up to court standards, Yuzhyu tried complicated rhythms on her little hand drum. Dartha danced, and one woman sewed a Damatran headdress for Taniva, who had taken off her distinctive riding boots. They were instantly recognizable to anyone who had met Taniva. Instead she went barefoot, something Rhis both admired and envied. Elda had never permitted her to step outside without proper princess shoes.

The last day, Dartha, who had nimble fingers, braided crimson piping into all their hair, creating multiple braids. She made them extra tight so they wouldn't have to trouble about their hair for a few days. Then they all bathed in a cold stream (which was very unpleasant, but certainly woke one up) and folded away their dirty clothes into their saddlebags.

Rhis's scalp pulled and she kept wanting to touch the parts in her hair and the tight braiding outlining her skull. But she couldn't. Taniva had warned them that fingers in their hair would signal to anyone who looked that they weren't used to wearing their hair like local girls.

Rhis's new clothes were loose and a little scratchy, made with a rough linen blended with cotton, instead of the silks and polished cotton fine-cloth she was used to wearing next to her skin. But she liked the outfit—it moved freely.

As they got into line to ride over that vast bridge, after Taniva had been giving them details on what to expect, Shera finally asked, "How do you know so much about Damatras? I mean, you said you were here before, but aren't these folk your enemies?"

Taniva told them cheerily how it was a requirement for chieftains' sons and daughters to make one raid before they could ride the plains as heirs. "I am king's daughter. I must make mine a raid for kings and queens, do you see? So I lie up in the mountain above the waterfall, over there, and watch for a week. They never see me because I move around at night. Then I find my way in." She smacked her hands together. "And when I am in, it is easy enough to find where king and family have rooms. Not so easy to get past guard, but I found good disguise. So snick-snack! I take Jarvas's ceremony knife. Very old. He does not take it on training rides."

Rhis gasped. "That knife with the blue jewels on the handle?"

"Yes! He sees me wearing it at Eskanda. He knows I took it," she said with cheer.

Rhis listened in dismay. *"You stole it from him?"*

"Oh, from his room. He is not there. If I fight him for it, and win, then there is a feud from his father. If he win, a feud from mine. Many people die. Used to be, in the bad days of old, you fight to the death for your heir raid. Too many died that way." Her eyes crinkled as she brandished the elegant, lethal-looking silver and black handled knife with the blue gemstones. They flashed blue sparks in the sunlight. "Now, we just make the raid when they are not there. So they do not lose honor." She smacked her chest. "Jarvas takes two years ago my father's favorite bridle, the one for parade. But we are not at our tents, we are away on a scout run. But everyone else is there. When we return and Father find it gone, and nothing else gone, how Father cursed and cursed!" She shook with laughter.

Shera cast a glance at Rhis, then said, "You look funny. What are you thinking?"

Rhis said. "I just realized I'm grateful."

"For?"

"I didn't think anything could make me glad to go home to Elda's lectures again. But hearing about this custom just did it."

Shera smothered a nervous giggle.

Taniva finished tucking the blue-gemmed blade back into her waistband under her smock, where it stayed out of sight. "So this is why I am only stable girl when we go inside, and why I hide my face when you speak. And why I will be one to find pest-princess. I already know my way around."

Then she kneed her horse and dropped back in line.

"I wish she'd told us that before," Shera muttered. "I hope they don't have posted signs about royal thieves all over the place, with her face painted on, and her name in big letters."

"Shh," Rhis whispered, trying hard not to laugh.

When they reached the foot of the bridge, suspicious guards eyed them, one even poking through their saddlebags in a cursory way as Dartha did the speaking. All the High Plains people knew Damatran speech, as they were taught to know their enemy. A few words seemed familiar, Rhis thought.

They were waved on.

Rhis had thought the subliminal rumble she heard was her heartbeat, but as they slowly moved to the middle of the bridge, the mighty waterfall came into view, white spray reaching as high as the ridge. And above the enormous mountain, and behind it, ranges of even higher mountains, their ever-snowy tops gleaming coldly in the sun. Just like in Nym.

She did not find the sight comforting:

There isn't a whole lot of possibilities for escape, she thought.

*D*espite Rhis's worries and tension, at first everything went pretty much as Taniva had outlined. They rode in without more than a glance from the many guards. Not all of them had yellow hair and pale skin, as Rhis had feared—she did not want to stand out and be considered suspicious. But there were dark-haired Damatrans as well as light, and a variety of skin colors, though mostly on the pale side. There were plenty with the golden skin of the High Plains, which made Rhis suspect that, even though the two kingdoms were enemies, people had probably been mixing over time, so it wasn't so unusual to have a mother from one kingdom and a father from the other.

Anyway, no one seemed the least interested in Shera and Rhis's browner skin, or their round eyes, so unlike the slanty ones and broad faces to be seen in infinite variety around them. Still, Rhis was glad of the unusual clothes and braids. She suspected that her own clothes might have caused some second looks.

They followed the traffic down the broad street between slate-roofed stone buildings (shops below, living quarters above) that led to the castle, and at those gates, again Dartha did the speaking for them. Rhis, this time stepping close enough to hear all the words, was interested to discover that the Damatran and the High Plain languages did sound a lot alike.

They were shunted off into what appeared to be a servants' area inside the huge stone castle, again reminding Rhis of home. Only this one was enormous, with far more people than hers.

Rhis looked around—smelled the familiar tang of slightly moldy stone—and discovered for the first time in her life that she really didn't much *like* stone castles.

The horses were left with Taniva at the stable, and they followed a group of people whose clothes were a lot like theirs—in a variety of colors—to an entry-way lined with doors. The people in front, all laden with enormous bags of foodstuffs, were waved off in one direction. The guard looked them over with a slightly puzzled frown, his brow clearing when he saw the tiranthe and hand drum. The girls were waved another way.

Eventually they ended up in a room with a miscellany of people, all of whom shared only one characteristic, they were to be interviewed before being sent along to whatever they'd come for.

Rhis was again reminded of home. Nym had had too many troubles in its past for wandering players to be admitted to the king's or queen's presence without an interview first. There had been more than one assassination attempt by pretend entertainers.

But by the time the harassed woman in charge of such things got to them, the lamps had all been lit, or glowglobes clapped on, and the wafting smells of spiced rice and braised fish made it clear the castle workers were all going in to supper.

"We will see your offering tomorrow," the woman said slowly in two or three languages, adding grimly, "We are now in need of such." She made a warding sign at the window—which afforded a view of that enormous tower.

Rhis was surprised at her tone, and the gesture, but said nothing as they were shooed off to a long barracks room with narrow wooden beds and bumpy hay mattresses. They were offered blankets, which looked too thick and scratchy (they were wool) for summer, even the cool summer of the mountains. So, after each of them had gratefully stepped through the cleaning frame and felt grit and grime snap away from their bodies and clothes, and after they'd passed all their travel clothes through, they curled up in now-clean cloaks and lay down beneath the wide-open arched windows. The Damatrans seemed to believe in plenty of fresh air, and the summer's heat evaporated very fast so high in the mountains.

Rhis tried to compose herself to sleep, but she was far too nervous and excited. Also the room was full of noise. Not loud noise. But here a wooden bed frame creaked as someone tried to find a comfortable position on what had to be an extra-bumpy mattress, and there someone snored; farther down the long rows of beds someone else coughed, and at the other end a pair of girls whispered—and everyone around uttered sharp "Sh!"s which were much louder than the whispers.

Rhis finally realized what made it impossible to sleep: though the three High Plains guards were with the other two princesses and her, Taniva still had not joined them.

She was worrying about Taniva's saddlebag and dreaming about searching for it without realizing she'd dropped into a restless sort of sleep, when a hand on her shoulder jerked her awake.

The dormitory was silent now, except for the sounds of deep, heavy breathing. Weak silvery light in the high windows barely outlined a face with looped braids.

"Huh?" Rhis mumbled.

The shadow bent close. "It be me," Taniva whispered, her breath warm on Rhis's forehead. "You come. Now."

Rhis rose, reached for her saddle-bag. Sleepiness vanished as she joined the others, all carrying their gear. No one spoke. With soundless steps they made their way out of the dormitory.

Taniva led them down a couple of twisting, turning halls, past an area that smelled of baking bread. Light leaked from below closed doors, behind them came sounds of people moving about.

Twice they stopped, each time to wait for slow-walking sentries to wander past. Taniva kept them pressed still and flat against the cold stone walls until the sentries rounded corners, then she sped off in the other direction, followed by the rest of them, Rhis and Shera laboring under their saddlebags. Yuzhyu and the High Plains people did not seem to notice the extra weight.

Though Rhis's mind bloomed with questions, Taniva did not speak until they'd traversed what seemed to be an entire city's worth of plain stone hallway. Again they waited for sentries to pass, and then started up the narrow stone steps of a tower.

On a landing, Taniva stopped.

"Guards outside now. She is up here." A jerk of the thumb toward the top of the tower.

Rhis understood at once. Iardith was imprisoned at the top of the tower. They'd get her out, take their stuff to the stable, and as soon as the gate opened, they'd ride out. Nobody, she hoped, would care whether or not a bunch of girls had had their audition—not if they could get away before the princess was discovered to be gone, and the alarm went up.

"Hurry," she said, and Taniva whirled around and started up the stairs three at a time.

The others trundled after, soon breathing hard and sweating under their loads.

But at last they reached the top landing, which was just a narrow space before a sturdy wooden door. Taniva gestured to one of her guards, who brought something out of a pocket, edged past Yuzhyu, knelt, and inserted something into the lock. In the faint moonslight lancing down from the slit window above, Rhis couldn't make out what she was doing—but a few heartbeats later the guard gave a grunt of satisfaction and the big door swung open.

The tower room had windows all around, flooding it with silvery-blue light.

Iardith sat up in bed, her long black hair braided for the night.

She clapped.

"No—too late at night for light—guards get suspici—" Taniva began, but it was too late.

The light from the wall-mounted glowglobe was blinding to their dark-adjusted eyes. And of course the light would be visible to anyone outside who cared to look up at that broad arched window.

But that was only a fleeting thought. Because though Rhis had from time to time imagined Iardith's reaction to their appearances as rescuers, she'd always thought the princess from Arpalon would welcome them with relief . . . fear . . . joy . . . all expressions difficult to imagine on that beautiful face.

What they got was sardonic disgust, as Iardith said with cordial sarcasm, "You *idiots!*"

SEVENTEEN

"We're here to *rescue* you," Shera exclaimed.

Iardith flung back a shining loop of braid. "Do you really think that *I* am stupid enough to need rescue?"

The group stood there aghast—except for the guards, who didn't follow the rapid conversation. One of them stood at the door, the other two outside on the landing.

Then Taniva burst into laughter, slapping her knee. "*You* abduct *him!*"

Iardith gave a kind of sour laugh. "Let's just say that I let him take me away."

The Damatran guards outside were definitely efficient enough to care to look up: Dartha entered, saying, "They come up stairs." And gripped something inside her clothes, her face grim.

There was no way out; would the women really fight?

Rhis felt dazed and sick as she looked down at her—

Moving fast, she pulled her tiranthe from the saddlebag, and while the others stared at her as if her wits had flown, she began to strum in a fast, crazy manner.

Before she could speak, Taniva snapped her fingers. She laughed silently, beckoning to her guards. "Sing! Dance!" she ordered.

Yuzhyu, breathing fast, pulled out her hand drum and began to tap it; the two older guards were blank-faced as they clapped, but Dartha grinned, a quick flash that was a lot like Taniva's grin. She began twirling in between the others, dancing round the handsomely furnished cell as if she did this sort of thing every day.

Shera began to sing the song that Rhis played. Rhis joined in, ignoring the dryness of her throat.

And so, when four guards entered, swords in hand, it was their turn to stare in amazement.

Iardith still looked sardonic, but at least she played fair. She crossed her arms across her front, not the least discommoded to be found sitting up in bed in her nightgown, as she said loftily, "I wanted some music."

The guards turned eyes of various pale shades from the regal princess to the group of players who plied away, ending a song and plunging into another. Dartha danced toward them, forcing them to lift the ready swords and step back.

One of them gave a faint shrug, said a single word, and they withdrew—relocking the door behind them.

Rhis lifted her hand, but at Taniva's quick gesture, she resumed playing.

"Do not stop," she said, pointing to the open windows.

"That was fast thinking," Iardith said cordially. "But if Jarvas is the one to come up here to investigate in the morning, he'll recognize you at once."

Taniva retorted, "Then will ask why you do not recognize us."

"I will of course say that all servants look alike," Iardith snapped back.

Rhis glanced at her group—how very different they were from one another—and snorted a laugh despite her wildly beating heart.

Iardith added, "Besides, it won't really matter what I say. Jarvas does what I want."

"So you can want him to send us away," Shera said, as Rhis kept strumming the tiranthe.

"Oh, yes," Iardith said with an indifferent shrug. "At least you did come. Though I wonder why? No matter. You can go right back, with some messages to the rest of those fools. Beginning with that disgusting little toad, Dandiar the Scribe. So I shall always think of him."

Rhis felt her sympathies swinging—quite unreasonably, she reminded herself firmly—to the real Prince Lios. Beside her, Yuzhyu looked down at her drum, her face crimson.

Iardith never even glanced her way.

"So you find out," Taniva said. "Hah!"

"He told you?" Shera asked curiously, her brow crinkled. Rhis wondered if Shera, like Rhis herself, imagined Dandiar confessing the truth before a marriage proposal.

But Iardith said, "*He* didn't." She looked up at the windows, her long, pretty fingers twiddling with her braid in a rare fussy gesture, then she dropped her hands into her lap, making one of her graceful poses. "Lios did. Or whatever that lackey calls himself." And in a calm voice, as if describing an everyday occurrence, "The party was about to end, and the fool had yet to come to the point. Since the world knows I cannot go home empty handed—I have to marry a crown, and my own honor demands that it be a better one than my father's—I followed him to his room after the concert. I thought a little flirting and romantic talk would hurry him along. But as soon as I tried to kiss him, he panicked. As he should! He knew right well what my father would do if some servant tried to flirt with *me*."

Shera's and Rhis's eyes met. *Marry a crown*, Rhis thought. Lios might have been a stick of wood or an old hedgehog, just as long as he would get her a crown.

As though her thoughts paralleled Rhis's, Iardith said, "He is a handsome enough lad, that I will say. Though dull as can be. All he likes is sport—racing—shooting—wrestling—fencing. Tchah! Anyway, he panicked. It was quite funny, really, though at the time I was just angry. Told me who he really was, and who Lios really was. When I stamped out, ready to murder that snake of a scribe for daring to lie to *me*, there was Jarvas. I'd been ignoring him, though he's almost as easy on the eyes as that Lios-lackey. Damatras might be big, and everyone is afraid of them, but the truth is, they are almost as poor as Arpalon. I want to be rich," she finished. "But beggars cannot be choosers, and when he started trying to argue with me about not having danced with him—that I was playing with his feelings—I cut through the rot and said I wished someone would take me away."

She shrugged, and smiled. "So he did." She laughed. "I must say, he catches a hint fast. Better, he organized everything himself. I didn't have to do a thing, yet we were gone by sunup. Though that journey left much to be desired—I can see it will take some time to teach them how a monarch ought to travel. And be treated. But I can wait to civilize these barbarians first. I need that crown on my head."

She huffed out a breath, then went on briskly, "So, that brings me to my messages. You must see to it that my father knows that this was my idea. He can bluster all he wants—he may get a better settlement that way—but he's not to rubbish up my plans by sending an army."

Taniva said in a low, rough voice, "So at least you think of those who must fight in your cause. And of the lands trampled in the fighting."

Iardith shook back her braids. "I don't like fighting and blood, no. Especially when Arpalon would come out the worst of it, I dareswear. I do not want a disaster associated with my name." She pointed imperially at the floor. "So now they've all heard you plinking that thing, and no one has come back upstairs to investigate further. Unless you want to knock and deal with the night guard, they've probably forgotten all about you. I suggest we get some sleep. They can let you out in the morning."

Taniva gestured to Dartha, who dropped to the floor, peered beneath the door, then rose, shaking her head. She held up six fingers. Six guards now on the landing, where there'd been none before.

Taniva sighed. Rhis suspected she wanted to break out the way they'd broken in. They sure couldn't now. *If it were home*, Rhis thought, *someone would be wanting to know who let us up here. I don't think they're going to forget by morning.*

"Tomorrow will be another long, no doubt ghastly day. It's going to take real work to make this place half-way civilized enough to spend my life in."

Iardith flung herself back on the bed, and clapped out the lights, leaving everyone else to dispose themselves as best they could on the floor.

Rhis did not want to ask her to share the bed. She realized everyone else felt the same when Shera said accusingly, "You might at least spare us a pillow or two. You don't need all those."

Fluff! Fluff! Two down-stuffed pillows landed, one on top of Rhis, the other farther away. "Shut up," Iardith said.

Summer or not, the tower room was chilly, open as it was to the outside air. When the sounds of footsteps clattering beyond the door woke Rhis, she found Shera's hair tickling her nose. They'd curled up together, under both cloaks. When Rhis raised her head, her temples panging, she discovered Yuzhyu's bright hair just behind her; she'd shared their pillow, facing the other way.

Taniva and two of her guards had taken the second pillow, the oldest sitting up beside the door. From the steady gleam in her eyes, reflection from the bleak dawn light in the window, she'd sat up all night; later Rhis found out that indeed, she'd kept checking all night to see if the massive guard placed round the tower had diminished so they could sneak away, but it never had.

The girls rose, rubbing eyes, yawning, shaking heads, clothes, cloaks. Everyone went still when the door swung open and Jarvas stopped abruptly on the threshold, several of his Damatran guard crowding behind him.

He no longer wore the sinister dark velvet she'd seen him in at Eskanda. He was dressed like his guards, in sturdy tunics of practical brown, belted at the waist, with loose riding trousers stuffed into their boots. They all wore knives and swords— including Jarvas.

His scowl turned into a frown of perplexity when his gaze reached Taniva, and then cleared. "You? Here?" he exclaimed, and grinned.

Taniva scowled.

"Give it back," Jarvas said, advancing into the room. He hopped over saddlebags and pillows and cloaks, taking up a stance directly before Taniva. He held out his hand.

Taniva snorted. "I buried it in the forest."

Jarvas said something that made Dartha choke on a laugh, and Taniva fight a grin. But she just crossed her arms. "Give it," Jarvas said. "It's on you. I wouldn't set to horse without my bridle. You have my knife. I want it back—and I won it fair-and-fair," he added. Then waved a hand around the room. "You can't get out. If you want to fight me, I'd be more than happy to. But you'll lose."

Taniva tipped her head. "Maybe. Here. Not on the plains," she added with a darkling glance, as she put her hand inside her blue smock and withdrew it reluctantly. Then slapped the silver-and-black handled knife onto his palm, the blue gems winking in the rainy morning light.

Iardith had been watching with an increasingly dire frown. It was immediately clear to Rhis, at least, that she expected to be the center of attention, and did not like her betrothed talking to anyone else. "What's this about?" she demanded. "Never mind, it's already boring. Where's my breakfast?"

The look of disgust that Jarvas sent her made Rhis gasp. She remembered quite well how besotted Jarvas had been with the Perfect Princess at the Eskanda party—a besottedness that, if his expression was anything to go by, had long since vanished.

"You can all come downstairs," he said.

Iardith said, "Once I am properly dressed. And you had better remember that whatever you decide about them, *I* am a hostage, not a prisoner. And I want at least some of them to take messages back, that will be to the benefit of us both."

Jarvas jerked his thumb over his shoulder, and his guards retreated, clattering back down the steps. "My father will sort all that out," he said only, and banged the door shut behind him, leaving the girls alone.

Iardith lunged out of bed, flinging off her nightgown with an impatient rip. As she moved to the vanity table across the room and snapped her fingers over the silver pitcher (which began to steam gently) she said over her shoulder to Rhis, "You can stop with the disapproving frown any time, Princess Perfect," she said nastily. "I plan to get you out first. I remember quite well how much you toadied up to Prince Scribe. You'll take my messages, and Prince Scribe can do what he does so well, and write the letters."

Rhis recoiled. "Princess Perfect?" When she remembered having called Iardith the Perfect Princess, her face heated up.

Iardith, meanwhile, had splashed the magically heated water into the silver basin, and bathed her hands and face, making no attempt to spare any water for the others.

Then she stepped through the cleaning frame on the opposite side of the room—belatedly followed by the others, one by one. They might not get to warm up faces and hands in the herb-scented hot water, but at least they would be clean.

"Oh, aren't you just so innocent, my dear," Iardith said, toweling her skin vigorously until it glowed a dusky rose. "Save it for someone who will be impressed with your model deportment and good behavior." Iardith yanked her way into a soft linen under-dress of pale yellow, then flung a heavy, ribbon-flounced over-dress to Shera. "Here. Help me with that. Jarvas, the idiot, wouldn't travel with my maid. Well, he paid for it," she added with a small smile. "Go ahead." She pulled the expensive velvet gown of ochre impatiently over her head. "Lace up the back." The golden embroidery glimmered in the watery light.

Shera complied, pulling the silk laces with a hard yank that made Iardith gasp, and spin around.

Shera said sweetly as she tied the knot, "I'm sorry, did I hurt you? I'd never done anyone's laces before."

Iardith flounced around and began to finger her hair out of its night braid. Shera sent a wink at Rhis, whose eyes had teared up as she waited for her turn to step through the cleaning frame. Behind were the soft noises of the others fixing hair, changing, repacking.

Rhis stepped through the cleaning frame, wishing it would whisk away tears the way it did grime. But Iardith did not pay her the least heed as she marched out and down the stairs, leaving the others to follow.

"Am I really like Elda?" Rhis whispered to Shera.

"Of course not," Shera whispered back indignantly. "Do you think I would ride in a carriage willingly with a prating, pompous Elda?"

"I'm sure Elda doesn't think she prates—"

"Oh, yes she does," Shera said briskly. "She *likes* prating. She told me once that she spends the last time of the day before she falls asleep arranging useful things to say, and she trusts her daughter is writing them down for the benefit of future generations. You wouldn't do that. Ever."

Rhis gulped on a watery laugh.

"Oom," Yuzhyu said, quite distinctly. Rhis realized the Ndaian princess hadn't said that for a very long time. "Yiss, om! Time to zee king."

Iardith sighed. "I so detest awkward accents."

"Om!"

Shera giggled.

Rhis followed, surreptitiously wiping her eyes on her shoulder as she hefted her saddlebag. With a mischievous grin, Yuzhyu said "Om!" every step they took all the way down the winding tower—and there were a lot of steps. Iardith muttered in affront, but when the other girls muffled laughter—Shera whispering "Om, om," under her breath—she gave a sharp sigh and remained silent.

When they reached the ground floor, the Damatran guards closed around them, carrying spears, with swords worn at their sides. The girls walked down the flagged hall surrounded by these tall, fierce-looking fellows. Though they looked far less sinister, the way they kept sneaking peeks at Iardith, who marched first, head held high, her shining fall of black hair streaming smoothly down to her heels. Rhis's feelings swooped. She fought a flutter of giggles.

The urge to laugh was gone all too soon. They marched down a hall with a high stone ceiling, then stopped outside two massive iron-reinforced doors. Rhis tightened her arms around her saddle-bag, dreading a barbarian throne room, complete with bloody weapons mounted on the walls, skulls used as dishware, maybe a torture instrument or two as decoration, and a lot more fierce-looking guards.

They passed inside a narrow room. A tall, massive man who had to be Jarvas's father sat near a huge arched window, beyond which rain poured. The king of Damatras was eating his breakfast as he listened to reports from soberly dressed men and women, all with looped braids. As Jarvas led his party in the king paused with his spoon in the air to give orders, whereupon the man or woman spoken to bustled out and the next in line moved to his table and began their report.

The kingly signs were his golden cup, and the diamond drop he wore in one ear. Otherwise he was as soberly dressed as his minions; the only color was that provided by nature, the silver-streaked pale hair lying on his shoulders, and in his braided beard.

Jarvas stepped up to Rhis's side. She gave him an uneasy glance; they had never spoken before. She was scared enough without any Damatrans coming right up to her.

"Don't tell my father who you are," Jarvas muttered. And dropped back before she could answer.

Yuzhyu's eyes flicked between them.

The king looked up from his eggs and toasted bread. When he saw Iardith, his thick eyebrows contracted. "What is she doing here—who are these others?"

Jarvas pointed to Taniva. "What *were* you doing, anyway? You didn't really go up there to dance and sing?" He sent an accusing look at Iardith. "Despite what was said."

Iardith just shrugged. "I hope," she enunciated, "there is a breakfast ordered for me—and I am not required to eat it in front of a gaggle of lackeys."

The king and Jarvas ignored her. Despite the situation, Rhis felt another butterfly-wing of laughter behind her ribs: it obviously had not only been a hideous journey for the swain, but the king didn't seem any more enamored of the Beauty of Arpalon than his son now was.

"We come to rescue Princess from Arpalon," Taniva said, confronting the king, arms crossed.

The king frowned. "You are High Plains?"

"Taniva of—"

"Heh," the king said, and grinned. It was a humorous grin, but there was far too much gloat in his voice when he said, "Your father is going to just hate the ransom I'm going to demand."

Taniva said something that made the king throw back his head and laugh. "You've got courage, girl, but then we knew that." He glanced wryly at his son. "Got your blade back?"

Jarvas pointed silently to the blue gemstones winking above his belt.

"And these others? Potential ransoms, I trust?"

"Shera of Gensam," Shera said in a small voice.

"Yuzhyu of Ndai."

Rhis couldn't figure out why Jarvas had said what he'd said. Did he mean her ill? She'd been the most afraid for Taniva, royal descendant of this king's worst enemy. But so far, the king seemed reasonable.

Besides, she refused to lie, unlike Some People.

She lifted her chin. "Rhis of Nym."

The king pushed his chair back. It squeaked on the flagstones, making several people wince. "*You* are? You *are?*" He began to laugh.

Jarvas sighed softly just behind Rhis as the king got to his feet and approached them. He was even bigger than Rhis had imagined. She fell back an uncertain step or two as the king approached, grinning down at her. "You are? By all that's rich— and that means your father. Jarvas!" He swung around. "You can put all these over in the garrison prison. The guest cells." He chuckled as he wagged his hand at Shera, Taniva, and Yuzhyu. "Including that one—" He jerked his thumb at Iardith.

"What?" she snapped. "I told you, I agreed to your marriage terms. You only have to get my father to agree—"

"Your father," the Damatran king retorted, "is as poor as a miller in a drought. You might have been good for a cushion alliance, but that's it. This little thing—" He flicked Rhis's hastily made, lopsided braid. "—comes from a land that might be as big as an ink blot on the map, but Nym is richer then Arpalon, Gensam, and the High Plains together! Maybe even as rich as Vesarja. Who knows? Though I mean to find out! She goes into the guest tower, boys. We want her comfortable, we want her safe. Very safe. If she gets down those stairs past you, every one of you will wish you'd chosen to be bricklayers before you die." He laughed again, somehow sounding both jolly and quite heartless. "Don't forget writing implements. Her father is going to pay a smacking good bride price, or an even bigger ransom! She can think about her choice while uninterrupted." He swung around and glared at Iardith. "You, we'll get rid of as soon as I squeeze that strutting rooster of a father of yours. Hah!"

Rhis looked around, dazed. Taniva winced, Iardith looked cold and unconcerned, Shera's eyes had filled.

Jarvas lifted a shoulder, as if to say: I warned you.

Rhis's eyes stung as the guards advanced.

Just before they closed around her, Yuzhyu stepped close. "Remember, Lios comes," she whispered.

Oh, wouldn't *that* make things much better! Remembering with painful clarity what she had said to Lios the last time she saw him, Rhis felt the tears burn down her cheeks as she was marched away.

EIGHTEEN

She was shut up alone in Iardith's old room. Right behind her (and her comet-tail of guards) came a row of servants to whisk away Iardith's belongings. As she watched three servants pack up and carry all those dresses and accoutrements, she wondered if Iardith was the best-equipped abducted princess in history.

The bed was changed, the silver ewer refilled, the basin cleaned.

Nobody spoke to Rhis, who dumped her saddlebag at her feet and sat on a hassock out of their way. She'd thought once about trying a dash for the door—then remembered the guards. A quick peek at the half-open door revealed at least half a dozen brawny fellows—each carrying a sword or spear—crowded onto the tiny landing or standing on the stairs, all peering in with serious faces.

Rhis remembered what that horrible king had promised—they'd all be killed if she got past them down the steps—so she sat tight, hands on her knees until they left, the door shutting with a thud, and the lock tumbling.

Rhis stood up and took a look around. The cell was quite spacious, a perfectly round room, the walls behind two pretty tapestries (imported, from the style, all the way from Charas al

Kherval) built of the light gray stone she'd admired from the bridge what seemed a thousand years ago.

The windows were arched like all the rest. Below them a sheer drop to the stones far below.

She glanced at the bed, then sighed. This tower was the highest point in the entire city. How many bed sheets would it take, all tied together, to reach the ground? Say . . . 100? 150? And all she had were two.

Not even being left with the magical silver basin with its water that heated up cheered her. It was obviously a precious gift since the Damatrans had no resident mages—but Rhis just saw it as evidence that she'd stupidly made herself a prize in the king's game, rather than a rescuer of a princess she didn't even like. She sat on a hassock, chin in hands, feeling thoroughly sorry for herself.

That only lasted a short while. She was too mad to get in a good self-pity wallow: also, much as she disliked Iardith, and the king of Damatras, she knew most of her mistakes were her own.

She simply had to think of a way out.

She moved to the windows, surveying escape possibilities. She peered at the right, beyond the geometric jumble of towers and crenellated walls. Through the back window was the waterfall thundering into the river, white water rushing upward. As the sun gleamed briefly between the clouds, it struck a rainbow over the clouds of mist.

A rainbow! Usually the sight of one made her smile. But her heart ached too much for smiles. To the left was the mountain slope. The Damatrans had cleared a wide space all the way up the slope beyond the sheer cliffs, probably for defense. Nym had always done the same, she'd learned at her lessons. This clearing meant that no invading army could sneak up under cover of the trees. Supposing an invading army had managed to sneak across the river below the front window without being noticed, that is, or had managed to scramble like a bunch of spiders down from the sheer cliffs behind the city walls.

She gazed upward at the tops of those cliffs, far above the tower. From her relatively high vantage she could just make out firs growing along the edge, most of them twisted from the wind. Teensy tufts at the ends of the branches caught another stray sun gleam—the rain clouds were breaking up—where new fir grew. These tufts always looked like candle flames, she'd always thought.

The reminder of home just made her sadder. Not that she hated her home, but . . . somehow she wished life would go on like an Eskanda party—or rather, life would go on at Eskanda—

She turned her back on the window and stared down at her hands.

At Sidal's little opal ring, worn faithfully every day.

Cold chill tingled unpleasantly through her nerves. Sidal was just a simple spell away. Or was she? Rhis remembered what Taniva had told them about Damatras having some kind of mysterious magical ward. Well, if anyone knew what that meant, it would be Sidal.

Rhis shut her eyes and performed the spell her sister had taught her.

She opened her eyes expectantly, but Sidal did not come.

Rhis waited one long breath, two. Three. Then gave up, and turned sadly to unpack her saddlebag. At least she could play her tiranthe to keep herself company. She'd sing all the most tragic, miserable songs she knew, she decided; if the guards beyond the door could hear her, she hoped they would feel as glum as she did.

So she sat down on the hassock, warmed up her fingers and her voice, then began to sing, accompanying herself on the tiranthe.

She was on her third verse of Eranda Sky-Born's Lament—

> *"Here I lie,*
> *wounded, cold, and alone,*
> *in this great fortress*
> *of solid stone . . ."*

—when a whish of air blew against her cheek, and there stood her sister!

Rhis stuttered to a halt.

Sidal staggered, then sank onto the bed as she blinked away the residue of magic transfer. When she'd recovered a little, she held up a finger to her ear. Rhis understood immediately: *Anyone outside?*

Rhis whispered "Guards," making sword-fighting motions with one hand.

Sidal pointed to the tiranthe, mouthing the words, *Keep playing!*

Rhis gave a couple of loud fake coughs in the direction of the door, then resumed her song.

Sidal smiled a little, her eyes closed as she listened. Rhis came to the end of the song and began another, playing as loudly as she could, but this time she did not sing.

Sidal knelt next to her hassock. "I am in Damatras, am I not?"

Rhis nodded, trying not to falter in her playing.

Sidal pursed her lips. "This ward, though enormous, is ancient, and thus easy to break. But I cannot leave it broken— any powerful mage doing a scrying sweep will notice at once. Any powerful mage like the Emperor of Sveran Djur."

Rhis grimaced. Every child learned about the sinister threat looming over the western sea—the enormous island empire of Sveran Djur. Its sorcerer king was considered the world's worst threat, ambitious as he was. And what lay directly to the east of his main island? Vesarja. Directly below and a little west of Vesarja, the smaller island of Ndai. Surrounding Vesarja, which was the largest kingdom on that part of the continent, lay Damatras to the north, the High Plains adjacent, and then the rest to the east, including Arpalon and Gensam, all the way down to Nym at the southernmost point, across from the smaller island of Wilfen.

Sidal said, "Sveran Djur is always scrying our way, looking for a momentary weakness. The only hope I have is that it's before dawn there, but I have to be fast. Now. Finish that song, and give me the tiranthe."

Surprised, Rhis brought the piece to a hasty conclusion. She handed the instrument to her sister, whose left hand spread over the chord dampers in a practiced manner, as her right began strumming. Rhis stared in amazement. She never knew her sister played. And ballads! She realized what it meant: that Sidal, knowing Elda's disapproval, had kept quiet on the subject, probably for family amity.

Rhis sighed. There was so much she just never saw! Feeling very young and ignorant, she bent her head close to her sister's, and as quickly as she could began outlining what had happened.

She faltered only when she came to Lios's masquerade. Deciding that that had nothing to do with the present difficulties, she skipped right past the confrontation in the garden, and all references since, continuing right up to the king's command.

"Good enough," Sidal said, strumming a few chords. "We can go home right now, then I can fix the ward—"

"No," Rhis said.

Sidal was so startled her fingers paused, but she began strumming again, faster than before. "Why?"

"I—I don't want to just leave the others. I need to see this awful mess through. I helped make it, after all. And I know they're all looking for me," she added quickly. Though she knew she wasn't being honest. That is, those things were true, but she had to—somehow—resolve things with Lios. Confront him. No, what she meant was—

"I hadn't considered that." Sidal let out her breath out in a long sigh, blowing a loose strand of hair off her forehead straight up. The hair fell to her cheek unnoticed as she finished a song. She handed back the tiranthe.

Rhis promptly launched into another melancholy ballad as Sidal said softly, "I wish I had time to ask Mama's advice. But I don't dare take any more time. What do you want to do? I take it you wish to escape in order to rejoin your friends?"

"Yes!"

Sidal said, "I have at home a cloak that shrouds you from being seen directly. If you wait until they come with a meal, you slip out—"

Rhis shook her head, thinking of those guards. They were all someone's brother, or cousin, or friend, and she suspected that the king, jolly as he sounded, would keep his word. Kings had to keep their word. Even if it was a rotten word.

"No," she said. "I can't go down the steps. The king said, if I get past them, they all die."

"Ugh!" Sidal pressed her fingers to her forehead, then dropped her hands, returning to her usual efficiency. "Then you must escape by magic, which the king cannot blame them for. Not if the door is blocked. He'll know magic was at fault. It'll also warn him that his ward, though powerful, is terribly outdated," she added. "I think even Emperor Dhes-Andis of Sveran Djur, terrible as he is, would think twice about attacking *this* kingdom, but we'd rather not find out, right? Very well, then."

Sidal rose, extended her hands, and began whispering. A faint glow shimmered in the air, reaching from her hands to the bed—which lifted, heavy as it was, sailed grandly toward the door, and then—very slowly and quietly—tipped upward until it rested against the door. Sidal rubbed her hands down her sides, whispered—and the bed returned itself to its place. It still shimmered; Sidal made a pass over it with her hand, whispered more, then stopped, wiping trembling fingers over her brow.

"All right," she said. "When you are ready for the bed to move again, all you do is pass your hand over it—just like I did—and say these words." She repeated the magic words, which made little sense to Rhis.

But she said them over and over until she had them in memory. Sidal nodded, saying wryly, "Just as well you inherited the family talent for magic."

"One more thing." Sidal paused and drank off half of Rhis's water. "And luckily, I have this one all ready. All I need is a transfer." She breathed in and out a couple of times, then muttered—and after a soft *paff!* of air, a piece of what looked like black ribbon lay on the floor.

Sidal bent, picked it up, and dropped it into Rhis's hand. It was slightly sticky, and heavier than fabric.

"When full dark comes, you step on it, and it becomes a bubble around you. It will rise. You direct it by movement. Practice in here first," Sidal said, as Rhis strummed two chords over and over as she concentrated. "You really don't want to try it while sitting in a window."

Rhis shivered. "No."

"As you'll see, you only have a certain amount of time. As you breathe the air inside the bubble, it gets smaller and smaller. And each time you use it, you get less of a bubble. I'm afraid I daren't stay here long enough to layer on more spells of use," Sidal said, and paused for more water. "If you are careful, once you've escaped if you find yourself still in trouble you could always use it to rise away to safety, and then just use your ring again. I will come and take you away." She tipped her head to one side. "I really wonder, though, if I ought to leave you. Mother might be angry. Just why is it necessary to rejoin these girls? Are they all so incompetent without your help?"

"No." Rhis's ears burned, but she just shook her head. "Taniva is the bravest of us, at least in adventuring. And Yuzhyu is—"

Noises outside the door caused them to turn startled glances at each another.

Sidal whispered, made a sign, and just before the door swung up, she vanished with another soft pop of displaced air.

Rhis shoved the ribbon-thing into her sash and began another ballad as one of the guards elbowed the heavy door open and entered carrying a big tray. At once familiar spicy smells filled the room, spices she'd learned to use in making High Plains dishes.

Rhis's mouth promptly began to water—she hadn't had any breakfast.

But she forgot her hunger when she was surprised by a familiar pale-haired figure entering behind the guard: Jarvas.

The guard set the tray on the side table and left. The door shut. It didn't lock.

Rhis turned in question to Jarvas, who grinned. "I don't think you'll fight your way past me."

"No."

"So they don't have to lock us in," Jarvas said, with a slight shrug, no more than a tightening of his splendid shoulders. Then he chuckled. "Taniva would probably make a run for it."

Rhis had to laugh, despite everything. Jarvas so obviously wished Taniva were here—or that she might come and try battering down the door.

She stood up; Jarvas sat down on the hassock, his brown and dark gray Damatran clothes a contrast to his pale hair and skin and eyes. He still wore that blue-gemmed knife through his belt, but he hadn't come clanking in with a lot of other weapons, for which Rhis was grateful.

"My father sent me in to try to talk you into a betrothal," Jarvas said. "I did try to warn you."

"I know." She laid aside the tiranthe and sat on the edge of the bed. "Thanks. I didn't believe you—I thought it was a trick."

Jarvas ran a hand over his head. His hand was big, long-fingered, his palm as callused as Taniva's. "Yes. I saw that." He dropped his hand to his knees. "Why did you girls come here?"

"To rescue Iardith." And on his laugh, she said shortly, "It would have worked, too, if Iardith had just come with us."

He flashed a quick grin. "Taniva would have seen to that. She's already been in and out of here once before. Did she tell you? And I raided her father's camp over in High Plains." He grinned again.

"She did tell us," Rhis said, finding the conversation surprising. While she did not want to marry Jarvas in the least, handsome as he was, she did appreciate the lack of threats, or worse, gloating.

"I don't want to marry you," Jarvas went on, his thoughts obviously galloping a parallel path to hers. "Though I will say this. Rather you than Iardith." He grimaced slightly.

Rhis gasped. "You kept following her around at the party, and glowering at all her partners, and—"

"I know. Lios—or rather, the other one, the one pretending to be Lios—tried to hint. Good fellows," he added. "Both of 'em. But I was blind." He gave her a wry smile. "No. Problem was, I *wasn't* blind. Deaf, say."

"I guess being really beautiful will do that," Rhis said. She didn't gloat—not when she could so clearly remember her own blindness over Andos the false prince.

Jarvas gave a soft laugh. Then tipped his head. "You are unexpected. No tears? No threats? Iardith is crying now—what a storm! I pity those girls. She sure had a nasty tongue when we didn't have hot meals for her, on silver, while on the ride. At first she laid on the sweet words when she tried to bribe 'em to get her a carriage, and silver to eat off, and this and that. They kept coming to me, but I said no. We needed speed. Not comfort. Then came the tears. Some of the boys got mad at me, but when I didn't change the orders, she got mad at them. Her father would have them all hanged for serving her cold food, my father would have them flogged for letting her get wet in the rain." He chuckled, a husky sound Rhis found unexpectedly attractive.

"I take it the magic of beauty wore off?" Rhis asked.

"By the end of the ride no one spoke to anyone else. She was in a constant sulk, and my boys didn't know whom to blame. Then we got home at last, and she lit right into my father." He pointed a finger. "I'd rather have you, all told, but if you don't want me, well, your father's good for the ransom, right?" He hesitated. "You do not seem at all disturbed."

Though his voice was admiring in a cool way, she could see in the slight narrowing of his eyes that suspicion was not far away.

Would she have been more worried if Sidal had not given her the ring and the ribbon-thing? No—she would have been ashamed, because her sister would have had to find a way to rescue her anyway, she knew that. Though Sidal could not have used her magic for political reasons—that was a vow all mages made. The ring bypassed that, because it had been a personal gift, given out of love.

But Rhis didn't need Jarvas reminding his father that half of her family were accomplished mages.

She said, "My father is rich, that's no secret. I suppose if he has to, he'll pay. But I think he'd rather I solve my own problems."

Jarvas looked puzzled. But got to his feet. "I'm supposed to give you the night to decide, and tomorrow my father will send someone to your Nym demanding either betrothal or ransom."

"Wait," Rhis said, curious.

He had been moving away, but paused, looking back over his shoulder.

She said, "You don't want to marry me any more than I want to marry you."

He didn't deny it—he was no courtier to flatter her with false compliments.

She went on, "I'm a prisoner, I have only the two choices. But why are *you* doing it?"

"I only have two choices, as well. I made the mistake of bringing Iardith," he said. "You made the mistake of coming here to rescue her. My father thinks using the situation to Damatran advantage is just common sense."

He rapped once on the door with the back of his hand. It swung open. He said, "See you in the morning."

She just smiled.

He left. The door swung shut and locked.

She moved to the table. There were flat corn cakes, and boiled grain with spices and browned onions, grilled fish, and a variety of greens topped with a tart sauce that tasted of peppered lemon. In a bowl was a sliced peach with cream and honey. She devoured it all, then sat back down to play the tiranthe and wait for dark.

But just as the sun had begun its slant toward the west, sending shafts of golden light from the extreme end of the window to paint golden color up the edge of the wooden door, there was a flicker of color in the shaft of sunset light.

Dust motes, she thought, but when the flicker happened again, this time looking like a face, she stared into the shaft.

And to her astonishment a face—not solid, but made of light—formed in the sun shaft.

It was Prince Lios.

NINETEEN

The familiar smile, snub nose, and warm brown eyes made her
throat constrict painfully.

She heard a whisper in her head, as if a ghostly voice had
spoken just behind her ear.

It was his voice.

Rhis. The girls are out. Now we're trying to find a way—

"How am I seeing you? By magic?" she asked, looking
away and back again.

The voice faded, as did the flicker. Rhis stopped,
glowering at that shaft of light as if she could force the image
back with her mind.

To her surprise, the image did return. Lios frowned into
the dust motes as if concentrating. *Think about me*, he asked.
Please! It will make it easier for Yuzhyu.

"Yuzhyu?"

*She's a mage—can tell you later. I just want to reassure
you, we're forming plans to get you out.*

Rhis said, "I can get myself out. Where are you?"

His eyes rounded in surprise, then narrowed in worry.
Don't do anything dangerous—

"Where are you?" she asked, whispering fiercely so as not to be heard behind the door, but his voice and face were fading.

Pottery—He turned his head sharply, and the image winked out.

Rhis sank onto the hassock. Yuzhyu—a mage? But—

She shook her head hard. No use in asking herself questions she couldn't answer. Instead, she wondered how to find out where the pottery was. For a short time she considered various questions that she could ask the guards outside the door, questions meant to sound innocent, but she knew that once she went missing, no matter how plausible she'd made a question about pots, potteries, clay, or dishes, the guards would remember her question. They might even get in trouble for it, though they could not have known her purpose.

So she had to find it on her own.

The back window gave the best view of the main part of the castle and city, and half of the vistas to left and right.

She pulled the hassock over and leaned carefully on her arms, then peered out. To the right, winding old streets between a jumble of roofs. Lots of shops and homes, but no clay, no kilns. A castle pottery was not a small thing; she peered to the left, where the sun was just sinking toward the mountain. It was difficult to see past—and when it vanished, so would the light— so she shaded her eyes and did her best. Was that a clay pile? And a round kiln beyond?

The lock rattled—the guards were back for her tray.

She flung herself down onto the hassock and strummed softly until they were gone, then she packed her saddlebag carefully and laid it on the hassock.

The golden light turned ochre, then began to fade as the sun vanished behind the mountain to the west.

Rhis's heart began to thump in her ears as she stretched out her arm and whispered the words. Just as it had for Sidal, the bed shifted to the door, stood upright, and settled there.

She pulled the ribbon-thing from her sash and inspected it. It was not black, but a deep, deep blue.

She followed her sister's directions. It snapped up around her in a blur of bluish light: suddenly she found herself standing in a gently bobbing bubble. She pressed the sides. They gave stickily. She hastily pulled her hand back, afraid to poke a hole in it. But then cautiously extended her hands, touched the sides, which shivered slightly, like a tapped jelly. She leaned to the right.

The bubble bobbed slowly to the right.

Rhis lurched to the left. The bubble shuddered, bouncing sickeningly. Ripples ran through the blue skin of it. All right, so she knew how to go from side to side. Slow and easy was the trick. Not bouncy.

A quick experiment with leaning forward and then back proved that she could now move in four directions—but what about up and down?

She stretched her hands upward, just touching the top— and the bubble rose until it bobbed gently against the stone ceiling.

Rhis gulped and tried not to look down as she crouched, touching the skin on either side of her feet. The bubble dropped down. When she patted, it dropped faster. She pulled her hands away, and it stayed where it was, in the middle of the air.

A little more experimenting gave her a better idea how to maneuver—but when she looked up, she was startled to discover that the top curve of the bubble was closer to her head. It was shrinking!

She collapsed it at once, and sank to the floor, breathing hard.

Another glance at the west window. The light was almost gone. And the bubble was blue, so if anyone looked up, they shouldn't see it against the twilight sky.

But she'd better go before all the light was gone, and she got lost.

And then ran out of air.

And plummeted to the—

No. Don't think about that. Just do it.

She stood up, pulled her saddle-bag over her shoulder, pushed the hassock to the back window, and climbed up. Then, sitting with one leg in and one out as cold night air ruffled over her face, she carefully extended the ribbon thing to one foot, and said the spell to form the bubble as she eased out of the window, her heartbeat now racing frantically.

But she landed safely inside, though the bubble bobbed up and down in a terrifying way.

She shrank down and the bubble began to drop precipitously; now thoroughly frightened, she lunged up, flung her hands to the top—and the bubble shot up above the top of the tower.

Rhis whimpered, bringing her hands down, pressing them to her front as she stared down at the stone ceiling of the tower, so high above the city—

And what she saw almost made her forget her danger.

There, in the very center of the tower roof, resting in a large stone cup, lay the biggest gem she had ever seen.

As she hovered there above it, even through the diffuse blue of the bubble-skin she could see lights glinting inside the stone. Instinctively she collapsed the bubble onto the top of the tower. She knelt down, staring into the stone. The lights flickered brilliantly, drawing her deeper in, deeper, her entire mind straining to find the pattern there as her awareness spread through a vastness that could not possibly be held in a stone—

Just in time she shut her eyes. *Magic.* This huge, glittering gem was one of those rare things, a diamond scry-stone. Most of them were made from quartz or crystal, but this was a single diamond, bigger than her two fists put together. The biggest diamond she had ever seen. Sidal had told her once that diamonds held immense amounts of power, far more than any other clear stone, but that much power was dangerous to anyone not trained to handle it.

She touched it cautiously, looking at it sideways: Sidal had taught her to be cautious around *any* scry-stones. Skilled mages were always looking through them, and could see one another unless one knew how to ward oneself from being seen. The searchers were not always benevolent.

She touched it again, this time letting her finger linger. The diamond seemed to sing on a very high, sharp note—sharp yet almost sweet. A compelling note; the stone vibrated with power.

And it lay in the hands of the Damatrans?

The singing changed to a melody painfully sweet and sad all at once. As if beckoning, or rather, holding out hands to the sky, yearning for freedom.

Rhis's other fingers gently closed around the stone. The thinking part of her mind—almost overwhelmed with the beautiful song of yearning—only had room for one thought: *I hope you don't turn me to stone.*

Free, the stone sang. Free, free, free! It seemed light in her hand, almost as if it wanted to fit there. So she lifted it, and the song soared with golden, joyous trills.

She tucked it into her sash, pulled her white blouse over the sash to hide the bulge, and then held out her bubble-ribbon again. The shortness of the previous ride seemed not to have diminished it much.

She would have to trust it—or stay on the top of this tower forever.

As if warning her, a few raindrops stung her face. The wind was turning cold, and picking up strength.

She made the bubble and stepped inside. Then leaned up to clear the crenellations of the tower.

She stood—and the bubble slowed, suspended in the middle of the air above the castle. The wind then began blowing it east.

East, not west.

Biting her lip hard to prevent a whimper from escaping, she leaned her hands against the western side, and it began to move westward, gradually picking up speed. But when she tried looking down through the skin, the lights below were blurry, and if she angled her head down, her hands shifted, making the bubble tremble and bob.

So she slowed and tried again, lowering herself little by little until she felt a brush against her head.

The top of the bubble! It had shrunk!

She pressed harder, thinking over and over *Where is the pottery?* It was now too dark for her to see, but the bubble was so small she did not want to stop it from whisking so surely over the rooftops of the western part of the city.

She peered anxiously down as the bubble lowered, getting smaller and smaller until she was kneeling.

The bubble touched the ground, and she collapsed, and bent to pick it up. The ribbon thing was definitely smaller. How many more uses? Maybe only one, she reminded herself as she tucked it firmly into her sash.

Now to find the others—and not get caught.

It was full dark under a layer of thin cloud. She just barely discerned the jumble of out-buildings beside the clay field, and had just started toward it when she heard the rustle of light, running steps.

She whirled around, shoulders hunched—and then gave a glad gasp of surprise when Dartha whispered, "Princess Rhis! How did you find us?"

"Dartha? How did *you* get here?"

"Come. This way! They plan how to get you. Come, come!" She held out her hand.

Rhis took it, and, led by Dartha, ran over the rocky, weedy ground toward the storage sheds behind the kiln.

She stopped before they reached them, and whistled a bird call.

Seemingly from out of the ground two silhouettes appeared, silently approaching. They closed on Dartha and Rhis.

Dartha whispered a fast explanation to the shorter silhouette—one of Taniva's guards. The other whispered in Vesarjan, "Who is that?"

"I'm Rhis."

The boy whistled softly, long and low.

Dartha ran back in the other direction—on guard, Rhis realized.

The boy led Rhis swiftly between the storage buildings to a shed, said something out loud—and more figures emerged. They helped him open a rickety door meant to permit wagons to back inside.

A faint ruddy glow lit the back; when her silent guard led her around stacks of huge clay water and storage pots, she discovered Yuzhyu, Lios, Taniva, Shera, and some others crouched in a circle looking down at a model of the city crudely drawn on an old piece of paper.

They all looked up, but Rhis was aware of only one face.

"I said I'd get myself out," she said, and was gratified at Lios's wide-eyed astonishment.

"How did you manage that?" he asked, his admiration plain. "No—"

"Later," Taniva cut in, waving her hand in a sharp chop. "My suspicion makes more need to be fast. Come! We get out *now*."

The boys turned Lios's way. He looked unfamiliar to Rhis, wearing those guard clothes—like the Damatrans', sturdy tunic-jackets, though made differently, and dyed a sort of gray-blue. He said, "Let's," and they all sprang instantly into action—one dousing the little lick of flame, another sweeping up the map, and the rest falling in around the girls as they were led out of the storage houses and up a rocky, crumbling hillock behind the pottery.

They zigzagged up in the darkness, a very uncomfortable journey, especially when Rhis made the mistake of looking back once to discover how very far above the city she'd climbed. Its lamps and torches and glowglobes winked and glimmered far below.

She followed Shera, who was breathing hard. Up toward the city wall they climbed. From a distance the wall had looked uniformly smooth. Closer, they could see that it was much repaired—but still too high to climb. No guards walked it—but it glowed faintly.

Rhis pointed. "Magic?"

"Yizz, yizz," Yuzhyu whispered. "There is magic guarding the top. We cannot climb over."

Rhis scooted forward. "But if you are a mage, can't you transfer us over?"

Yuzhyu turned her way. "No. Is political cause. I can do nothing."

"But—"

"I have a better way," Taniva said. "Never mind the magic. I got in and out without it. Just a bit farther, above that stream."

A couple of people exclaimed "Where?" and "I can't see anything!"

But Rhis heard the high singing note. When she turned her face upward and to the left, the sharpness left the note and it turned sweet. Without any thought she began scrambling up in that direction.

"Rhis?" Shera called, then hurried behind—followed by the others.

Rhis kept going. She couldn't see it in the thickening darkness as the rain clouds built up, but she could hear the stream: a rushing trickle.

In silence everyone climbed. Though the strange singing in her brain sustained its chord, Rhis was not as aware of it when she concentrated on Lios. There he was, behind Yuzhyu.

No one spoke until they had gone a ways alongside the stream. They often slid in mud, but by now the rain had begun, so they were wet anyway.

The weird pull on Rhis's mind eased, and she faltered, murmuring, "Aren't we here?" just as Taniva said, "Hah!"

And took Shera's hand. Rhis followed. Mostly by feel she discovered she was to climb under the wall, where the stream had slowly been crumbling away the foundation of the stone.

One by one they all climbed through, and then there was another steep climb, in pouring rain, until they reached the forested area that had not been cleared away by the Damatrans.

Early morning light outlined the rocky hillside surrounded by forest.

Rhis was tired, gritty, cold, but at least she wasn't thirsty. Water dripped and trickled everywhere.

"My cave is not far," Taniva said, no longer keeping her voice low.

"They don't patrol up here?" Lios asked, catching up with her.

Rhis felt a brief flame of warmth inside at the sound of his voice—the magic singing faded away, and she breathed deeply, aware of her surroundings. But when she remembered those horrible words she'd spoken to Lios, the inward warmth turned into the prickly heat of embarrassment.

"Once a week or so a sweep. But they guard against army. Not one person."

"We figured that might be the case when we slipped in," Lios said.

"How you do that?" Taniva asked.

"Got some laborers smocks, bought a load of garlic. They eat a lot of it up here, did you know that?"

Taniva laughed. "We eat it too! And red pepper! Good spice in winter."

"We only dared the six of us. This was meant to be a scouting foray. The rest of the fellows are with the horses, down in the valley behind the river fork."

"I know where that one lies," Taniva said. "Now. Where . . . where . . ."

Rhis stumbled wearily; Yuzhyu closed in on one side. "Need you help?" she asked, extending one of her small hands.

Rhis sighed. "I'll be fine. But oh, I'm so tired." The singing dream world started closing in again. She forced her eyes open.

"I think we all are," Yuzhyu said.

"There it is. Still dry!" Taniva called.

Her women split up at once to search the surroundings as Taniva led the way through a narrow crack in two great rocks that slanted up a hillside. Some ancient landslide left the rock revealed, like the slanting layers in the great cliffs behind the city.

Rhis could see the rock. The peachy light that heralds the sun's first appearance lit the tops of the tall pines and the rocky mountainside.

Rhis followed Shera into the cave, which widened into a mossy area that was out of the storm. Though the rain by now dwindled to mist.

The cave smelled of mold, but that vanished when Taniva found her stash of wood and made a fire. She hung her cloak over the crack in the rock, blocking the firelight from glowing, and then hunkered down.

Lios gestured, and his young guards gathered around, sitting in a tired group. "That was a wonderful escape," he said.

"Maybe." Taniva smacked her hands. "But it was too easy."

Rhis did not want to call Lios's attention her way, so she whispered to Shera, who crouched beside her, chin on knees, ruddy hair hanging sodden down her back, her eyes closed. "Iardith?"

"Stayed behind," Shera whispered back, eyes still closed. "Said she had plans of her own, which did not include returning to her father empty-handed." She opened her eyes, and grinned wryly. "I think, from some of the things she said, she planned to oust you as Jarvas's new betrothed."

Rhis felt Lios's attention. Again her face heated up. "She is welcome to him."

Taniva said, "I do not like this. No alarm. No search. My escape, too easy."

Shera groaned. "If that was too easy, I'd hate to see what hard is."

Lios said apologetically, "Hard has to come next, I'm afraid. We cannot count on late alarms or searches. We had better leave and make our way to the horses. We'll rest as soon as we're safely over the border into home."

Taniva smacked her hands again. The sound hurt Rhis's ears. She felt the strangeness closing in again, like water seeping in under the door to her mind: her mind flickered with dream images, though her body was still awake.

"First we eat a little," Yuzhyu said. And frowned around. "I feel magic. Very strong."

Rhis turned her way, forming the words to tell her about the stone. But the singing was too loud, her body suddenly so heavy, so ready for sleep . . .

She jerked awake when Lios said, "Eating is a good idea. But I think we'd better do it while walking. I will feel somewhat better when we reached the camp and the horses. Glaen will be worried about us," he added.

Shera sat up, her eyes startled.

But she said nothing as Dartha handed out the last of the girls' stores, and they left the cave, walking single file out into the mist.

TWENTY

Shera did not speak once that long, nightmarish day. Rhis walked next to her, slipping in and out of dream. The stone sang sweetly, as if urging her tired feet to carry her on: it seemed to want to get away as badly as she did.

Lios walked with seeming tirelessness up and down the line, encouraging people, talking to keep them awake. But he stayed away from Rhis and Shera, and neither spoke to him.

At sunset the tired group shuffled down the river bank far west of the city, where the river narrowed to white water. Here was an old row of rocks that formed a hopping bridge, as Taniva called it.

Under pouring rain, as the light faded, Rhis faced those uneven wet stones. She wished she could just waft herself over. And though she did not know any magic whatsoever, when she hopped to the first stone, she seemed to move slowly through the air, as if it were water and not full of raindrops, and landed lightly. She hopped to the next, and the next—and almost stumbled when Yuzhyu took a crowing breath.

"Rhis," she called. "Have you a spell on you?"

"A spell? No—"

"You have zis magic light on you, ooom." She was so excited her accent was back very strongly.

Rhis's entire body tingled. She closed her forearms across her middle and fought away the strange sense of lightness.

And it withdrew slowly, almost reluctantly.

She almost fell at the next hop, she was so heavy. Like she'd taken one of the boulders upon her back.

Three, two, one. And then a thin, strong hand reached down and pulled her up the steep riverbank, and she looked up tiredly into Glaen's narrow face.

He dropped her hand, reached past, took Shera's hand in his grip. He pulled her up, but did not let go.

Shera said, "Glaen? What are you doing here?"

"You were gone," he said. Not *You were gone*, like the group was gone, but *YOU were gone.*

"I—we thought—" Shera sighed sharply. "We stupidly thought Iardith needed rescuing. Guess what?"

"We had a bet going on that. I won." Glaen drawled with the old irony. "Having bet five to one that she was the one who abducted Jarvas of Damatras."

Shera giggled, then choked on a sob.

"Hey. Don't start, or you'll get me at it," he said in a low voice. "We'll talk later. I hope you've saved up some of those insults," he added. He lifted his voice. "We got a hot meal all ready, so step up to the formal dining parlor as soon as you put on your jewels, your highnesses!"

Fast as they'd traveled, one of Lios's people had traveled even faster—making sure of the trail, and warning the others. In gratitude Rhis followed Shera up a trail into a clearing under spreading trees. The welcome glow of firelight drew Rhis stronger than any mere magic. She allowed her saddle bag to thump to the ground, the tiranthe giving a discordant hum of strings. For a time she just stood there, the warmth of the fire beating gratefully over her numb face and hands, and causing faint curls of steamy smoke to rise from her clothes.

Hearing soft laughter, she looked around. The Vesarjans had set up tents; while she'd been in her reverie, someone had picked up her saddlebag and borne it away.

Reverie. She felt the weight of the magic stone on her mind, which caused a warning prickle. She caught a fleeting memory: Sidal's face. *Diamonds are much stronger than any other stone . . .*

She forced herself to move, poking her head into tents, all of them open to the firelight, until she recognized her own saddlebag.

She pulled the stone from her sash. It was strangely heavy. She could barely lift it. The singing changed to a high, skull-rattling whistle. But Sidal's warning voice in memory was louder, and so, using the last of her strength, she shoved the stone into her saddlebag.

At once the singing lessened. Then it turned sweet again, a lovely chord so faint, so beautiful. If she just got closer, she could—

Gravel crunched under feet right outside her tent. She knew it was Lios. A rush of feelings chased through her as she backed out of the tent and straightened up.

"Rhis, are you still angry with me?" he asked.

He didn't mean the disastrous rescue plan. She knew he meant his masquerade. "I don't think so. I mean, I was, then I wasn't, then when I was, I think I was more mad at myself for saying those nasty things." There, it was out. And oh, she did feel such relief!

"Perfectly understandable," Lios said promptly, and flashed his quick grin. "The poets certainly say it's natural to throw blame around. Why, here I am, living proof. I blamed you for the fact that I was an arrogant fool, ignoring others' feelings with my witty 'joke' that wasn't witty or even much of a joke. Yes, completely your fault—"

She shook with silent laughter, though the tears still weren't far away.

"So how about we make a pact: we let our blames smash into one another, fall to pieces, and vanish." He clapped his hands lightly. "There! Gone. I don't feel any blame toward you any more, not a speck. Do you feel any for me?"

"No," she said, and somehow all her pent-up regret and embarrassment and anger were gone. She laughed, feeling much lighter inside.

"Good," he said. "Things are messy enough at home. Your words were good practice for what everyone else said when they found out. Hoo!" He gestured, his clothes jingling faintly.

"What's that noise?" Rhis asked.

Lios grinned. Then he flung his arms wide and hopped from toe to toe. "Isn't that a laugh?" He danced around in a circle. "Me in chain mail."

"You look—" She wanted to say taller, but that wasn't quite right. Intimidating. But she didn't want to say that, either.

"Silly? It feels like walking around with your own personal mattress—except sleeping on linked metal is not comfy."

"You said things are messy at home. I take it they were mad, too," she said tentatively.

"Why did I think it was a great idea? One good thing: I'll have to think really hard to come up with anything more stupid."

"Does Queen Briath know?"

"Oh, yes."

"Is she—"

"Angry? Yes." Lios turned his face up to the dripping branches overhead. Then brought his chin down. "Don't blame my mother—there are reasons—but she doesn't really like me much. Still, she made me the heir. I worked hard for it. I really don't want to lose it all if I can possibly prevent it."

"But you came to rescue Iardith anyway?"

He sighed. "We came after you all. You saw Glaen, I know. Breggo is with the horses."

Rhis wondered for the first time if someone might have left behind a clue. At the sound of a familiar fluting voice, she suspected who might have left a note for her cousin.

She frowned. "It seemed such a good idea at the time."

And was grateful when he didn't gloat, or scold, or laugh. "How did you get away from that tower? That was a mighty stroke of genius, by the bye. I hope you'll do that a lot in the future. I also wish Iardith had seen you walk into camp just as we were going over our desperate rescue plan for the last time. It might even have impressed her. Or maybe not."

He'd seemed tireless from the distance she'd been careful to maintain, but up close, the firelight revealed marks under his eyes. Her heart lurched in its accustomed tread. "I—" For just a moment she hugged to herself the thought of keeping that impression of genius.

But she'd already had plenty to say about liars. "My sister," she said, discovering her voice had gone hoarse. "Magic." She pointed to her ring. "In case."

He frowned a little—looking plainly worried. "Where are my wits? Come over to the fire. The food might not be courtly, but there's plenty. Actually, a couple of the boys make really good trail cornbread. And Andos was smart enough to grab a pot of honey in the scramble to leave Eskanda."

Talking in his low, pleasant voice, he described their journey, making it sound funny, like when he started out—the mighty prince at the head of his noble minions—his horse skidded in a slimy puddle and he did a perfect somersault and landed face-flat in the mud. From then on one of the noble minions on a hill horse did the leading. But, tired as she was, Rhis sensed that he was hiding the anxious effort it really must have taken, especially since the boys did not have a map with Taniva's shortcuts.

He drew her toward the fire, where boys and girls sat on rocks and in a row along a fallen log, everyone busy with bowls and spoons.

Rhis was too tired to feel much of anything when the pretend Prince Lios appeared round the fire, twin flames reflected in his beautiful dark eyes as he smiled at her and handed her a bowl. "For you, the last of the honey," he said. "I'll never forget you were the only one to spare a fellow's feet."

"Don't. Remind us," Lios said quickly. His face was far ruddier than could be explained away by firelight. Then he bowed grandly, indicating a mossy rock. "Your throne, Princess?"

Rhis felt weak laughter. "Princess. We haven't done a single princess thing for so long." *Except when the king of Damatras—*

Shera gave a loud sigh. "It was stupid to come running up here," she admitted. "We don't even have Iardith, after all the trouble we went to!"

Rhis tasted the cornbread. It was delicious, the moreso with clover honey drizzled over it.

Lios sighed, staring down the bowl in his hands, and the untouched food. Rhis looked at his tired profile. She was glad that they were friends again, that she'd gotten past feeling angry and awkward and horrible. But getting past the awkwardness between them hadn't fixed everything. For the first time, she considered Lios's masquerade from his perspective, and what she saw made her feel awkward and anxious all over again. A lot of people—his own mother—seemed angry with him. Would they even be here if he had not traded places with Andos? Probably not. Though it was hard to say whether Iardith would have arranged her own abduction if the real Prince Lios had turned her down instead of the false one.

In fact it was hard to think at all past the singing chord in her mind. It seemed to have gotten louder. Being away from it helped a little, but not all that much. The stone seemed to want to be moving, and its note was restless and anxious.

The rise of voices broke her reverie: she recognized Glaen and Shera arguing. Was it mock or real? She tried to concentrate on the words, but all she could make out was the rise and fall of their voices on the other side of camp, where they sat a little apart on a mossy log. Maybe they didn't know themselves if it was real or mock anger, she thought sleepily, as she slid off her rock, folded her arms over the stone, and just leaned her forehead on her hands. Just for a moment—

"Up! Up!" Breggan ran through the camp, his chain mail jingling at every step. "We have to ride out!"

Heads popped up—many people had fallen asleep right where they'd been sitting—lamps were lit.

"They're up on the high road," someone reported.

"Who?" Yuzhyu appeared, hair wild, a lamp swinging in her hand.

"The Damatrans," Breggan said. "They're after us."

TWENTY-ONE

"We're too close to the border to give up," Taniva declared. "I know a footpath. It will take us straight to border."

"Is that how you got here so fast?" Lios asked.

"Yes." Taniva patted her travel bag. "Have special map."

"Let's go," Lios said, lifting his voice. "Fall in!"

Rhis gritted her teeth and followed. She longed for sleep, to escape the persistent singing inside her head.

The note seemed to climb higher and higher during the day-long dash along those narrow paths, ducking low branches and being smacked in the face by leaves. Always the sense of *Faster! Flee! Go!* sang in her head, making thought almost impossible.

So she didn't think, she just kept her sight between her horse's hairy ears as she followed.

She almost slid into a kind of dream existence, an uncomfortable one full of shrieking cries and weird whistles, when she was roused by cries of anger and dismay farther up the line.

She looked around. They seemed to have come a very long way in a short time. Sure enough, they emerged from the thick old forest growth of a shady slope into a clearing just below a cliff.

Rhis vaguely recognized that clearing, where she and the other princesses had paused to make their plan for entering Damatras.

Only now, ranged along the top of the ridge and blocking off the narrow path, was a very grubby-looking Jarvas, with a lot of fellows his own age. They'd clearly endured a very fast ride in order to skirt the fleeing would-be rescuers, and reach the border first.

"Well done, my son," the King of Damatras boomed, riding at the head of a force down a side path just above Rhis and her friends. The king paused under the shade of a spreading, leafy tree; that road was much broader than the path they were on.

"They were riding parallel to us the entire time," Lios said in disgust.

Several people sent looks Taniva's way.

"That is the main border road," she said. "It is much longer than my path."

That, and Jarvas's presence already at the border, meant that the Damatrans had to have started out about the same time Taniva, Lios, and Rhis and her friends left the cave—and they'd ridden all night.

"They knew all along," Shera exclaimed. "How?"

The answer emerged behind the King of Damatras, as Iardith rode between the guardsmen, looking cool and amused.

"We always respect a good run," Jarvas called, grinning.

"You betrayed us," Shera cried out, glaring at Iardith.

The magic stone was singing so loud, its note so high and sharp, that Rhis's head rang.

Iardith shrugged. "*You*," she drawled, "got in *my* way." And she pointed at Rhis.

The King clapped his gloved hands and rubbed them. "It seems I've most of the heirs of all my neighbors here," he said genially. "What a story this will make! Come along, my fine young friends. We'll do you all proud, I promise, while you are our, ah, guests."

Silently, but in unison, both Jarvas's guard and the king's men all put hands to the swords they wore at their saddles. They didn't actually draw their blades, but they were clearly ready for a command to do so.

Breggan's hand drifted to the sword hanging at his own saddle. Lios already had his hand on his hilt; Glaen, muttering under his breath, smoothed his hand over his horse's mane and then dropped his hand to his own saddle sheath.

Taniva and her guard had already drawn their steel. They held those sharp knifes pointed toward the sky—they weren't even pretending that they weren't ready to leap into battle as soon as Taniva gave the signal.

Rhis pressed her fingers to her head as the stone keened *Flee! Flee! Flee!*

She struggled to think past that incessant message. The Damatrans and her own party were getting ready for a fight. Not a practice one, but a real one. A fight in which people could get stabbed, even killed, in order to force the others to give up—but they wouldn't just give up. She could see it in Lios's thin, white mouth and jutting jaw, in Breggan's sober gaze from which all the shyness had vanished.

And in the Damatrans' eagerness.

She didn't want a fight. Nothing good came of fights—despite the old ballads. Maybe the old ballads became fun only after everyone's cuts had healed, but one thing for sure . . .

The stone vibrated against her knee, the sound intensifying as if to wrest her attention solely to the magical diamond and its need to be free. Rhis fought against it and darted a quick glance around. There was the tiny bridge joining the rocky cliff edge of the main border road, along which Jarvas and his troop had stationed themselves. The king's road, above them on the same slope, curved away around the side of the tree-dotted hill, past one of the waterfalls falling into the chasm that formed the natural border, to the bigger bridge a small distance away. The bridge that joined Damatras and Vesarja.

Rhis and her friends just had to get to the bridge.

The king and his men would have to dismount in order to slip and slide down the steep, treacherous incline to their path below. Jarvas and his men would have to cross the bridge one by one.

The king gave the nod to his son.

If she acted now, they couldn't surround her. So—just as Jarvas nudged his horse forward, his hand gripping the hilt of his sword, Rhis slid her hand into her saddlebag and grabbed the stone.

The singing intensified, almost deafening.

She sucked in a breath, fighting the urge to *flee! Flee! Flee!*

She leaped off her horse and stumbled onto the little bridge over the chasm.

As Jarvas started his horse down the little path toward her, Rhis yelled, "If you move, I will drop this thing!"

The stone had begun to sink sweetly again when she started over the bridge, but when she held the stone over the rickety wooden rail of the bridge, it shrieked on so piercing a note her knees almost buckled.

Yuzhyu gasped. "That is what I hear! It is magic stone!"

"I know that noise," the king shouted, and, "Hold!" to his men.

"What?" Jarvas called across the chasm to his father. "Hold?"

"Yes," the king returned grimly. "That girl from Nym has the kingdom protection!"

Jarvas stared, mouth open, at Rhis. She could see his wide pale eyes. "That thing was on the roof of the High Tower!"

"Don't I know that," the king said, even more grimly.

Rhis was trembling all over, vaguely aware of Yuzhyu whispering steadily behind her. The stone shrieked unmercifully; Rhis closed her eyes as tears of pain escaped, and yelled, "Let everyone pass! Or I drop it!"

She could no longer see, but she heard the creak of gear, the clop of hooves, and then the little bridge shook as people passed by her to safety, one by one.

The angry king shouted, "You can follow them, girl, but we're going to be right on your heels. I will never stop until I get that stone back, and then personally wring your neck." He added, somewhat spoiling the effect of his threat, "*After* I find out how you got to the top of that tower in order to grab it."

Rhis was too frazzled to care about mere kings. The stone was taking over the world, turning sound into screaming pain.

But just before she could no longer bear it, a hand brushed over hers, and the terrible inner shriek changed so suddenly she half-collapsed against the bridge rail.

"Safe, safe," a soft voice spoke next to her. Yuzhyu.

Now the stone began to sing again, a soft, gentle harmonic that made Rhis stagger again, her body so tired she nearly dropped the stone.

But Yuzhyu's small hand supported hers. Without touching the stone, Yuzhyu helped her get it back over the rail. And then the stone sang again, this time sending a stream of images: soaring high against the clouds, faster than any bird could fly. The rise of a castle—a sudden glittering cloud descending toward an army, and smiting it away—

A great wave rising to smash over a line of ships—

Yuzhyu gasped. She jerked her hand away. "Stow it," she said urgently to Rhis. "At once!"

Rhis used the last of her strength to stumble to her horse, its ears twitching; she thrust the stone into the saddle bag and leaned tiredly against the horse's sturdy shoulder.

As soon as she wasn't touching it, the stone's allure faded to the old faint singing note.

"That ver-ry dangerous," Yuzhyu said in a low voice.

Rhis crumbled onto the ground, dizzy, weak, and thoroughly miserable. She didn't even care when Jarvas edged his horse cautiously down the trail, dismounted at the other end of the bridge, and started across, step by step.

Yuzhyu stretched out her short arms, blocking Rhis, the horse—and the stone. "Do not ze touch. Or I take stone. Use." She smacked her front.

"Grab 'em," the king called to his son, who took another step on the bridge, his face even more grim than his father's.

"Then I make you ze mushroom on log," Yuzhyu said fiercely, and Jarvas promptly backed up, hands out.

"Jarvas," the king warned. "Take those two prisoner."

Jarvas lifted his head. "You do it. And if she turns you into a hoptoad—"

"Mushroom," Yuzhyu said. "Worse."

The Damatrans did not disagree. The king sighed. "That's why I really, really hate mages."

"And they hate ze pipple with ze swords," Yuzhyu muttered, as the king motioned to his guards to dismount and start down the hill, swords at the ready, to surround the girls.

Rhis struggled to her feet again, though it took almost all the strength she had left. She was careful not to touch the saddlebag. So far they had not been taken prisoner, but neither were they on the safe side of the border. Meanwhile, had Lios and the rest had the sense to ride away? No. They'd halted a little ways from the Damatrans, on the Vesarjan side of the road. Except for Lios and Taniva, who stood at the edge, Taniva with her knife in her hand, her brows a long furrow over her eyes.

The horse twitched at a nearby crunch of gravel. There was a short exclamation as one of the guards almost slipped on the slope.

Yuzhyu clenched her fists. "I stay wiz you," she said to Rhis.

Rhis tried to straighten. The guards, slowly closing in, did not look any too happy. Menacing, certainly, holding their swords, but the way their eyes kept flicking to her saddlebag almost made Rhis laugh.

It was that tiny bubble of laughter that enabled her to straighten up. She gulped in a breath, and that helped, too. The stone was still singing, which echoed through her skull, but not nearly as horribly as before.

She looked up at the King of Damatras there on the road, his own sword in hand.

Rhis's mind cleared a little more. She saw how much danger she and Yuzhyu were in. But beyond that, she understood why she was in danger—because she'd been a thief, for the first time in her life. And she'd stolen the protection magic for an entire kingdom.

"I'll give it back," she called to the king. "I'm sorry. I just wanted you to let us go. I'll give it back."

The king raised his sword, and the men halted. Some of them with quiet exhalations of relief.

"Why did you take it in the first place?" the king demanded.

Rhis shook her head. "I don't know. I didn't mean to. But it—well, it just sang at me."

To her surprise, the king did not scoff at that answer, silly as it sounded in Rhis's own ears. He waved his sword in a lazy circle, rounding up his men, and then put the sword back in its sheath. "Go on home, young Princess from Nym," he said. "You've got guts, I'll tell you that, and I admire guts. But I wouldn't sleep of nights if you married my son, wondering what you might be up to next. I just *really* do not like mages. And if you can stomach handling that stone, you may's well be one."

"We're free," Yuzhyu whispered, smiling.

The king lifted his head, addressing his son, who still stood at the other end of the bridge, ten paces from Rhis, Yuzhyu, and the patient horse. "Jarvas, I have done picking wives for you. From now on, you're on your own."

"Then this subject is finished for at least ten years," Jarvas called back promptly. "Twenty!"

"What?" That was from Iardith, still sitting on her horse, looking perfect—except for her angry expression.

"I don't know why you insisted on riding with us," the king said to her in his hearty boom as he climbed back into his saddle. "But now I'm glad you did. You can ride right around the road there, in perfect safety, and return to your father in the same safety. All honorable and right," he added in a louder voice. "Do we agree on that, young Vesarjan prince? Everything perfectly honorable, no harm to anyone?"

Lios called across the chasm, "Agreed."

"What?" Rhis said, hopelessly trying to follow. But her head ached, her body felt worse, and she longed to just lie down and sleep for a year.

"Pest cannot make trouble," a new voice said just behind Rhis, and suddenly Taniva was there, having run down the old trail past Jarvas and all his young guards, to join the two girls. "Up you go," she said kindly to Rhis. "Give bad thing to king, and we get out."

With her strong arms she boosted Rhis back into the saddle. She held up one of her kerchiefs, rescued from her own saddlebag for the purpose. Rhis took it, reached into her saddlebag, and eased it around the stone, which rang mercilessly inside her head.

But she captured it inside the kerchief, and pulled it out.

Meanwhile, the king himself had urged his horse down the slope. He rode up next to Rhis, Yuzhyu and Taniva backing away. The two animals sniffed curiously at one another as, with care, Rhis handed over the stone, and with equal care, the king took it. "That's one of the duties of the Damatran monarch," the king said in a low voice, for Rhis alone. "Checking on it, once a year. And I will tell you what until now I only told my son—it's the one duty I really hate."

Rhis looked unhappily into the king's face. "I don't know why I took it."

"Oh, that much is clear," the king said. "Or as clear as anything is, around magic. That thing lured you in. Your mother's a mage—you've got the same head for magic or that thing would have complete control of you by now. That's why I hate checking on it. You'd think that stone is alive." He hefted the kerchief. "Well, now to find a better place for it." He grinned. "Where even a princess from Nym wouldn't look."

Rhis smiled back, feeling worse than ever.

The king motioned to his people, who mounted up again. The king's horse clambered in a rustle and clatter of stones back up to the main road.

Jarvas and his young guards also mounted up, and rode past Rhis into the lower path toward the forest. Jarvas lifted a friendly hand to Rhis in passing, but then he stopped and cast one glance back—at Taniva, who stood in the middle of the bridge, arms crossed. Jarvas grinned just a little, and patted the hilt of the jeweled knife in his sash.

Taniva's mouth curled up at one corner, as she gave him a look that so clearly said, *I'll get it yet!*

And Jarvas sent her one back that said, *I'll be waiting.*

He called to his father, "Race ya back!"

"Done," the king said, and within moments all that was left of the Damatrans was a cloud of dust, and the rapidly diminishing thunder of hoof beats.

Rhis, Taniva, and Yuzhyu proceeded the rest of the way up the old trail.

And when they reached the main road and stepped into Vesarjan territory, there was a weird flicker in the air, and one—two—three—five mages appeared, standing in a circle around where the Damatrans and the young rescuers had been earlier.

One of them was Rhis's own sister, Sidal.

The tallest, oldest, and most forbidding was a gray-haired woman. "And now that the political questions are resolved," she said to Rhis. "You will answer to *us.*"

TWENTY-TWO

"Not until the child has had rest and something to eat," Sidal said firmly.

"We will transfer to Hai Taresal," the gray-haired mage responded, and no one argued.

Rhis found herself wrenched away into a kind of non-space. It felt like someone had shoved her through a wall and then out the other side. She staggered, finding herself in a small room with the patterned tiles of a Destination on the floor.

Sidal appeared a moment later, and took her arm. Yuzhyu was gone—all her friends were gone, leaving her surrounded by mages.

But Rhis was beyond questions. She listened to the swift murmur of voices without comprehending a word, walked with her sister, and finally she reached a room with a nice, soft bed. Sidal helped her through the cleaning frame, helped her get rid of the Damatran rider outfit. Someone had brought a soft nightgown, which Sidal slipped over Rhis's head.

Then she slid into a cool, soft bed, and that was all she remembered for quite a long while.

She actually woke several times, but each time it was just long enough to drink down the waiting steeped listerblossom, and then she ate a few bites of bread and cheese, then back she went to sleep again. Next couple of times she woke she ate a bigger meal, and stayed awake long enough to watch the rain against the windows—but before she could consider whether or not to get up, she fell right back to sleep again.

When she finally woke up, Sidal was still there. Someone had brought her a little desk, at which she sat, that familiar, dear little strand of hair falling over her forehead as she worked at copying something from a book.

Rhis watched her for a while, just enjoying lying still without having to do anything. But slowly the questions floated up from the murk of memory, like little bubbles when water begins to boil—and then they began to pop.

"Sidal," she said.

Her sister glanced up, smiled, and dropped her quill. "You look much better now," she said. "How about a real bath? There's one right through that doorway. It's a sunken pool, big enough to swim in!"

"Oh, that sounds so good." Rhis got out of bed. She was slightly dizzy but otherwise felt so much better.

Sidal kept up a calm, pleasant stream of chatter as Rhis got a bath, one of her dresses to wear (Sidal said, "We had your clothes brought here from Eskanda"), and a good, hearty meal.

When she was done, Sidal said, "Do you want to sleep some more?"

Rhis considered. "I think I'm all slept out. Now I'm full of questions. How long has it been, anyway? Where is everyone else? Um, where am *I*?"

Sidal touched her fingers. "You've been sleeping for four days—this is the morning of the fifth. Most of your 'others' are here, having arrived yesterday. Except for Lios, who rode ahead, and arrived the day before. 'Here' is Queen Briath's palace in Hai Taresal, capital of Vesarja."

"Oh," Rhis said. She made a face. "The queen who hates Dandiar—ah, Lios?"

Sidal said, "What the queen thinks or doesn't think is her business to tell. But we are her guests. And in case our own parents are your next question, yes, they do know you are here."

"Uh oh."

Sidal's smile was ironic. "I am here to see that in all the questions of magic and state that have been flying about, you yourself are not forgotten." Sidal tipped her head. "So far, everyone's been fairly reasonable. Despite that very close call."

Rhis smacked her hands up to her forehead. "I can't believe it. I think I hoped if I slept long enough, that whole thing about the diamond would turn into a dream. But I really did steal it, didn't I? And it was the magical protection of a *whole kingdom*?"

Sidal nodded once at the end of each question, and Rhis groaned, hands still over her eyes.

Sidal leaned forward, forearms on her knees. "There are things you'd better know before your interview with the queen."

"Interview with the queen?" Rhis repeated faintly.

Sidal gave another of those firm single nods. "Rhis, you girls didn't just catch the attention of all the local rulers with your mad dash, you yourself managed to catch the eye of every mage within a month's hard travel."

Rhis moaned from behind her hands.

"Now. Do you want the bad news first, or the good news?"

"There's *more* bad news?"

"I'll take that as a 'bad news first.' Unless you're not feeling ready?"

Rhis sighed, and dropped her hands into her lap. "I supposed I'll just sound sulky if I say I'm never going to be ready. I feel fine, Sidal. Go ahead. Get the worst over quick."

"Well, you did manage to resolve the state question very neatly, at least. Everyone attests to it except for Princess Iardith, and, of course, her father. But since the King of Damatras upheld what everyone said, that's that. The biggest question is the magic aspect. Now. The bad news is, you somehow discovered one of the old Singing Diamonds, left over from the ancient days. The mage council has been seeking those and trying to get rid of them, one by one, for centuries. To be fair to the King of Damatras, he didn't know he had one—none of his immediate ancestors did. They don't know anything about magic. They don't even like magic. And they didn't have to learn about it, because they had this very, very powerful protection. Understand so far?"

Rhis gave a cautious nod.

"The reason a single object could contain so many powerful spells is that the Singing Diamonds seem almost alive. Some think they *are* alive, in a way impossible for us humans to easily define. So the mages have been collecting them, one by one, for many, many years. They replace the protections, and send the stone back through the World Gate to another world where such things are more common—and can be dealt with. Understand so far?"

"Yes."

"Then back to us. That stone had been atop the tower in Damatras for hundreds of years, and it was . . . well, it was bored. It wanted to be doing more interesting things than just protecting a kingdom. So when you came by, it did its best to get into your pocket, and it tried to get you to run away with it. Am I right?"

Flee! Flee! Rhis rubbed her forehead. "Yes."

"It wanted you long enough for it to be carried to someone more interesting—someone with a lot farther reach in magical power. Someone . . . like the Emperor of Sveran Djur, who—the council thinks—may have already found one of those stones once. It would explain his incredible powers. But what we don't know is if he controls the stone—or if the stone controls him."

"It was trying to control me," Rhis said.

Sidal had been watching her closely. She said, "But you managed, somehow, to fight off its effects. Not many can. Yuzhyu knew enough not to touch it. She said she almost lost herself in just the few moments she held your hand to keep you from falling off the bridge."

Rhis let out a cry of alarm. "But what about that Emperor? Is he on his way here?"

"No. Now we can get to the good news. Your young friend Princess Yuzhyu, who is a very smart girl, figured out what that thing was, and she threw a protection around the stone, and just in time. See, when you held the stone over the chasm, it was fighting hard to stay in control of you. It fought so hard that every mage within five kingdoms in any direction 'heard' its cry in their scry stones. We could all feel its power, but we couldn't tell what it was, or where it was."

Rhis clasped her hands together tightly.

"Yuzhyu shrouded it just in time, because the council all agree that they sensed the Emperor using his own stone to seek this one. He would love, very much, to have two of those stones—if he can master them, and they don't master him."

Rhis shivered.

"And now we come to you. Who managed to keep your will intact."

Rhis said, "Just barely."

"And that despite the fact that you have no training. Some think that having no training helped you. I don't think that's quite true, but either way the matter remains that you have an enormous potential for magic. Yet you are quite ignorant. The mages are very worried, let me tell you."

Rhis was still thinking about Yuzhyu. Now she understood all those images, ending with the huge wave swamping a line of battle ships: those were the stone trying to lure Yuzhyu. "It promised to kill any enemies that came to Ndai," she whispered.

"You *heard* that?" Sidal asked. "Oh yes, you've more ability than ever we thought." She patted the front of her robe, grinning. "That's our family!"

Rhis said dismally, "So what, are they going to put me in mage school?"

"Not unless you want to study magic," Sidal said.

"No." Rhis wrung her hands. "You know I admire you ever so much, Sidal. But the thought of doing magic spells all day, not having music, and gardens, and plays, and, well, *people*—"

Sidal patted the air between them. "Calm down, calm down. Papa and Mama are keeping the promise they made when you were first tested: nobody is going to force you to do anything. Including becoming a mage, just because you have an enormous talent for it. History is far too full of disgruntled mages who were forced into magical studies because they had the talent for it—and ended up doing some terrible things."

"I don't think I'd turn evil," Rhis said. "But I don't think I'd be happy."

"I agree," Sidal said. "And so I told them, and they accepted it. The question is really about any children you might have some day." And at Rhis's uncomprehending look, "If you were to, say, marry a prince, and your children have this ability, including one who might be picked as heir—"

"Oh," Rhis said, feeling prickly heat at those words *marry a prince*. Because she didn't think of any prince, her first thought was of Prince Lios who had once been Dandiar the Scribe. She forced her mind back to the subject. "I get it. This is about the problem of magic and politics, and no ruler can be a mage. What did they decide about that?"

"They didn't. That's where we are now. There are many debates going on—the queen of Ndai insisting that it makes sense for queens, and kings, to know how to protect their kingdoms, and others arguing about too much power in the hands of a single person. The Emperor of Sveran Djur being the ready example of just how bad an idea that can be."

"Ndai's ruler knows magic because they're an island?" Rhis asked.

"That, but also because they are the island closest to Sveran Djur. Everyone agrees that Ndai needs a strong magical defense as well as a strong navy."

Rhis brought her knees up under her skirt and hugged them against her chest. "So what will happen now?"

"What happens next," Sidal said, "is your interview with the Council, and then with Vesarja's queen."

Rhis hardly had time to feel the constriction of worry around her heart at that before an impatient knock at the door brought Sidal to her feet. "That has to be Shera," she said. "This must be about the fifth time. Today." She looked over her shoulder. "I take it you feel ready for visitors?"

"Oh, please let her in," Rhis exclaimed, leaping up.

Sidal laughed as she opened the door. Shera raced impatiently in.

"Rhis!" she cried in a tragic voice. "It would have been *too horrible* if they didn't let me see you before I have to go home—"

Sidal called over her shoulder, "I'll tell them you're feeling better, Rhis. Stay here, mind."

"Stay here?" Rhis asked, but her sister was gone. "Am I a prisoner?"

Shera slammed the door. "There! *Now* we can talk. You're not a prisoner, but the queen won't let Lios come see you until she—oh, never mind that. Rhis, I have to go home tonight! Isn't that horrid?" She flung herself face down on the bed, her ringlets wild.

Rhis had gotten so used to seeing Shera with her hair pulled back into the simple braid she almost did not recognize her sister-by-marriage. Shera wore one of her prettiest dresses, her hair dressed beautifully, with ribbons binding up curling locks.

She raised a tearful face.

Rhis said, "Sidal told me you got back yesterday. Is Glaen angry with you again?"

"Yes. No—yes. Oh, I have to tell you everything." Shera flopped onto her back across the bed, her feet in their embroidered slippers kicking her lacy petticoats up and down. "I'm so mad I can hardly think! Glaen and I came to an agreement on the ride, and everything was *soooo* nice. If you didn't count Lios looking all sad and grim before he just plain left us to ride ahead. And Iardith being *absolutely hideous* to everyone. Especially Andos, who is the sweetest fellow—if you don't mind a sword master's son. But Glaen and I talked it all over, and we agreed that Rastian really didn't count—I was far too young, and had no experience yet. Of course I'd fall for the first familiar fellow I saw."

"So what happened?"

"Well, we arrived yesterday—and who do you think was right there in front, waiting?" She did not give Rhis time to guess, but wailed, "Rastian!"

"Oh." Rhis winced. "Uh oh."

"Glaen and I were holding hands, see, and well, he got all formal and distant and just horrid. Called me a heartless flirt, said he couldn't trust my word. Demanded to know this and that, but would he listen? No! I tried to explain, but he heard everything wrong, and finally I told him that Glaen and I both thought he was a blockhead—which wasn't true, I was just so mad—and *then* he ran off to challenge Glaen to a duel!"

"No!"

"Oh, yes. So there I was, yelling like a wet cat, and Rastian full of *honor* and *my promised word* and all that rot, and Glaen got ever so nasty, and started making jokes out of every silly, pompous thing Rastian said, and they were about to get into a fight before they could even go to their rooms to fetch their swords, but then Lios came in and shut them up like that." She clapped her hands.

"What did he do?"

"He didn't do anything. He just said—you know how nice he is—that the west tower was where they used to keep the political prisoners, and the two were welcome to move in and continue their quarrel. He'd provide whatever weapons they wanted, from pin-whistles to arbalests."

Rhis gulped on a laugh. "Pin-whistles?"

"That's what he said. Everyone was in there by then. He told us about a couple of dukes two hundred years ago who each claimed to be experts in playing the pin-whistle, and they had this duel—well, anyway, everyone was laughing too hard by then, and then he took them all downstairs for iced punch."

"Phew!"

"Rastian said I wasn't worth a pin-whistle, which I think quite horrid, especially as he's to lead the escort home, and Glaen said *he* wasn't worth a pin-whistle, and when Lios showed up and said he could call for the escort to the tower, they both stomped off in different directions. I was crying, and Breggo escorted me the rest of the way, and sat next to me while we had the ice, and was so nice to me. I mean, he'd been so kind all along, despite his being disappointed about Taniva."

"Breggo?" Rhis repeated, trying to imagine him comforting Shera.

"He's very, very sensitive," Shera protested, her cheeks glowing. "Did you ever notice how long his eyelashes are?"

Rhis gazed at her, instantly suspicious. "So . . . Glaen was angry at Rastian, or at you?"

"Well, at us both," Shera said, sitting up and fussing with her hair ribbon as she gazed out the window at the lifting rain. "Afterward. After dinner, I mean. It was nice out last night, before this horrid storm moved in. And Breggo was sitting with me on a balcony. Oh, Rhis, you cannot conceive how pretty this palace is. Eskanda is nothing to it. Little grottos and balconies with views, and the most wonderful—well, anyway. I told Breggo all about them both, and he was sympathetic. And so kind, didn't I mention that? Anyway, I told him I appreciated fellows who have a sense of kindness, and—and so what if some of the things I said were the same words I'd said to Glaen? They were nice words, and *true*."

"And what, Glaen heard you, right?"

"He came round looking for me. To apologize. He *said*. He interrupted us, just like that. Made a sarcastic comment about how I must use the same words on every fellow, and he'd go apologize to Rastian, instead, who had his sympathy—"

"Uh oh."

"It wouldn't have worked anyway," Shera said miserably, plonking her elbows onto the bed and her chin into her hands. "I mean, Glaen is like lightning, so quick and bright. But being around him every day would be a little like having a thunderstorm every day, don't you think?"

Rhis considered nervy, quick-moving Glaen. "Oh, yes," she said. "But he's so sensitive. I think he gets hurt easily."

Shera sat up, fingering one of the bows in her ringlets. "So you're feeling sorry for him?"

Rhis sighed with exasperation. "Shera!"

"Well, it sounded like—" Shera waved her hands, then bounced up off the bed. "Anyway, I have to go home, and Sidal told me last night that I am expressly forbidden to get engaged to anyone before I leave. Isn't that *nasty*? It's like *everyone* was spying on me."

Rhis said, "It doesn't sound like a very pleasant night."

"No, and it'll be an even worse journey. I just know my mother will be angry. When I said that she'd probably lock me up until I was twenty-five, Rastian said, *Ha ha*."

"How mean!"

"At least your sister is fair with *her* nasty comments. She told him that if he could not behave courteously he could be sent back by magic, and he could retire and think about what an escort of honor means." Shera wrenched at her hair ribbon, then finally said, "You think I'm fickle. Just like Rastian said. And Glaen."

Rhis exclaimed, "I don't think anything. Except that I really hate magical things, and I never want to see another diamond, singing or not."

Shera looked contrite. "I'm sorry. I forgot all about that. It's just, you were gone for all the days we traveled, and Glaen was so nice, and then Breggo, and then we met slap up with

Rastian—well, never mind all that. I do have to go tonight, but you'll write to me, won't you?"

"Of course! Now we can write real letters to one another," Rhis said.

"Good," Shera exclaimed. "Then you can let me know what happens with Lios—"

The door opened, and Sidal rejoined them. "Shera, they are waiting for you."

"We can't leave now, it's raining." Shera pointed to the window—where, just then, a shaft of light reached down between the clouds, lighting up a pretty carpet of different shades of rose, outlined by green leaves. The figures looked like dancing rabbits.

Shera put her hands on her hips. "Where is rain when you want it?"

Rhis laughed as Shera flung her arms round her, gave her a squeeze, then backed away tearily. Then, with a sniff, Shera marched out.

TWENTY-THREE

Sidal waited until her rapid step had diminished down the polished parquet floor outside, then said, "Rhis, are you ready for your interviews?"

"I guess they're ready for me," Rhis said. "I think I'd rather get it over than sit here worrying."

Sidal said, "That's my sister! Head into the wind, that's what Mama always told me. Eventually the storm has to pass on by, but if you try to run, it follows you."

Sidal led the way down a long hall with windows all down one side. These windows overlooked a spectacular garden cut into a sloping hill, with a complication of gnarled flower-vined archways and little paths crossed by graduated waterfalls. The paths led over tiny arched bridges, each decorated with fine carvings.

Rhis found the sight so intriguing that the journey seemed far shorter than it would have otherwise. At the end of the hall, a waiting pair of footmen opened tall double doors. Inside an enormous room, seated in tall-backed chairs upholstered with midnight blue velvet, was a half-circle of robed figures who had to be mages, probably from all the important countries in their part of the subcontinent. Plus representatives from the magic council.

This was no cozy room, it was a formal one, for state purposes. Thoroughly intimidated, Rhis took in the high walls with their long midnight blue curtains, now drawn to shut out the beautiful garden. Above was a gently domed ceiling on which was painted a scene of clouds and comets and flying horses. Glowglobes gave the room light.

One of the mages stood up. Rhis recognized the tall gray-haired woman from the border of Damatras. "I am Taunsan, Royal Mage of Vesarja," she said. She did not introduce any of the others.

Sidal indicated a chair sitting all alone in the middle of the marble floor. Rhis sat gingerly upon this as Sidal moved to the extreme edge of the half-circle.

"Tell us," Taunsan said, "exactly what happened from the moment you first had access to magic, until our arrival."

Rhis turned to her sister for support, received an encouraging smile, and began. At first she interrupted herself, going back over the same words, stumbling, sometimes struggling to express the weird, piercing note of the Singing Stone when it tried to force her to its will. She finally came to an end amid a morass of questions as she watched the silent, sober-faced mages for hints of what they thought. But they neither spoke nor moved, except for Taunsan, who said, "Thank you. We will deliberate. Sidal, please conduct Princess Rhis to the next room."

Sidal led her to another door, opposite from the circle of mages. "I wish I could have prepared you but she wanted it this way," she whispered, opened the door to an even more fantastic room than the one they'd just left, gave Rhis a pat, and then shut the door soundlessly behind her.

The room was enormous, oval in shape. A shallow curve of tall, arched windows overlooked the waterfalls. The rest of the room was cut from silver-veined marble, with an elaborate fountain carved of white marble into a complicated tumble of winged shapes, like a flock of fantastical birds all caught in a moment of time as they launched toward the sky. The water spouts were cleverly hidden, so it seemed that the flow was a splash kicked up by the departing birds.

On approaching this fountain with slow steps, Rhis realized the fountain did not just fall into a pool, but ran down a very shallow stream, where it passed under the windows and joined into one of the ordered flows outside, leading to the waterfalls.

"This is my summer interview chamber." A woman's voice came from behind Rhis. "Enter, child."

Rhis turned in a circle, still trying to take in the stylized wings in the tapestry and chair backs, the ceiling painted over with faint flying horses as if seen from below, blending at the edges with the painted clouds. Covering a portion of the inlaid wooden floor was a spectacular rug of midnight blue, woven with a border of stylized flying herons—white, silver, pale blue, gold.

A short, round woman rustled toward Rhis, her step brisk. She wore a gown of heavy watered silk. But that was not what captivated Rhis's attention any more than the complicated strands of pearls at her neck, or the diamond-and-pearl drops at her ears.

What caught Rhis's attention was that the woman's eyes were exactly like Dandiar's.

Queen Briath smiled a little. "So I look like my son, do I?"

Rhis tried to gather her wits, but even so she couldn't help noticing details and differences; the queen was about the same age as Rhis's mother. Her elaborately dressed hair was very dark, with silver streaks at the temples. The queen did not have a snub nose. Hers was pointed, as was her chin.

Rhis belatedly performed a proper court curtsey, but the queen only made an impatient movement. "Come, come, sit down. They tell me you are still recovering from this magical mystery of theirs. I mislike the sound of it, truth to tell. Though I trust Taunsan with my life. But some of those others? Hah!"

Rhis followed the queen. Now that her back was turned, Rhis realized how short she was—Rhis was the taller by half a head. But one certainly didn't notice that when facing Briath of Vesarja.

"So. It seems I have you to thank that my son's disastrous plan was not such a disaster after all."

Rhis's face heated. "You mean his masquerade?"

"I do not," Queen Briath said. "I thought that was quite clever, actually. I understand you were of the opposite opinion."

"Oh," Rhis said witlessly. "Um."

Queen Briath plumped down into one of the fine silk-covered chairs that were placed at the four corners of the heron carpet. She motioned Rhis to take the one opposite. "There's water, and a very good iced punch if you like that sort of thing," she said, indicating a low table of wood and etched glass that had been placed next to Rhis's chair. On this table sat a golden tray filled with food and drink.

Rhis busied herself with a goblet of water as the queen said, "You seem to be far more careful with your tongue than your sister-by-marriage." She chuckled, the pearls in her ears dancing. "I'll tell you this. If I could have tried such a masquerade thirty years ago, I would have."

Rhis looked up, startled.

"Think about it. You grow up the heir, and even if you're short and fat with a needle-nose—" The queen tapped her own nose significantly, as her rings glittered and flashed. "—all you hear is how lovely you are, and how smart, graceful, clever, and ever so beautiful—whatever they think you want to hear."

Rhis said cautiously, "We don't do that. In Nym."

"Aye. That's because Nym is small enough to avoid a court. All you have to face every day are your family, and the people who work for you. I can't get rid of my court: having all my nobles here dancing attendance on me as I entertain them keeps them busy enough not to be plotting, as some of them would be if I left them alone on their estates to live like pocket kings and queens. The half a year they aren't here, they're busy enough tending to their lands so they'll have enough money to spend next season." She grinned. "And I make certain court is expensive. For one thing, you'd be surprised just how many artisans a palace like this requires. That's a lot of livelihoods."

Queen Briath gave Rhis that sudden, ironic smile, but with so much laughter in it that Rhis smiled back.

"Now. Back to me. When it was time to marry, the princes came flocking. And there I was, thinking myself so clever because I could speak three languages, I knew the rudiments of magical theory, I could tell you the names, principle actions, and dates of all the kings in each kingdom around us, to five hundred years back. But did I know anything about young men? Hah!"

Rhis set her goblet down, and clasped her hands together.

"There are three of us who ended up married to pretty faces. The Queen of Gensam is one, though at least her consort is a poet, and has some brains, even if he's useless for matters of state. Iardith's father married a pretty face without a vestige of wit behind it. The greatest tragedy of the Queen of Arpalon's life was her realizing her teen-age daughter was prettier than she was."

Rhis's mouth dropped open.

Queen Briath snapped her fan open, then shut, and pointed it at Rhis. "And then there was me. The Prince of Ndai was living a masquerade, only I thought it was real. My sister-by-marriage, Yuzhyu's mother, knew very well that her younger brother was spoiled rotten because he was so boyish, so charming, everyone always believed everything he said. Maybe he would have been more honest, if not more bearable, had they given him some kind of training, and seen to it he didn't charm his tutors into doing his work for him so he could run out and play."

Rhis gazed at the queen in surprise. This conversation was nothing like any she'd ever had with an adult, even her mother, who could be very matter-of-fact. But she'd never gossiped. And here was this queen, gossiping about her own consort as if it was everyday chat.

"But his entire life he had only two things to do: throw orders around for his own entertainment, and spend money. I thought I was so smart, waiting until my middle thirties to marry. It just means you fall harder, if all you've experienced is court flatterers. As soon as we were married—and I mean that very day—he swept through this very palace, handing out orders like *he* was the king. Within a week, he managed to offend half of my court. I had to send him home or I would have been at war with every one of my neighbors."

Rhis said, "I didn't know any of that."

The queen gave her a wry smile. "Of course not. Who would tell you the unvarnished truth? Your own father was older than all of us, and we never really knew him. Your mother is a mage, and tight-lipped. Your friends all talk about each other—just as my generation did. And Lios likes his father, even knowing he's a rotter. Anyway, so I had a son, and he looked, and sounded, just like his father. I didn't trust my feelings for him. I didn't trust *him!* So I sent him to his cousins, with strict orders to put him to work."

"He works hard," Rhis ventured. "I saw that by the second day we were there."

"I know he does," the queen said with obvious approval. "I also know he's smart. This party of his was in the nature of a test, though he didn't know it. I didn't want him coming home and using his father's boyish charm to tell me all the things I wanted most to hear. So I told him he could arrange this party to meet all the eligible young females—and of course he'd invite all the local young fellows, because he needs to know them, too. And then I watched from afar—yes, that means I had my people spying on him—to see how he would handle being crown prince without me being anywhere nearby."

"Oh." Rhis nodded. "So you didn't mind his pretending to be a scribe while Andos acted like a prince, but you didn't like him riding after us when Iardith and Jarvas disappeared?"

"His plan of running off after you girls was foolish, and very nearly painfully embarrassing for me. So, no. I did not like his plan, but I *did* like his reasons. He told me everything, you see. Not in person—he felt he had to move too fast for that—but by letter, before he rode off after that silly wench from Arpalon. And of course I had my most trusted steward there, in the guise of the head footman, who corroborated everything Lios told me. Lios took the blame for everything squarely on himself. Even offered to resign the heirship, if I deemed him unsuitable."

The queen paused, frowned, and then pointed the fan at Rhis again.

"What I found surprising was that every other sentence, it seemed, was about you. What you'd done, what you said, what you thought. Where he thought you'd gone, and why."

She threw the fan onto her own little side table, and sat back, her beringed fingers laced over her plump middle. "So now I want to hear about that, but from your perspective, and without your talking to any of the others first. You can skim the magical stuff. I want to know who said what, when, where, and how. And what you did. Go ahead. I cancelled my entire day's work, though I'll be making it up far into the night." The queen leaned forward and poured herself a big glass of punch, then sat back again, smoothing her skirts with one hand. The rings on her fingers winked and gleamed. "Don't stint on the details," she added, sipping.

And so for the second time Rhis told her story, beginning with her arrival at Eskanda. She talked about the party, the masquerade ball, the play, and finally, Iardith's mysterious disappearance. Then she described the girls' decision, the ride, what happened in Damatras. What the king said. What Lios said. The long ride back, and her threat with the stone.

At the end, the queen set her goblet down with a snap so that it rang on the glass. "One last question. Some of the other young ones think you should be rewarded for saving their skins so well the other day—ah, ah." She raised a hand. "Never mind about the theft of that stone. Sometimes the heroism of ballads and plays is happening to catch the right way to avert disaster at just the right moment. Everybody likes a triumph, and moreover, everyone loves a party. So you can be celebrated for your heroism. Old Damatras can't make a peep because he's going to be too busy making nice with the mages, as they replace his protections for him before taking away that stone. So. If I were to grant a wish of yours, what would you ask for?"

Rhis shrugged, vaguely uncomfortable. She already had plenty of wealth, and as for mysterious magical objects—phew, she'd had enough experience of *those*. She finally said, "I think what I want most isn't anything I can ask for."

"You're talking about people, am I correct?"

Rhis blushed, but said determinedly, "It would be stupid to ask for Lios's hand in marriage. He would hate it that way. I would hate it that way, if someone went to Papa without talking to me first. Besides, I don't know if he wants to get, well, married. I don't know if *I* do—"

"Ah," the queen said, snapping her fan. "Smart girl. Most sixteen year olds rant about *forever or I'll die* until everyone around them is ready to begin hurling dishes."

"Well, maybe if I was sure. But things went so fast, and then I haven't had a chance to sit down with him and talk. I think, if I had any reward, it would be the chance to just sit with him so we could talk, like we did at Eskanda. And maybe with everyone there we could have our play after all." Rhis finished somewhat wistfully.

"That is a reward that, reasonable as it sounds, I cannot give you," the queen said, not without sympathy.

Rhis looked up, startled.

"Most of the guests are on their way home. As for Lios, you're not going to see him."

Rhis's lips parted in dismay. "Oh, Queen Briath—is it my stealing?"

"Ta, ta, ta," the queen cut in, snapping her fan open again, and waving it to and fro. "Spare me the tragedy. If Lios saw you right now he'd be wild enough to call out half the guard, and would probably rant all manner of foolish things. The fact that my son thinks you're beautiful, and what I'm seeing is a girl as plain as a sparrow, makes this matter far too serious. If anyone can take seriously the 'love' of a twenty year old boy—"

Rhis pressed her fingers over her mouth, and the queen snapped her fan again.

"—or a sixteen year old girl. I know the two of you can hardly wait to get together, and before you both know it, you'll be hugging and kissing in the garden."

"What's wrong with that?" Rhis asked.

"Nothing! Except that hugging and kissing only tells you you're attracted to one another, and you already know that. What it *doesn't* do is tell you if you can run a kingdom together."

"But—"

"The King of Arpalon and I each had plenty of kissing and holding hands in the garden, and look what *we* married! And we were twenty years older than you are now."

Rhis could not prevent tears from burning her eyelids, blurring the queen's image.

The queen said, "I know you think me heartless. My son already told me I am. He's got my temper, that boy does! But at least he was honest. I like that. Though I won't change my mind." She shook out her skirts. "Now. This is what is going to happen. After a nice big party in celebration, a party that everyone is going to hear about, you are going home to Nym. And Lios is on his way to Eskanda right now, so he won't be here to see you or you him. What you two *can* do is write letters, each year on this anniversary. Oh, beginning now, since I never let you say good-bye. I'm not as heartless as I seem! In between times you may study magic, or statecraft, or whatever you like, or not study at all, but sit at a window and count the days. But you'll not see one another until five years pass."

"Five—"

"Years. Yes, it's cruel, and yes, it seems forever, but five years pass in a blink. I still think twenty-one and twenty-five far too early for certain kinds of decisions, but if you two are still of the same mind in five years, then we three will sit down and talk. Because Lios is a smart boy, but he's got a lot to learn about kingship. If he wants to be king, he's going to learn it."

Queen Briath stood up. "Are we understood?"

Rhis's throat tightened. She wanted to protest, *We'll see what my parents say*—except she remembered her mother's admonition before she left: that nothing could happen until she was twenty.

It was a grownup conspiracy! They were determined to treat her like a baby, but she was determined not to cry like one.

So she curtseyed, and walked out with her most dignified step. Not until she shut the door and walked into Sidal's arms did she let the tears come.

TWENTY-FOUR

A Week Later

Dear Shera,

I'm on my way home, so I thought I may as well write, though I'm so unhappy I could—well, no, I won't say it. I can still hear Queen Briath making fun of sixteen year old girls. What I <u>will</u> say is, I counted up all the days in five years, and it does seem forever. A very long forever.

Let me finish with Vesarja. The mages declared that I am to go away for at least a season to Erev-Li-Erval, to learn about magical theory. But at least I won't have to go until I turn eighteen, Sidal says.

After my interview with the mages, Queen Briath threw a huge court party in my honor, celebrating the safe arrival of all Prince

Lios's visitors. If I hadn't been so gloomy about not getting to see Lios I would have appreciated her speech more, but Sidal said that it was a work of art. How else could someone make it clear that we'd been in danger from the Damatrans, without insulting the Damatran ambassador?

I think I'll call Jardith The Pest from now on, the way Taniva does, as she was quite awful to me when she thought no one was listening— she asked where Lios was, and I told her, and then she said, "He can't have much interest in you to give you up like that," but when I said, "I hope some day you meet a prince who will give up his entire life just to live in a cottage with you somewhere," she said, "I would never marry anyone but an heir. Only a fool would pick life in a cottage." Why did I even listen to her?

Yuzhyu's part in our adventures got hardly a mention, but Sidal says that's because of the magical side of things—they don't want talk about Singing Stones going out—but she got some king of magical reward that made her happy indeed. Yuzhyu is a lot smarter than people thought—you should have heard her jabbering away in some magical language, and all those mages with the sour faces were listening like she was their chief.

As for me, no one quite came out and said what I'd done, only that I'd done it well, that I had, 'with my quick actions, cemented future alliances' and so forth. The food was very good, and the musicians even better than the ones we had at Eskanda, and I danced every single dance. Not that I cared all that much, since Lios wasn't there to dance with. But it was fun anyway...

From Shera to Rhis:

> ... oh, Rhis, you can have no idea how _tedious_ this court is. But Mother is _still_ angry with me, can you _imagine?_ Every time anyone even mentions my visit to Vesarja, my brother just laughs, and says things like, 'At least I haven't managed to get myself engaged to three girls at once!' And I DIDN'T get engaged three times! But People Think They Are So Clever...

Lios to Rhis:

Dear Rhis.

     This is my first letter, but the tenth try at a first page. I was going to keep a journal for you, except halfway through describing my yesterday's breakfast I thought, Lios, you lettuce-head, this is the best way to ensure she never wants to see you again. I guess I will end up each day telling you what I did, and pretend I'm hearing your answer. In fact, I think I'll put your answers in this blue ink here. I remember you saying you like blue. You can tell me if I guess right. *Lios, don't be a clotpole. I wouldn't say that!* How's that for a ridiculous idea? But you've no idea how much it cheers me right up: if you can't be here, then I'll imagine you. I won't look at another girl. Well, maybe look. I like looking at girls. But if they try to talk to me, I'll have them banished, and anyone who mentions marriage will be locked in a tower until she turns ninety. How's that? Five years! Who needs magic, when the possibility of five years feels like fifty?

From Rhis to Lios:

. . . Five years! How awful! Your mother must really hate the idea of marriage. Or maybe she just hates people our age. I <u>know</u> I'll never feel any different than I do now. But I'm determined that I'm going to learn everything Elda knows in a single year, and just show them all . . .

A Year Later:

. . . and, oh, Lios, this will make you laugh—at the end of winter, Elda thought I was sick! She actually complained to Mother that she was afraid I was studying too hard. Mother was worried, and was asking all these questions about my health, until Sidal came in. Listened for a few moments, and then checked that the door was closed. She said that Elda's nose was out of joint because I was passing her daughter up in remembering historical dates, and working up numbers. Sidal added that it ought to be quite good for young Shera to have a challenge as she'd been getting just a little too smug about how much smarter she was than anyone, and how she's always right. Sidal told me after, she's been bossing the castle children.

One thing for certain. Elda won't let _me_ get smug. But she still is better than any tutor because she doesn't just teach one subject, and only that, but she puts them all together. How did I not notice that before? Well, she doesn't do it very interestingly—she has no interest in

why the people do things, just what they did,
but then I can always go ask Mama, especially if
there's any magic involved. She's given me
histories of the great mages, and suddenly a lot
of events in history are a lot clearer...

From Shera to Rhis:

> ... and he was so handsome! I simply could not help falling in
> love with him, though he's only the younger brother to a duke--
> but I have never seen a more handsome fellow, even Andos was a
> toad next to him. At least this time I had the wits not to go
> blabbing it All Over Court, but wouldn't you just know it, who
> would come out into the Rose Room and see us flirting but
> Rastian's mother—she told him—he pitched the most tiresome
> fit at me, and then he blabbed it all over. Don't let anyone ever
> tell you boys don't gossip. They are ten times worse than girls...

From Lios to Rhis

> ... your seventeenth birthday, and I tried to
> imagine you. Are you taller? If you grow as tall
> as me you'll just fit into my arms the better in
> four years. But I won't say any more as you'll
> be as glum about those long four years as I am
> in writing about them now. So, to more
> cheerful subjects. I heard from Glaen—oh. You
> did not know this, because it happened not
> long after I wrote you last year. My mother
> sent him off to Ndai to learn how they build the
> hulls on their ships. So much faster than ours.

Sail plans better, too. Glaen was miserable the first month, angry the second, frustrated the third as he wrestled with the language. I wrote to him in it, knowing how hopping mad that would make him, but it worked! He's been writing back in Ndaian, and Yuzhyu told me in a letter he stopped saying things like "May I hop your design of a banana?" and "I would like to meet your corn-cake." This would be a very good sign of success . . .

End of the Second Year

From Rhis to Lios:

. . . and you would never guess who I got a letter from—Iardith! She wrote to tell me—she also wrote to Shera—that she's being sent to Thesreve as her father's ambassador for the renewal of their silk trade treaty, and then on to the Court of the Empress in Charas-al-Kherval, at the same time I will be in the imperial capital, studying magical theory with the mages at Twelve Towers. But in and around all the bragging about the importance of her treaty mission—and how she will introduce me to some suitable fellows of respectable birth, if the mages permit me social activities—she managed to slip in a report of her visit to you in Hai

Taresal and how many pretty duchesses and the like you danced with. Especially Hanssa. But I'm remembering what you promised . . .

From Lios to Rhis:

. . . I know this letter is not even half the size of the first year, but I was afraid our couriers would have an uprising if I sent another book-length letter. No, I'm joking, the truth is, there was not the time this year. Yes, you are thinking that I found the time last year. That is true. It's also true I didn't this year. I can't say why. You are always in my thoughts. Anyway, I spent just about all summer all along the borders, with Taniva and a few of the others, doing a shared-alliance practice defense sort of thing, in case the King of Damatras declared war. But Jarvas sneaked into our camp one night, and got into my tent. You can imagine how that riled everyone up! He said his father is getting false information supposedly from the King of High Plains. But when Taniva and he compared notes, it sounds like most of the insults about the two kings came not from each other, but from the direction of Arpalon, who stands to gain if everyone has to buy steel from their forges for all the extra weapons a war would need. Jarvas and his boys stayed with us as a diplomatic gesture. It was actually fun. We were in mud up to our eyebrows, playing battle games every day. Battle is lots of fun when you know no one is going to get killed. Though it was more fun when Jarvas finally convinced Taniva and her girls from the

High Plains to stop making us lowland boys
look so bad in the riding-and-shooting . . .

Shera to Rhis:

> . . . so my mother sent me right back to the Eagle Mountain
> house, and this time for the <u>entire winter</u>. How can I help it if I
> fall in love so easily? I assure you, I did NOT set out to lure
> that fellow on. A minstrel! What happened was this. I told
> you my uncle sent me a tutor in tiranthe and harp, since there's
> nothing else to do in the mountains—as you well know—and I
> practiced and practiced. She played so beautifully, all I wanted
> to do was sound even a tiny bit as good as she did. But I kept
> hearing things I didn't like, and changing the music, and so the
> tutor taught me measures, and phrasings, and before I knew it,
> I was writing down all those little melodies I was always hearing
> in my head.
>
> And then the tutor said that I needed someone more advanced
> with music writing, because she was a performer, not a writer.
> So this minstrel came—oh Rhis. He was tall and slender, with
> the most beautiful black eyes. Well, next thing I know, he's
> making up songs about the tragic and romantic minstrels of
> history, especially Floridal and Jessin. I think Floridal was
> about as exciting as soggy bread, the way he <u>mourns</u> so in that
> stupid song! Of course Jessin would up and marry the prince!
> But Mother threw a tantrum, sent him out (after breaking his
> lute, which I must say, was quite horrid, and they talk about <u>my</u>
> lack of self control) and then she made it a Royal Order, that if
> any handsome minstrels even <u>try</u> to cross the border, she'll order
> the Guard to <u>shoot them on sight</u>. How mean is <u>that?</u>

End of the Third Year

Lios to Rhis:

I still talk to you in my head. My, you do say the most flattering things! There I go, joking again. You call me a clod and a fool when I am one, of course, because there were never eyes more true or honest than yours. I don't know if the imperial court has made you more sophisticated than me. While her father does his best to make trouble with everyone, especially between Damatras and the High Plains, Iardith has been sending Hanssa a stream of letters that include tidbits about how you've been dancing with every prince who comes by to do his world tour. Dance away, I say. I would rather you choose me from a wide selection in two years than from not knowing anyone at all. Yes, Hanssa is often at court, but you probably know by now that her parents raised her in hopes that she'd be a queen. And—away from Iardith's influence—she's turned into good company. But you know what we talk about most often? You . . .

Rhis to Lios:

It startled me to arrive home after a year that had never sped by so fast. Everything here seems so small and cramped after the vast spaces, the ancient artifacts and breathtaking arts from all around the world that make up the imperial city. What made me feel the strangest— and maybe a little bit sad—is that Elda's wisdom also seems a little cramped. She doesn't know even a quarter of the history I've picked up just through studying other matters. But it would not do to say so. I am very sure that, had she the chance to go to the imperial city too, she would have gained all that I gained, so I am not to claim any superiority. What I can claim is that I am lucky indeed to have these opportunities. Why, I can even cast a few spells! Oh, just party tricks, illusions, nothing real. They are very firm about that. But it does come easily to me. Speaking of easy, the influence does not go all one way. Shera sent me the music to one of her songs—and do you know, it's all over Erev-Li-Erval? Yes, everyone is singing it! She has a wicked way with a double melody sung in counterpoint, a song-style coming back into popularity now that the Imperial Heir seems to be about to marry one of the Snow Folk. I learned some of their language, just for a challenge . . .

End of the Fourth Year, and Last Letters:

Rhis to Lios:

For a long time after I got your last, I tried to think what to say. Jardith has been sending me reports of how much "everyone" expects to see Hanssa become the next queen of Vesarja, and I finally realized that this would not be so bad a thing, if one sets aside my sixteen year old feelings. How real are those feelings any more? Do we know one another, or are we writing to a cherished memory that won't change—but no longer exists? I don't know. What I do know is, the more I learn, the less I am sure about. But the better I listen. I don't even hate Jardith—not after I found out that she was writing to me because I am the only one who writes back to her. Yes, I know Hanssa doesn't write back to her, Jardith complains about that on one page while she tries to make me jealous by describing her as a future queen on another. Do you think she tries to make everyone feel like she does? At any rate, this letter is the shortest of all. I'm not going to bore you with bragging about what I've done, where I went, what I learned. Those things can wait until we meet—or until we write again, if you choose. Because you may have decided to court another, and if so, I know it will be because she is the best and most worthy person for you in all ways. You were my first friend, during those days at Eskanda, and my feelings about that have never changed.

Lios to Rhis:

I wonder what is in your letter—whether it will pass mine on the road between Nym and Hai Taresal. Don't think I'm drunk, how terrible my writing is. I just returned from the coast, where we had to join with Wilfen and Ndai in fighting an incursion of pirates, and my hand is still recovering. From a mighty duel with a terrifying pirate captain, you ask? No, from a lee lurch, when the ship gives a kind of hiccough and throws everyone, and more importantly every thing, askew, and my fingers were smashed by a barrel of flour. This was right before the attack—well, war stories are boring, that much I've learned having to listen to these barnacled old captains telling us how easy we young ones have it, and how tough things were in the old days. Even weather. All that aside, I wonder if I might be seeing you at a certain event next spring—or not. The thought of seeing you again makes me as clumsy as the boy I was. I think I'd better put down this pen and make certain there are no lurking barrels of flour.

A Joint Communique from Damatras and The Kingdom of the High Plains:

With Respectful Compliments to Her Highness, Rhis of Nym, from her Royal Highness Taniva of High Plains, soon to be Queen of Damatras: Your Highness is Requested by the Royal Pair to grace their Marriage Ceremony with your Royal Presence, on Spring First-Day

. . . Rhis. I finally learn enough of your alphabet so I write to you myself. I do not write much letters, but I remember you with good feelings. I want you to come if you can. I will tell you about my raid. We abducted Jarvas. Good fun by all, though some bumps and bruises until everyone was agreed. Including Jarvas. We made our fathers go to treaty table. Stop many threats. Maybe now we can have games again—our girls and boys, Damatran girls and boys. Too many have cousins on either side of border. My hand tired now. Taniva.

You will come? Hai, if you do, I have an idea. Taniva almost fell out of the window laughing. We will scare the braids off my father. He keeps dreaming you're going to come back and steal his crown. We've got to nick it—and the joke is, he's got it locked behind about twelve doors. Say you will come. Jarvas.

TWENTY-FIVE

"It is *such* a relief to be able to talk without spies," Shera exclaimed as she climbed into Rhis's carriage, plumped down onto the opposite cushioned bench, and disposed her skirts prettily, and began to fuss with her hair and her little travel bag.

Rhis gestured to the waiting escort-commander, and her cavalcade began to move. Rhis had thought that a troop of tough Mountain Riders as well as two carriages worth of servants, and another carrying baggage, were far more than a princess of little Nym needed to attend a friend's wedding, but her father had said, "No, no, you'll go as we see fit. You're not just a princess of Nym any more."

And her mother had agreed.

Rhis of course knew what was meant. And even though she was twenty-one years old, had traveled to the imperial court, had danced with three kings, had shared spiced ice with an emperor-elect, had talked with one of the Snow Folk in a language not native to either of them, she still blushed whenever anyone made reference to Lios. She'd begun to wonder during the last year if the blushes had just plain become a habit.

"He might not like me," she exclaimed, exasperated. "Or I him. I mean, we might like one another fine, but feel like brother and sister, or—or he'll like me but he's fallen in love with someone else."

"Have you fallen in love with someone else?" her mother asked.

Rhis had certainly been attracted to others. Especially to the emperor-elect, but she'd recognized early on that that was because he reminded her so much of Lios. Only he was a mage journeyman, not a scribe. But he'd had the same serious air that would change, all of a sudden, into a sense of fun. And he'd had the same regard for people, seeing them just as people, not as representatives of rank.

"No," she said finally. "But we all know that what one feels doesn't guarantee what the other will feel."

"Nevertheless," her father said. "Everyone in our corner of the world thinks of you as the next queen of Vesarja. Whether or not that is true, you may as well have the entourage of a queen, because you will be treated like one."

"That means the flatterers and falsity," Elda put in, for this discussion was at the family dinner.

"You must remember that you'll be hearing what they think you want to hear. If you believe any of it, that's at your own peril." That was Princess Shera, now turned sixteen, speaking with such an air of importance that Rhis smothered a laugh.

Elda nodded approvingly. "Well said, my dear. Well said."

Of course. Because that's what you have said, Rhis thought, but kept her peace.

Her reverie was interrupted when Shera flung herself back against the cushions with a loud sigh. "It's so *good* to get out of Gensam again!"

"I thought you got back together with Rastian again," Rhis exclaimed.

"Sort of." Shera shrugged her pretty, rounded shoulders. The new style was for wide, rounded necklines, tight bodices, and tulip-shaped skirts which looked wonderful on her. "Four times, all told." She grinned, dimples flashing in her cheeks. "But last night, when he said he wanted to sneak along as a guard just to keep an eye on me, we had a big fight. I told him he could go guard a tree or a rock, something that had the patience to listen."

Rhis said with sympathy, "I'm sorry he wasn't invited."

"I'm not. He only wanted to come so he could glower at anyone I might flirt with. Will flirt with," Shera corrected in a fair-minded tone. "I can't help it. I love to flirt. I love romance. Papa took me aside last year and told me that I'm a lot like his side of the family—more in love with the idea of falling in love than with a person. And though Rastian and I are friends—mostly—I don't want to marry him . . ." She fluttered her hands. "I still want romance. Rastian's as romantic as an old pair of shoes." She sighed. "Maybe when I'm older I'll settle down. Like Papa did."

She looked out the window and said in a casual voice, "Do you happen to know if Glaen was invited?"

"No."

"Well. Tell me about that robe. The embroidery is amazing, it's like brocade, so it doesn't look dull, but a robe? Or is that the fashion in Charas-al-Kherval?"

"It is," Rhis acknowledged.

"And you're wearing empire fashions *here*? Woo, even Iardith would be impressed—if she were coming. But I hear everyone wrote to Taniva saying they'd come only if she didn't, and then Taniva told, oh who was it? Oh anyway, Jarvas wouldn't have her, so that's that."

"I'm wearing empire fashions because skinny people look awful in those wide necked dresses with the tight waists and the skirts draped over hips I don't have. I love these robes."

Shera scanned the soft layers of gauzy silk with a critical eye, then gave a nod. "You do look good. What do you want to wager you start a new fashion?"

Rhis laughed. "We'll see! What I really want, though, is to hear some of your music. Come on. Our last journey together we made music, and were just beginners. Now you're leading musical fashions, and I want to be the first to hear your new songs."

Shera sat upright. "You can be the first to hear the song I made for their wedding gift! I think it's my best yet—I've got a triple counterpoint in a 5/4 rhythm—"

"5/4? That's impossible!"

"Oh, no it's not! It's a delightful rhythm, like galloping horses—they will *love* that." She demonstrated on her lap. "And just *ravishing* chord changes. Oh, if I don't have everyone singing it by the end of the week, may I turn into a croaking toad!"

Everyone assured one another that the wonderful thing about the weather so very high up was, you could wear your very best clothes and be certain you wouldn't wilt from the lowland heat.

Otherwise, the old fortress overlooking Lake Skyfall, which officially lay on the border between the Kingdom of High Plains and Damatras, was beautiful in a grand, austere way. An army of servants had done their best to make it more festive for the noble and even royal visitors arriving from as far away as the Island of Wilfen. Brightly woven cushions softened the stone benches, and colorful territorial banners hung everywhere, rippling in the brisk mountain winds.

Jarvas and Taniva together received most of the guests, when they weren't seeing to other matters. Rhis's arrival caused no little stir, and the royal pair were both on hand when the six matched horses galloped round the last bend into a grand courtyard lined with stone statues of rearing horses.

Shera, face to the window in order to thoroughly enjoy the commotion their arrival caused, gave a loud gasp. "I see Lios! There he is!" She jabbed her finger against the glass, almost breaking it. "Ow. He's there—and with *Hanssa!* G-r-r-r, the rotter!"

Rhis felt her heart constrict. She did not lunge at the window, but nothing in the world could have prevented her from sending a fast glance past Shera's shoulder. There was a tiny lady, dainty and graceful as a butterfly, her gold-touched red hair pulled back on either side of her head as she laughed up at the man on whose arm she leaned. He was partly hidden by a press of spectators. A moment they both were poised, the lady laughing, and then they turned away and were immediately swallowed in the crowd.

How strange it is that one can travel for five years, and meet hundreds of people, but a flickering glimpse of no more than the shape of a shoulder, the way his brown hair waved back over his ears, and she knew him immediately. And once again the sun poured its light right out of the sky and through her bones.

". . . that rotter." Shera sniffed. "He's *worse* than Rastian! He—"

"Wait," Rhis said. "Wait. There has to be a reason for what we saw."

"Yes," Shera said, fuming. "Unless what we saw *was* the reason."

Like screaming nightmare creatures, all the worst explanations ran through Rhis's mind, but she'd learned not to latch onto what hurt worst, just because it was too easy for pain to impose its own logic.

"Lios," she said, "was never mean."

Shera said, "Unless he's changed."

"If he's changed that much, as well I find out, right?" Rhis retorted lightly, but Shera wasn't listening. "There's Glaen," she said softly, as Shera gasped.

Shera isn't trying to make trouble, she loves drama, Rhis reminded herself as the carriage rolled to a stop. Tears and laughter, anger and forgiveness, rush forward and fade back— romance for Shera was like a dance, or like her music, with all the rainbow of emotions. But like a rainbow, they were soon gone.

Rhis felt a little wistful as she stepped out, and then she couldn't think at all because Taniva gripped her wrists and pulled her into a rib-cracking hug. Then, exclaiming so fast that Rhis could not understand her, Taniva pushed her at Jarvas, who thumped Rhis heartily on the shoulder with such enthusiasm Rhis hoped she'd be able to use her arm afterward.

But it was good to see them both—even Jarvas. Even Jarvas's wily old father, still hale and hearty, lumbering forward himself to offer Rhis his arm. "I'll take you in," he said.

"I promise I'm not going to steal anything," Rhis replied smiling up into the king's ruddy face.

He gave a great laugh as he waved aside the waiting guests, and they scattered like chickens in a yard. "No, no! Seems to me you'll be too busy to steal! Come along, Jarvas," he called over his shoulder. "You've done your duty until the next one comes along—now lend a hand, lend a hand."

He pointed a massive finger, as the guests over on the other side of the room parted, and there stood Lios and Hanssa. Rhis scarcely had time to register Shera's loud sniff before Jarvas thrust his way amid the guests, stopped in front of

Hanssa. He then stuck his elbow out in the most approved courtly manner, and Hanssa slid her arm round his. And they started off—the red-haired duchess's daughter hopping at every other step.

And though the Damatran queen was waiting to be introduced, and there were half-a-dozen old friends to be greeted, Rhis had eyes only for the slim fellow of medium height now left alone, whose smile was the old smile she'd cherished so dearly, a smile she did not know was mirrored brightly in her own face.

Then they were next to one another: all she heard was her own name on his exhalation, "Rhis."

She held out her hands, he took hers, slid her arm within his, and she sensed in his wheeling about that he became aware of their surroundings at the same moment she did. And so they blended into the crowd as new arrivals clattered into the courtyard beyond the double doors, all of whom had to be greeted and exclaimed over. Lios introduced Rhis to Jarvas's mother, who had returned to Damatras to see her son married: that had obviously been a treaty marriage, but it had stayed friendly enough.

Then there were many old friends to see and to catch up on. Some Rhis had seen in other places over her five years, others—all the Vesarjans—she had not seen since she left. Glaen was the first one to greet her, grabbing her up and swinging her around before setting her down: his courtly manners were all but gone, now that he was a second in command of a merchant marine fleet. He was as skinny as ever, his hair, nearly bleached white, still hanging in his eyes. He wore his green officer's coat with more pride than he'd ever worn velvet or lace, and showed Rhis proudly each pin or medal he'd earned in working with the allied fleets to beat back the waves of pirates infesting the coast.

"Princess Yuzhyu wanted to be here, of course," Glaen said. "She told me to personally greet you, and beg you to visit her in Ndai."

"She can't get away even for a short stay?" Rhis asked.

"Not with things as they are," Glaen said with a brief scowl. "But I'm not going to spoil this wedding with talk about the Djurans or their evil allies."

Breggan was also there, two years married to Thirash, who greeted Rhis like an old friend. And so the day flitted by, filled with talk and laughter, then music and dance, always within arm's reach of Lios, who seemed to want to be as close by her as she wanted to be by him.

And despite Shera's dark prognostications, it turned out that Hanssa had accompanied Lios's travel party—along with four others. They'd stayed at royal posting houses all the way north, a staid, proper party as different from a certain mad, desperate dash as could be. Rhis even had some conversation with Hanssa, who sat next to her at dinner. She discovered that she was not the only one who could change over five years: Hanssa's sixteen-year-old passion for royally-born people had switched to a passion for royally-born horses, especially those with a pedigree for speed. Though she had learned to be charming—her taste in clothes was exquisite—when left to choose her own topic, it was horse racing. As soon as her broken toes (gotten in a fall when she tried one of Taniva's high-bred hunters) healed, she proposed a royal horse race.

After dinner, she hopped away on an ambassador's arm.

And so Shera did not get her drama after all but neither did she look for it. When the dinner was over and the guests wandered off to explore the mountain retreat or to gather for various forms of entertainment, Lios held out his hand—and Rhis knew their promised moment had come at last.

Her last glimpse of Shera was at the other end of the room where she sat in quiet conversation with Glaen, all drama forgotten.

Rhis was chuckling to herself as she and Lios walked out onto a long balcony bathed in the cool blue light of both moons, one rising, one setting.

"Did you think about what to say on the long ride to the mountains?" Lios asked. "I know I did."

"I was singing too much," Rhis admitted. "And talking."

"Time for my speech. It was a good one, too—I had quotes in at least four of the languages you probably speak better than I do, and I got in a couple of impressive metaphors that I lifted from the latest play from Siradayel, but you know what my mother said just before I left? She said, *Bring that girl back, my boy. When I get old and my court shoes pinch too tight to wear, it's her I want to hand my crown to.*" He shook his head. "Somehow I can't better that. Though the court heralds won't like that about pinched shoes, if we ever tell them about tonight."

Rhis swept her gaze once over the soaring mountains, their crowns of ice gleaming in the soft light. *I want to remember this day forever*, she thought. Out loud she said, "That's your mother, and that's Vesarja. What about you?"

Lios held out his hands. "But don't you see? There isn't any me, or just me. I come with my mother and Vesarja, they are an inescapable part of me. I wish I could say that my mother's temper will be so benign every day, but the truth is her shoes do pinch—or so she says when she gets mad in council and throws insults around like crashing plates. And as for Vesarja, I wish I could give you the play's version of being a queen, with boxes of gems and a new gown every day, and an endless series of courtly plays and surprises. You can have those things, but the truth is, our part of the world is unsettled. Sveran Djur is restless. He wants more land."

"I know."

"And Arpalon is in terrible straits. His spending reached a crisis because he kept thinking he'd recoup by marrying his daughter to a very wealthy king, but—so far—it hasn't happened. So he's stirring up as much trouble as he can among our neighbors, and Shera's own mother is listening to him, because she doesn't need him making trouble on her border."

"I know."

"And the silk traders are unhappy because Thesreve's silk is better, so they are gaining ground in world trade, and in short there is greed and ambition and danger aplenty out there in the world, and our job will be to ceaselessly guard against it. We will work hard."

"I know," she said.

"But it all changes if I can believe that you will be there, every day, every night, by my side. I've had five years to get to know other girls, and I have, and I liked many of them, but finally none of them was you." Lios gave an uncertain laugh, his feelings as whirled as hers. "All right, I've talked about what mother wants. What the kingdom wants. What I want. What do you want, Rhis?"

"You," she said, and took his face between her hands, and drew him into a long and lingering kiss.

The End

Printed in the United States
152889LV00002B/28/P